FOR LUNA

BY

DON ABMA

For Luna

About the Author

I began writing in the 1980's and enjoyed it. Writing became an outlet for me. I've written short stories, eulogies and memorials. I've sent articles to my local newspaper under a pen name. But I've never had the courage to share any of my writing with a wider audience, until now. This book took many years to write because life got in the way, often. Writing a novel could always wait. After all it was a dream, wasn't it? Now it's complete and I am eager to begin another.

I want to dedicate this book to my family. To my grandchildren, Lily & Brennen Bruce. To them I am Papa. To my two daughters, Carey Webster & Lindsey Bruce, who make me proud and I marvel at the wonderful women they've become. To my wife and best friend, Sandy, who has shared in a life well lived. Along the way she has helped me grow. To my stepsons David & John Kyes and my stepdaughter Dr. Jennifer Kyes, they've have added much to my life. And to their brother Jamie, who we remember every day.

I hope you enjoy reading this book as much as I did writing it. Please don't take as long to read it!

Don Abma

Chapter 1

A low groan escaped his lips, his head pounded. His tongue felt twice its normal size and stuck to the roof of his mouth.

Where am I? he thought. He got up from the bed gingerly so the pounding in his head wouldn't worsen, sat there and took in his surroundings. At this point he had no idea where he was or how he got there and in the fog of his mind he tried desperately to remember.

What had he done last night? Where had he gone? Who had he seen? It all seemed a blur.

A quick survey of the room revealed a pile of clothing draped over a chair. He recognized the jeans as being his and felt relief when he found his wallet still in the pocket. What he felt no relief from however, was his horrific hangover so he fell back on the bed, buried his head in his hands and moaned from the dull throb behind his eyes.

"Holy shit" was all he could muster as he slowly rolled over and placed his feet on the floor. He hadn't had a hangover like this in months, maybe even years. Certainly not since his days as a pro hockey player, toiling in the minors.

The question came to his mind once again. "Where the hell am I?"

Slowly, the fog lifted and his senses came to life. He smelled freshly brewed coffee, he heard the distinct crackle of frying bacon somewhere nearby and he felt soft footsteps as they fell across the hardwood floor. Someone approached the bedroom. As he looked up he was awestruck by the vision of loveliness that crossed the threshold.

"Hi" said the vision. It bounced onto the bed with such a youthful energy it made his head pound and his eyes water.

"Feeling a bit under the weather, are we?" she chided, giving him a radiant smile. "After what you drank last night I'm surprised you're still alive" she laughed.

"Hi" he said awkwardly.

He gazed at this young beauty and couldn't believe he had no recollection of how they met. She looked to be twenty-two or twenty-three and though she wore a flannel pair of pajamas he could tell by the swell of her breast and the curve of her bottom she had a great body. She also had the most hypnotic green eyes, gorgeous mop of red hair and a set of pearly whites any actress would kill for. She was a natural beauty and as he looked at her his mind reeled.

Who is she? What's her name? Where the hell am I?

No matter how he tried he could remember nothing about last night and so, for now anyway, he decided to bide his time.

"Was that coffee I smelled?" he asked, sheepishly.

She smiled, tilted her head and looked at him with a knowing grin.

"You can't remember last night, can you?" She smiled and hopped off the bed. "Well, I think I'll let you sweat a little" she laughed, as she left to get his coffee. Over her shoulder she asked, "do you think your stomach can handle some breakfast?"

"Just the coffee thanks," he answered and groaned softly.

Chase Adams, ex-pro hockey player was now a semi-pro private investigator. He was also a part-time counselor to teens at a neighborhood drop-in center. For some unknown reason he had this crazy illusion of being in control. For five years as a pro athlete he struggled in the minors. Then, after making it to the NHL, he suffered a career ending knee injury in his fourth game. After those experiences you'd imagine he would know better than to think he was in control of anything? Unfortunately Chase was a slow learner. He was a washout at twenty-eight. And just like those old war vets, he could tell when it was going to rain by the ache in his left knee. Though he hadn't played professionally in five years, Chase still worked out three times a week and played shinny on Monday nights. Even with his bum knee, Chase could skate circles around the boys and relished the chance to show off whenever he could. Chase Adams had never been what you'd call a ladies man, but he'd always been a head turner when it came to women. He was a quiet type with steel blue eyes and a tousled mane of blond hair that made him look more like a surfer than a hockey player.

"Here's your coffee, Chase"

She sat on the bed beside him, put her arms around his muscular neck and nuzzled in close.

"You were wonderful last night," she whispered as she flicked her tongue along his ear. She was toying with him now and giggled.

"Just thinking about it makes me horny," she sighed. She moved to face him and kissed him tenderly with just a hint of tongue and pulled away.

"Lisa!" he said, suddenly remembering. "I'm sorry Lisa," he apologized. "My mind went blank there for a minute."

"So you *do* remember me?" she smiled.

"Of course I do, who could forget?" he replied, just a little embarrassed.

It was all coming back to him now, slowly. So he sipped some coffee and started to feel human again.

He remembered they'd met at Quigley's, the neighborhood bar he and his buddies went to every Monday night after their game of shinny. He'd been feeling good last night since he'd scored eight goals and, as was the tradition, the boys bought him a boilermaker for every goal he scored. He thought of himself as someone who could handle his booze, but five was his limit.

Lisa had introduced herself at boilermaker number three and his buddies were howling as he was making his moves after number six. The unbelievable part was she took him home after number nine. That was the one she'd bought him.

The rest of the night was a blur and he doubted he could have been anything close to 'wonderful'. But he'd let that slide for now, deciding breakfast might be a good idea.

They sat across from each other at a small, wooden table at one end of a galley kitchen. The apartment was small, composed of a sitting room, one bedroom and a small bathroom with shower. It had furniture you'd see in a House & Home magazine with an assortment of floral prints and puffy throw pillows. And more scented candles than you'd find at one of those girly gift shops.

Nothing like my place Chase thought. A small balcony was accessible from the sitting room and overlooked a busy street. For a time they sat quietly, eating breakfast and sipping coffee. He looked at her, bewildered. He didn't know why he was here but he knew there was something more to this than met the eye.

"Chase, I have a confession to make," said Lisa, breaking the silence. A serious look came over her face.

"Okay," he said, looking at her over his coffee cup, "what's up?"

The plot thickens he thought and tried hard not to break into a grin.

"Last night was a set up," she confessed. She paused, looked at him with pleading eyes as a tear trickled down her cheek. "But you *were* wonderful," she said and smiled. "But not in the way you might think."

"So you're telling me nothing happened last night?" he asked.

There was relief in his voice and he sighed audibly. Chase Adams was no saint and he'd had his share of one-night stands but he was happy nothing happened, at least not yet. There was something different about Lisa. She intrigued him and he wanted to get to know her.

"That's right, nothing happened. I picked you up last night because I know that you help the kids on the street turn their lives around and I need your help."

She moved her chair closer.

"My sister," she paused, as another tear rolled down her cheek, "my younger sister Julie, she's in a lot of trouble and I don't know what to do."

Lisa put her head in her hands and sobbed. Chase sat quietly, allowing Lisa time to compose herself. She got up, swore and sat cross-legged on the living room sofa. He followed her to the sofa and sat beside her. Then she told her sister's story as he held her hand.

Julie had fallen in with the wrong crowd a few years ago. And what started as recreational drug use was now a serious addiction. And it threatened her life. She was part of a Russian gang running a large-scale ATM scam. Lisa didn't know all the details because most of the time her sister wasn't that coherent. But she knew her sister was in way over her head.

Chase listened as Lisa told her about the jam Julie was in. Because of her drug habit she'd found herself in debt to a man named Vladi Cherkov. He financed her drug supplier. At first, he suggested she could pay off her debt by being a drug courier for him, which she agreed to. This went on for a while but then, two months ago, he told her she needed to do more. Her new job was to make withdrawals from various ATM machines using the cards and passwords he supplied her. Every day she received 50 cards. She had to withdraw the maximum amount allowed by each card.

This meant she'd be carrying thirty thousand dollars or more by the end of the day. More money than she'd ever seen. Then she delivered the money to one of Vladi's henchmen at a different location each day. Julie said they gave her a new number to call each morning and that was how she knew where to meet. According to Lisa, Julie had been doing this for six weeks.

"They said they'd kill her if she didn't do what they told her to do," Lisa said.

She was shaking as she explained how Julie had come to her apartment two nights ago, frightened to death.

"Chase, I'm scared" said Lisa, her voice quivering. "Can you help us?" she looked at him with tears in her eyes. "Please."

"Shit, Lisa." Chase was just a little miffed. "I don't know. The Russian mob? I mean those guys are crazy."

Lisa told Chase that Julie came to ask for Lisa's help after she saw a news story on T.V. the other night. The story was about a young girl found dead in a dumpster behind a local hotel. She was in her early twenties and showed obvious signs of drug abuse. The dead girl had over twenty ATM cards in her pocket. And withdrawal slips totaling forty thousand dollars. But she had no money on her. When they showed the young woman's face on T.V. Julie freaked out. She couldn't believe it! It was one of the girls who worked for Vladi Cherkov! According to Julie this girl had disappeared about a month ago.

Then, two nights ago Lisa had come home to find her sister huddled on the floor at the front door of her apartment. After listening to her story she called a close friend. It took some convincing but this friend agreed to let Julie stay with her for a couple of days. Once her sister was settled, Lisa decided to go to Julie's apartment and pick up some clothes and a few of her personal belongings. As she approached Julie's building she noticed a man hanging around the front door. She slowly strolled by the building to get a good look at him. He was a large, muscular man with a long, ugly red scar on his left cheek. He had long greasy hair and a scruffy beard. He looked like he was waiting for someone and eyed her closely as she passed. Lisa was suddenly afraid and decided to forget about Julie's stuff and headed straight home.

As Chase listened intently to her story he could see the fear in Lisa's eyes and hear the trembling in her voice. He already knew that, despite the danger, he would help both Lisa and her sister.

"Chase, I don't know what to do." She got up from the sofa, walked to the window and hugged herself. It was 75 degrees in the apartment but she shivered as if the room was below freezing.

"Listen Lisa," Chase moved behind her and put his hands on her shoulders. He couldn't put the feeling into words but there was something stirring. Something stronger than anything he'd felt before. Chase Adams didn't believe in love at first sight but Lisa was pushing all the right buttons. "At this point I don't know what to do either. But I'm willing to help"

She turned, placed her hands on his bare chest, and looked up at him with her beautiful green eyes.

"Thank you Chase. Thank you so much. I knew you'd help."

For the next hour Chase and Lisa talked about what they could do. There had to be some way to get Julie out of her predicament. Lisa went over everything again and Chase kept asking questions, pressing her on details. To the point where Lisa became irritated. It was becoming painfully obvious they needed more information than Lisa had. Chase needed to speak with Julie and he needed more details on the girl's murder.

"Lisa," said Chase, finally, "I need to take a shower."

As he toweled dry he asked her to write down both her sister's address and the address of the friend. He told her he was going to do some research and wanted to meet with Julie later. He asked Lisa to give her friend a call and set up a meeting for later that evening.

"Ask her if there's a bar or restaurant we can meet at," he said, "somewhere crowded but discreet."

"What time should I tell them?" she asked.

He could see Lisa relaxing now that she had someone in her corner and a certain confidence came back in her look. It made Chase happy to see her this way.

"I'll be back around six, but I think we should wait until dark. Tell them to meet us at eight."

He headed for the door and as he reached for the handle he suddenly realized something was missing.

"Where the hell are my car keys?" he asked, giving Lisa the eye.

She smiled and gave him a sly look.

"I had to drive your car here last night, since you were in no shape," she laughed. "Here you go," she said, as she tossed him the keys.

"I'll see you at six."

He grabbed the door handle once again, stopped and turned to Lisa.

"By the way, where did you park the car?" he asked.

"It's out back in the parking lot."

"Great! See you later."

As he headed for the car, Chase wondered what the hell he was getting himself into.

His next move was to talk to his buddy Nigel. He'd need more information on that murder and he felt Nigel Waters could help.

As he exited the building he smiled. Parked on the far side of the lot was his cherry red '65 Mustang convertible, gleaming diamond-like in the radiant sunshine. The top was down, so he jumped in, started it up and listened to the purr of the powerful engine. He loved this car. When he'd bought it four years ago it had been ready for the scrap heap. But he and his good friend Nigel worked on it together, spending hours in his garage and developing a true bond of friendship. He'd met Nigel back when he was still playing hockey on, what he considered was, the luckiest night of his life.

~

"License and registration, please," demanded the officer.

In his drunken stupor, Chase Adams, local hockey hero, looked up at the cop with a stupid grin.

"What's the problem, occifer?" he laughed. "Was I going too fast for ya?"

The cop ignored him. He asked for his license, registration and insurance information and waited patiently as this drunk rifled through the glove compartment.

What was this guy thinking? thought the cop. He had no doubt the guy would blow double the legal limit. He was angry with this jerk for being on the road but he also noticed the guy looked familiar. He just couldn't place him. Finally, the guy turned to him and handed over his ownership and insurance papers.

"Where's your license" the cop demanded.

"I musta left it at home," he replied.

"Then you, my friend, are in a whole lotta trouble," said the cop, opening the car door. "Please step out of the car."

As he waited for the man to exit the car he glanced at the registration and he suddenly realized.

"You're Chase Adams?" he asked.

"That's me," Chase said with a goofy look on his face.

A look of admiration came over the cop's face.

"You played a great game tonight."

"Thanks," said Chase, feeling good about himself.

He was about to start with the excuses when suddenly the cop cried out and pushed Chase to the sidewalk. As he fell to the ground, he heard squealing tires and the revving of a car engine. That's when the cop flew across the hood of Chase's car and landed face down on the lawn beside him.

"My God!" screamed Chase as he scrambled to his feet watching the offending car peel off down the road and out of sight. He hurried over to the cop, who was bleeding badly from a deep gash on his head. Chase could see he had a broken leg too. He couldn't believe the rush of adrenaline he felt and how it sobered him up so quickly. The cop moaned and was losing consciousness when Chase reached for his cell phone and called 911. He gave his location to the operator, ran to the trunk of his car to get his emergency kit and a blanket he kept in the back. Removing a compress from the kit he applied it to the cop's head wound, stemming the blood flow. He then checked for any other obvious signs of injury, saw none, and waited until EMS arrived.

"Listen Chase, I've thought it over and I've decided not to give you a ticket this time," smiled Nigel.

He was lying in a hospital bed with his leg in traction. He'd also suffered a severe concussion. The doctors told Nigel he shouldn't sleep for several hours and Chase volunteered to stay and keep him company. Nigel's leg was broken in three places but the doctors were confident he would recover fully from all his injuries.

"I think you should lock me up and throw away the key," said Chase. "I feel so bad. What happened to you was all my fault Nigel."

"Bullshit, Chase," said Nigel, waving that thought away.

"You saved my life," Chase insisted. "If you hadn't pushed me out of the way it'd be me lying there, not you."

Chase paced the room. Under normal circumstances he could have cared less about this guy. Cops, had never been his favorite people. In the past he'd had a few run-ins with them and had always come out on the losing end, most of the time winding up with a night in jail to show for it.

"I owe you, big time," said Chase, sitting down for a long visit with his new best friend.

~

"Nigel, it's me," Chase said. He was already feeling a little guilty about getting Nigel involved.

"Hey buddy, what's up?" asked Nigel.

He explained he was in the car and wanted to meet. Nigel suggested a coffee shop about two blocks from the station house and said he could be there in ten minutes.

When Chase arrived Nigel was already waiting for him in a quiet corner. Nigel was well aware of Chase's penchant for privacy.

"I've already ordered a triple, triple for you, buddy," laughed Nigel. "How in the hell can you drink that shit, man?"

"Leave me alone, will you," said Chase, as he sat down.

"Speakin' of shit man, you look like a piece of it. What the hell happened?" asked Nigel.

"Listen buddy, I need your help," Chase said, ignoring the question.

He glanced around the room and lowered his voice. Giving no specifics Chase filled him in on what had happened so far that morning. Nigel kept interrupting him with questions but Chase ignored him and told him only as much as he felt he needed to.

"So," said Nigel, pausing for affect. "You want me to tell you everything I know about this murder but you won't answer even one of my questions? Is that it?"

"Nigel, I'm sorry, but I can't tell you anything more at this point," insisted Chase. "You've got to trust me."

Nigel reluctantly agreed and told Chase everything he knew. Which wasn't much since the case was not his. But he did promise to get more information and meet later for a beer.

"Thanks buddy," said Chase as he hopped out of the booth and hurried out to the street. "I owe you another one," he shouted over his shoulder and was gone.

"Hey," said Nigel, calling out to his friend, "what about the coffee?"

The waitress came over and gave him a smile.

"These are on the house, Nigel," she said.

"Well then I guess I owe you one, don't I?" he laughed.

"My name's Crystal," she said, in a shy way, "maybe we could have a drink sometime?" she added.

Nigel blushed and stammered.

"Uh, yeah, that'd be fun. Listen, I'll catch up with you later, okay?"

Nigel left the place just in time to see Chase's car turn south, heading downtown.

What he didn't notice was the black sedan that followed him as he left to continue his investigation. Chase was meeting another important friend.

Chapter 2

The phone rang, jarring Vladi from a deep sleep.

"Who is this?" he screamed into the phone.

After last night he was in no mood for an early call.

"Vladi?" was the timid response on the other end of the line. "It's me, Goren."

"What the fuck do you want?" Vladi yelled in his thick Russian accent.

Vladi had come to this country from Russia just two years ago and was already gaining a reputation as a serious player in the Russian mob. In the past year he'd brutally murdered three people and had ordered the slaying of several more. He placed no value on the life of any human save one, his own.

Many people feared Vladi Cherkov. His enemies and allies alike. Born in Moscow to a poor family, he was an only child. His father had been a hardworking man who earned extra money running black market goods for the Russian mob. Unfortunately, at 14, Vladi was sent to an orphanage when the state police took both his parents away because of his father's mob ties. He never saw them again and was forced to live in an orphanage run by the state. He was forced to endure the torture and humiliation of the people who ran the orphanage as well as his fellow orphans. He realized quickly if he was going to survive it would be up to him. Here, no one cared whether he lived or died. Most of them would be happy to see him suffer. As far as he could tell, they would all rejoice in his death.

At first no one took notice but the killings started soon after Vladi arrived at the orphanage, his fourth in the past two and half years. First they found small rodents, like rats and squirrels tortured. A dog was found hanging from a tree in the children's playground. Whoever killed it had tortured it viciously. They'd cut off the dog's paws. They removed its eyes and drilled a hole through its tiny skull. The staff suspected Vladi but could never prove it was him.

Only one year later Vladi Cherkov graduated to taking human life. With the overwhelming evidence in the murder case there was no doubt he was going to jail. The judge deliberated for less than an hour and Vladi received a fifteen year sentence. The killing had been gruesome and Vladi's reputation preceded his arrival at the prison in Leningrad. At the tender age of 17 he caused even the most hardened criminals to cower when he stared into their eyes and flashed his menacing smile. Though he was often held in solitary, he met an older man his first year in prison and they became unlikely friends. The old man saw something in Vladi and took him under his wing. The old man also knew he was responsible for Vladi losing his family. He'd hired Vladi's father to help him smuggle contraband into Russia and watched the state put him in prison. His father died there three years later. So the old man showed him the ropes, teaching him the skills he would need to survive his days in prison. The old man talked of when the Russian mob ruled the black market. He regaled Vladi with tales of the time he'd been the leader of a group of men who ran the docks in Moscow. But Vladi never made the connection to his father. He boasted that his vast network enabled him to smuggle anything into the country. And out. Others in the prison told Vladi his friend was a powerful man in the Russian mob. He'd become a wealthy man before the government crackdown caught up to him. Charged and convicted of a series of crimes, the old man had to spend the rest of his life behind bars. But, as he often said, he had plans for Vladi.

"When you get out of here I want you to go see a friend of mine," he told him. This friend was an important man in the Russian mob and would help him said the old man.

"His name is Alexei Rodnovic. I have told him about you and he will help you when you get out."

Vladi stared at him and laughed.

"But your friend will be dead by then," he said.

"You just remember that name," said the old man solemnly.

The old man died two years later but he had taught his pupil well. Vladi never forgot the lessons he learned and knew he would be ready when it was his turn to get back into the real world.

~

He hesitated. Unsure of himself, but he bravely knocked on the thick wooden door. He waited. After a few minutes the door opened and a burly man stood in the doorway.

"What can I do for you," the man said in a surprisingly polite tone.

"I would like to see Alexei Rodnovic," said Vladi, in his thick Russian dialect.

With no warning the man laughed out loud.

"Alexei Rodnovic?" he asked, as he turned and yelled into the house. "Hey Viktor!" he shouted, still laughing. "There's someone here who wants to see Alexei Rodnovic."

"That would be difficult," said Viktor, coming to the entryway. "You see, Mr. Rodnovic has been dead for almost 6 years," he added as he and his friend shared a belly laugh.

Vladi Cherkov began to feel the rage he often felt while in prison and wanted to choke the life out of both these men but instead, he smiled and politely asked what had happened.

Composing himself, the man named Viktor explained that Alexei had died of complications following a major stroke. He was 87 at the time.

"I see," Vladi said quietly, trying hard to remain calm. "I am sorry to hear this."

It was time to tell these men about his friend in prison. He explained how the old man had told Vladi to come see Mr. Rodnovic when he got out of prison. At the mere mention of the old man's name both men immediately stopped laughing. They looked at one another and in a respectful tone invited Vladi in. They asked him to sit in the den and wait, telling him they'd be right back.

After a short wait a tall man, dressed in an expensive suit, came into the room.

"Hello Mr. ah," said the man hesitantly.

"My name is Vladimir Cherkov but please call me Vladi."

"Well Vladi, my name is Gregory Rodnovic," as he held out his hand. "And I am pleased to meet you," he said and sat down in a chair next to Vladi. "I understand you were a friend of my uncle's," he smiled, "and that you met him in prison. Am I correct?"

Vladi looked the man over. He looked to be about 50 years old with salt and pepper hair cut short. He had the muscular body of someone who worked out regularly and he could tell by his handshake the man was strong.

"Yes, that is right," Vladi said and looked at him, puzzled.

"He was my mother's brother," smiled Gregory. "I am Alexei Rodnovic's son."

Gregory turned and whispered something to the man called Viktor, who left the room immediately.

Vladi watched the exchange and became wary. He tensed, sensing something was about to happen.

"My father told me that you would appear someday," said Gregory, explaining how his father had kept in touch with Gregory's uncle while in prison. He also explained the man, known as Mr. C to Vladi, was the head of the Russian mob in Moscow and controlled the mob in three other major cities in Central Russia. "My uncle was a powerful man Vladi," explained Gregory and turned as Viktor walked back into the room holding an expensive leather briefcase. He handed the package to Gregory. "My father told me that if you ever came here I was to give you this." He paused and handed the case to Vladi. "This is a gift from my uncle."

He looked up at Gregory surprised. He hesitated, not sure what to do next.

"Go ahead, open it," said Gregory.

Inside the briefcase he found a handgun and a pair of daggers. He smiled as he examined the delicate instruments. Gregory explained these were not ordinary instruments of death. He said the handgun was a silver-plated 357 Magnum with an ivory handle. He told Vladi the daggers' titanium blades were balanced perfectly and the hilts of each made of rare black rhinoceros tusk. Vladi was speechless.

"My uncle made it clear that you knew how to use these gifts. He said you could be a valuable asset to me and my organization. He asked me to offer you a job Vladi". Gregory, once again, sat down in the chair next to Vladi. "Would you like that?"

"Gregory. It would be an honor." Both men stood and shook hands.

"Then it is settled," said Gregory, "you will begin work tomorrow."

The next morning Vladi was on a plane headed for New York City. He would be working for Gregory's cousin Stephan Corolev. Stephan was the son of Vladi's old friend.

~

"I have information on that missing girl, Julie," said Goren. Vladi sat down and listened carefully.

"Where is she?" asked Vladi, a touch of excitement in his voice.

"I don't know that yet," Goren replied.

"Well, what the fuck do you know," he spat into the phone. "Goren, I want that bitch," he screamed.

Goren tried to calm Vladi down by using a soothing tone. He'd often succeeded using this technique with Vladi. He explained that while he'd been watching Julie's apartment he'd noticed a woman who looked a lot like Julie. He saw her walk by the apartment building two nights ago and he followed her to another apartment.

"Probably her apartment," Goren explained. He told Vladi he'd stayed outside the apartment the entire night and the next day. When she left the next evening he followed her to a local bar and watched as she spent the evening with a group of men. They were celebrating something but he didn't know what. At the end of the evening she left with a man. It was clear the man had been drinking and Goren followed them to the woman's apartment and again stayed there all night.

"Why the hell didn't you call me then," screamed Vladi.

"I'm sorry Vlad, I just wanted to find out a little more before I bothered you," Goren said sheepishly. "Right now I'm following the guy she was with."

He paused.

"Something strange is happening Vladi."

"What's that?" he asked.

"He just met with a cop."

Vladi stood up and paced the room.

"Listen to me Goren. I want that whore alive. I need to know who she's talked to and what she has told them."

Vladi paused, took a deep breath and continued.

"Goren," he said. "I am counting on you to find this woman for me. Please continue to follow this man," he ordered. "And I want you to update me regularly, understand?" Vladi insisted.

"Of course Vladi," said Goren. "I am sorry for not calling earlier but I promise I will tell you what I am doing, and will do so regularly from now on."

Vladi grabbed a piece of paper and asked Goren several questions, all the while taking notes.

"Damn it," he screamed, as he slammed down the phone. He was pissed. He hated it when Goren spoke to him in that soothing tone of his. One of these days he would smack him around for talking like that but for now he would let Goren think his antics were working.

"What is wrong Vladi?" said a soft voice from over his shoulder. A beautiful black haired Russian girl came up behind him. Her name was Sonja and she did not look a day over nineteen. Naked under an open silk pajama top, she crawled sensuously onto the sofa. The curve of her breast was evident as the translucent material clung to her lithe body. She had long legs, and her elegant arms wrapped delicately around Vladi's neck. She moved in close and nuzzled his muscular neck with her soft full lips.

Out of nowhere Vladi grabbed the young girl and pushed her away violently, yelling obscenities in her direction.

"Get away from me you whore," he screamed. "There is only one thing wrong," he said. He shoved her away and let her fall to the floor, "and that is that you are still here."

He turned, grabbed her by the hair and pulled her to the bedroom screaming, swearing at her as he slapped her face.

"Now get the fuck out of here before I kill you," he bellowed.

His face showed a look of rage that told Sonja he was angry. Angry and dangerous. Sonja grabbed her clothes and scurried to the bathroom, locking the door behind her. Her life was in danger and she had to think quickly.

Just a few weeks ago she'd witnessed the brutal murder of one of Vladi's couriers. The young woman had become nervous at one of the ATMs when a man from the bank approached. She panicked and ran away, leaving a card in the machine. When she returned to the apartment to explain what had happened Vladi hit the roof. He slapped her several times and punched her repeatedly, then grabbed her by the neck and brought her face close to his. He smiled and whispered to her softly. The others in the room relaxed, thinking the worst was over when without warning he pulled a knife from his waistband and viciously stabbed the girl several times, finally slitting her throat. His face had the same look of rage Sonja just witnessed and when he finished, he simply dropped her on the floor like a rag doll. Turning to his men he told them to toss her body in the dumpster behind the Newbury Arms Hotel. She could still hear his voice, cold and bloodless.

"Get this piece of shit out of here," he spat as he walked into the bathroom to wash the blood off. "And clean up the fucking mess!"

~

"Sonja?" he whispered, using that same soft tone she'd heard before. "I'm sorry baby."

He tapped at the door.

"Sonja, come on out. I am sorry," he spoke calmly, "honestly I am."

Sonja's stomach turned. Her body shook uncontrollably. She feared for her life, certain that if she opened the door he would kill her. Yet she knew if she refused he would smash his way in and kill her anyway. Sonja surveyed her surroundings, desperately searching for a way out. There was a small window above her but it was too small for her to escape through. She moaned quietly, knowing there was no other way out. She closed her eyes and walked to the door. Sonja said a silent prayer and opened the door.

Chapter 3

Chase Adams thought about his next move. He was confident Nigel would get more information about the girl's murder. Chase's job was to learn as much as he could about the Russian Mob. He had always been good at making friends and this ability helped him build an extensive network of people he could call on. He could get information on just about anything.

His next stop was the Hocking Building over on Tenth Ave. It housed the offices of the FBI and he felt a visit to his old friend Matt Hanson would be helpful.

Driving down Main, he made a left on Tenth. When he made the turn he noticed something in his rear view mirror. Just two cars behind, a big black sedan also made the left onto Tenth. He wasn't one hundred percent positive but he remembered seeing a similar sedan when he left the meeting with Nigel. Was someone following him? He had to be sure so instead of pulling into the parking garage, he continued down Tenth Avenue and watched in his rear-view as the black sedan followed.

Not wanting to alert his tail, Chase kept the car moving at a leisurely pace. He made his way across town to the Main Library to see if the sedan did the same. Even the most direct route would cause him to make several turns so he knew this would be enough to confirm his suspicions.

Twenty minutes later Chase pulled into the library parking lot, grabbed his cell phone, and quickly made his way to the main entrance. Out of the corner of his eye he saw the black sedan enter the parking lot. The driver pulled into a position that gave him a full view of the front entrance and the entire parking lot. Chase had to give him credit. He was no amateur. This guy knew what he was doing. Chase didn't know it yet but his tail made one fatal mistake!

Chase entered the building and looked back to make sure the driver didn't follow. As he suspected, the driver stayed put. He watched as the man lit a cigarette and slid back in his seat. He wasn't going anywhere and now it was confirmed! He was following Chase! But who was it? And why? He'd have to get answers to those questions later.

Right now, Chase needed two things to happen! First, he needed to ditch his tail. And second he had to ditch him in a way that wouldn't tip him off. He couldn't know that Chase knew. He moved away from the window and used his cell phone to call Lisa.

"Lisa, it's me," he whispered.

Chase told Lisa what was happening and what he needed.

Lisa, asked hesitantly, "what does this guy look like?"

As Chase described the man, Lisa heart pounded.

"Chase, that's the guy I saw in front of Julie's apartment. He looked creepy so I just walked right past him. Remember I told you about him?"

She hesitated.

"I know it was dark Chase, but he stared right at me so I'm positive he'd recognize me."

"Shit," he said. He thought he could slip away after Lisa 'accidently' hit the man's car. But if he recognized her that wouldn't work.

Damn it! He wasn't a hundred percent sure about Lisa's assertion but he couldn't take the chance. He didn't want this guy to know they were on to him so he told Lisa to sit tight. He needed to think.

He couldn't use Nigel. Surely the man saw them together at the restaurant. Maybe he could create a diversion! Deep in thought he gazed out the window at the dark sedan and noticed the fire hydrant nearby and suddenly, the idea came to him. He smiled. It was risky but it was the only way. And this is where his tail's one little mistake would cost him.

He'd parked in front of a fire hydrant!

Chase moved away from the main lobby and went looking for a place to set his little diversion in motion. He'd seen a popular cop show recently where the Fire Department had demolished someone's car because it was blocking access to a hydrant. That episode was the seed of his plan. But he had to be careful. He didn't want somebody getting hurt.

"Where there's smoke there's fire," he said aloud as he entered the furnace room of the building. The safest way to create his diversion was to create enough smoke but not too much fire.

Goren was confused as he watched this guy enter the Public Library. Why had he come here, of all places? He did not understand. But after hearing Vladi there was no way he was going to lose this guy.

"He'd kill me," Goren said aloud, as if someone was with him.

So as he entered the parking lot, he pulled alongside the curb to get an unobstructed view of both the front entrance and the guy's car. He watched carefully as his target entered the building, then sat back and lit a cigarette. He thought about calling his boss but decided to wait until he had more to tell him.

As he sat in the car enjoying a cigarette a couple of girls passed by and smiled. He smiled back and began to relax. He waited.

Twenty minutes later he lit another cigarette and pushed the seat back slightly.

Then, all hell broke loose!

Dozens of people ran out the front entrance screaming at the top of their lungs as smoke billowed from the roof of the building. Smoke alarms were blaring. Goren bolted upright and looked at the building when, without warning, three fire trucks pulled up. One parked on a diagonal directly in front of him. One sped passed him to the front of the building and the other stopped right behind him. Fire-fighters jumped out of the two trucks closest to him and started unloading equipment. They pulled out their hoses and connected them to the hydrant beside Goren's car. The men were shouting orders. People were running everywhere and chaos reigned.

Goren jumped out of his car and protested. He screamed at the men, telling them he had to get out. The fireman had an emergency to deal with so they ignored him. Desperate, he looked around for someone in authority who could sort out this mess and move these trucks. Then, just as desperately, he looked for the Mustang he'd been following. It was gone! Goren slumped against his car, devastated.

"He's going to kill me," he said aloud, then slid down the side of his car and moaned.

Chase jumped out of his seat as he triumphantly pumped his fist in the air.

"It worked," he screamed into the phone.

"What worked?" Lisa asked.

"My brilliant plan," he laughed, "I've lost the creep. At least for now"

Chase calmed himself, knowing he had to concentrate on driving since he was in some heavy traffic.

"I'm on my way to pick you up," he said getting serious. "Change of plan, Lisa. I'll be there in twenty-five minutes and I need you to be outside waiting. Can you be ready?"

"I will be," replied Lisa.

Lisa was waiting as he pulled up and she ran out to greet him.

"Get in," he shouted.

"What's the rush?" she asked, as he sped away from the curb.

"I think the guy who followed me knows where you live," he explained.

"What do you mean?" she asked.

Chase looked at her with concern in his eyes.

"It's the only way he could've found me."

"My God, what are we going to do?" asked Lisa, looking worried.

"For now, you're going to stay at my place," he said, and as he sped away he looked over and smiled.

⁓

"Listen Nigel, I just can't give you that information," said the detective, sitting at his desk intently studying pictures of the young woman they'd found behind the hotel.

"Why are you so interested, anyway?" he asked, as he looked up from the pictures.

"Well," said Nigel, "we had a complaint filed this morning and I think there might be a connection."

Nigel looked down at the pictures on the desk and felt a wave of nausea.

"Are you sure?" asked the detective, eyeing Nigel. "Tell me about it," the detective demanded suspiciously.

Nigel had rehearsed his story and was almost certain he could pull it off so he told his tale. When he finished he looked at the detective and smiled.

The detective smiled back.

"You know what, Nigel," as he got up from his desk. "That is pure bullshit!!" Then turned away and laughed. "Who the hell do you think you're talkin' to, some rookie?"

He turned quickly and asked Nigel to follow him. They entered a large room with bulletin boards on three walls and it was obvious this was headquarters for a massive, ongoing investigation. There were maps and pictures on all three walls and four other detectives were sorting through newspapers, magazines and other material. They had set up wiretapping equipment in a corner of the room and one of the detectives was there with headphones on.

"You see Nigel, this is not just some random act of violence we're looking into." The detective paused and gave Nigel a serious look.

"What happened to this woman was the result of gang violence and we believe she was working as a runner for the Russian mob."

The detective told Nigel the scam involved forged bankcards. They were using them to withdraw the maximum amounts from hundreds of accounts every day.

"So far," he said, "they've stolen over four million dollars."

Another detective in the room walked over.

"And that's just what we know about," added the second detective. "We think they may be working in other cities as well, so we've called in the FBI."

Nigel knew he would not have much more time so he quickly scanned the room. He was desperately trying to commit the faces on the wall to memory. They all looked mean. And they all looked like they could kill someone without batting an eye.

"Alright, let's go Nigel," the detective said and took him by the arm. "I've probably given you more than I should."

As they returned to his desk, the detective turned and stopped. Then he gazed hard at Nigel.

"I don't know what you're up to Nigel," he said. The detective then paused keeping his gaze on him and added, "but you better be real careful."

Nigel watched as the detective's finger pointed to the pictures on his desk.

"These guys play for keeps, my friend. If you know what I mean?"

Nigel looked up from the desk, his face somber.

"Yeah, I see what ya mean."

As he turned to leave Nigel simply said, "I promise, I'll keep ya posted if I find out anything, okay?"

"You do that," said the detective as he turned his attention back to his desk.

Nigel hurried out of the squad room eager to find his buddy Chase Adams.

~

The phone in Chase's pocket vibrated.

"Hello," he said, looking over at Lisa and feeling confident.

"Hey Nigel," he smiled, "what's up?"

"Don't what's up me, you lunatic," Nigel screamed into the phone.

"Whoa, buddy," cried Chase, surprised. "What the hell's the matter?"

"The freakin' Russian mob," screamed Nigel, "that's 'what's the matter'!"

Lisa listened as Chase explained that he knew what they were dealing with. He also told Nigel someone had followed him.

"Shit Chase."

"Nigel, relax, I got rid of the guy. Don't worry." Chase was trying to calm him down.

He explained how he'd managed to elude his tail and said he was sure the guy would not be a problem.

"Chase," said Nigel and as he did Chase could clearly hear the trembling in Nigel's voice. "This is the Russian mob, man." He paused and took a deep breath. "These bastards are fucking crazy!"

"Listen Nigel, you've got to calm down," said Chase in a soothing tone.

He told Nigel what the next part of the plan would be and suggested they meet at his apartment in twenty minutes.

"Listen Chase, my shift doesn't end for another hour. I'll meet you at my place at four thirty, okay? You know where I keep the spare key, right?

"Yeah I remember," he said as he sped along the highway. "See you at four thirty, and don't be late," Chase added.

They had some time to kill so Chase took a detour and stopped at the supermarket for some supplies. He made a u-turn and headed for the Winn-Dixie they'd just passed.

~

Goren watched as the firemen cleaned up the mess they'd made. He lit another cigarette and tried to think of a way out of his predicament. There was no way he could call Vladi! He had to figure out how to get back on the trail of this guy. How could this have happened? He knew he was in deep shit!

"Think man, think," he said to himself.

"How can I find this guy? Why didn't I write down the damn license plate number?" One fireman looked at him curiously but Goren didn't notice.

He closed his eyes and tried to imagine the plate number. He'd been following the car for close to an hour. Surely he could remember some of the plate number if he just concentrated. Then it came to him! He remembered how he thought it was weird that the letters in the plate were so close to the make of the car, a Ford. He clapped his hands together in triumph. The last four letters were FORG. Now he was in business! His contact at the Department of Motor Vehicles could help and he hoped with these letters and the make of the car he could get back on the trail. Grabbing his cell phone he dialed the number and said a prayer.

"You're in luck," said the voice on the other end of the line. "Only two red Mustangs have license plates that end with FORG."

The voice on the line paused.

"Okay," said Goren, excitedly. "Just give me the addresses, damn it!"

He jotted them down, hung up and breathed a sigh of relief. But then he looked and saw that the two addresses were at opposite ends of the city. He wasn't out of the woods yet. But now he had at least half a chance to get back on track. His heart was pounding and his palms were sweating. Looking at his watch he realized it had been just over an hour since he'd lost his target so he needed to hurry. Goren started the car and raced toward the first address on his list.

~

"Nigel," shouted Lisa. She was getting agitated. "Would you calm down and listen to Chase?"

She'd just met Nigel and her first impressions weren't positive. Chase was trying to explain the next phase in his plan and Nigel wasn't listening. He just kept going on about the Russian mob and how dangerous they were.

Lisa wondered how these two polar opposites could be such close friends. She looked over at Chase. A handsome, rugged man standing six foot, two inches in height, with steel blue, piercing eyes and a smile that most would describe as captivating. Confident but not cocky, Lisa had taken a shine to him from the moment they met.

Nigel, on the other hand, was not your typical cop. Looking at him, you might guess he was an accountant. He had a round, chubby face, with thick lips that turned down when he smiled. He was slightly shorter than Chase and had a thicker torso that made him look a little overweight, though he was anything but. At this point Lisa didn't know what to think. She worried about her sister and wanted to get her to a safer place so for now she would sit quietly and listen. Chase outlined their next move.

"Listen Nigel," said Chase as he grabbed him by the shoulders and looked him in the eye. "I need you to go with Lisa and get Julie, okay?"

Nigel nodded.

"While you're doing that I'm gonna go see my buddy at the FBI. We need to know who the players are. Got it?"

He turned to Lisa.

"Can you write out a description of the guy you saw?"

Lisa nodded.

Chase watched as she began writing.

"I'll try to get some pictures of these guys and maybe with Julie's help we can figure out who exactly we're up against."

Lisa handed Chase the description and walked toward the door to get her coat. Nigel was right behind her and quickly grabbed his jacket, moving past her to open the door.

"We'll meet at seven-thirty, okay?" said Chase, grabbing his coat and following them to the parking lot.

Before he could jump in the car Lisa hugged him and gave him a peck on the cheek. She looked up at him and told him to be careful.

He smiled.

"Don't worry Lisa. I know you're concerned, but I promise Nigel knows what he's doing. Frankly, I'd trust him with my life so I know I can trust him with yours. And your sister's."

He looked up and smiled at her.

"Right, Nigel?"

Nigel ignored him and got into his car.

Chase looked down at Lisa.

"Go!" he shouted and jumped into the driver's seat of his cherry red convertible.

Goren pulled up to the first address on his list. The apartment complex had a multilevel garage. And a security gate. To get into the garage with a car he had to have the security code.

He drove by the ramp and pulled into the parking lot of a small strip plaza next door. At the entrance to the parking garage he walked around the gate to have a look around. Goren checked each parking level but found few cars in the lot. And there was no red Mustang convertible. Frustrated, he realized most of the occupants were at work. He knew he could not rule out this address. He also couldn't afford to waste two hours waiting here to find out. So he hopped into his car and headed to the other address. It would take about forty minutes in traffic but he felt he could come back here to check again if he had to. Though he hoped he'd get lucky and find the car at the next address. He knew had to pare it to one address and do it quickly.

"I need a cigarette," he mumbled to himself and pulled a pack of Lucky Strikes out of his pocket. But when he looked inside the pack, he cursed. It looked like he was out of luck! Out of Lucky Strikes and he prayed it wasn't an omen.

"Shit," he cursed, and slammed on the brakes. He was just about to pull out of the parking lot, so he backed up and slipped his car into a spot next to the convenience store.

Minutes later he was speeding down the main drag pulling heavily on the cigarette and breathing a big sigh of relief. He knew it was impossible but Goren always felt the nicotine helped calm his frayed nerves.

After an uneventful drive across town he pulled up to the second address on his list. It was a small, rundown, three-storey building with an outdoor parking lot. At first glance he noticed a few cars but none were red. He needed to be sure and pulled over to take a closer look. But, like the other parking lot, he saw nothing to help him. There was no red Mustang. Goren looked at his watch. It was ten after four and Goren realized he had a problem. He knew he couldn't eliminate either place yet so he had to decide which place to stake out. He lit another cigarette and thought about it for a moment, becoming frustrated and worried.

Then aloud he said, "If I screw this up I'm a dead man."

Chapter 4

Sonja's heart was racing as she slowly pulled the door toward her. All seemed quiet and she began to relax when suddenly, the door slammed into her chest and she tumbled backward hard. She slid across the slippery tile floor and her shoulder smacked into the toilet bowl, stopping her abruptly. A sharp pain ran down her arm and her fingers went numb. Sonja tried to scramble to her feet but as she got to her knees she felt a hand grab a mass of her hair, pulling her out of the bathroom. She screamed at the sudden jolt as he ripped the hair from her head. Trying to ease the pain of having her hair pulled she grabbed Vladi's arm and held on as he dragged her into the living room.

"You fucking bitch!" he screamed, as he threw her onto the sofa. "Do you think you can hide from me? Do you? You whore!"

Sonja looked up at him and whimpered.

"No," she said meekly.

Vladi grabbed the robe from the floor and threw it at her.

"Put some clothes on, bitch."

Sonja took the robe, put it on and cowered at the end of the sofa, paralyzed by what she felt certain was about to happen. She was trembling and sobbing quietly. And though terrified her sobbing would make him angrier she could not control herself.

He sat down next to her and put his hand under her chin. Gently, he forced her to look up at him. He smiled.

"Sonja," he whispered. "Have I frightened you?"

Terrified, she tried to nod her head but his grip was so tight she couldn't.

"I'm sorry Sonja," he said in that voice so hauntingly familiar.

She continued to sob, tears running down her face.

He leaned forward and kissed her damp cheek.

He smiled at Sonja. She was so frightened she couldn't stop shaking. She was so sure he would pull out his knife and kill her she closed her eyes and prayed.

She held her breath, sure that her fate was death, when suddenly the phone rang. Shocked, Sonja shuddered at the unexpected sound and opened her eyes.

Vladi turned, looked at the phone and hesitated for a moment. He couldn't decide whether to answer the phone or deal with Sonja.

He just swore, took the phone and answered.

Sonja was frantic, convinced he would kill her. She watched him closely as he walked around the kitchen looking for a cigarette. He grabbed the pack off the counter and angrily threw it on the floor. She curled into a fetal position, so afraid he would, once again direct his anger at her.

Instead, Vladi pulled the phone down from his ear, put his hand over the mouthpiece, and calmly told

Sonja to put her clothes on and go buy him a pack of cigarettes.

"And hurry the fuck up," he said, as he turned back to his conversation.

Although her arm was stinging and her head ached she jumped from the sofa. She knew this might be her only chance to escape. She ran to the bedroom and threw on some clothes. As she did she suddenly stopped. There on the floor was an open duffle bag! Filled with money! She looked back toward the kitchen and, realizing that Vladi couldn't see her, grabbed a wad of bills from the duffle bag and stuffed them into her jeans.

As she came out Vladi threw two twenty-dollar bills at her.

"Here's some money!" spat Vladi.

Sonja grabbed the money and headed out the door. As she left she heard him yell.

"Sonja, grab a six pack of beer too! And hurry the hell up, you dumb whore!"

She didn't answer. She didn't stop. She just ran into the hallway, ran to the stairs and hurried down to the first floor. Sonja flew out the front door and hesitated for just a moment. He'd expect her back soon and she knew she'd have no more than a five or ten minute head start. She had to move quickly or she was a dead woman. She hailed a cab, got in and told the driver to take her to the bus depot.

Where should she go? Who could she turn to for help? Should she go to the police? They could protect her, couldn't they? Her mind was reeling and she was so afraid. She needed some time to think.

"Can you take me to the Broadview Arms Hotel instead please," she asked the cabbie. Knowing the hotel from her past, she knew it was far enough away that it would probably take Vladi a few days to find her, giving her time to think. Time to come up with an escape plan. Sonja took a deep breath as the cabbie turned at the next corner and headed for the hotel.

~

"That fucking bitch," Vladi screamed as he threw the duffle bag across the room. When he'd finally gotten off the phone he had wondered why Sonja was taking so long. While he waited, he went into the bedroom and saw the duffle bag full of money. Instantly, he knew she'd taken some money and was not coming back.

"God dam it," he said and picked up the phone.

Goren jumped as the phone rang. He'd been in deep thought so as he picked up the phone he looked at the call display.

"Shit," he thought, letting the phone ring one more time, trying to think of what he would say.

"Hello Vladi," he said, clearing his throat.

"What the fuck are you doing Goren?" questioned Vladi, "sleeping, you shit?"

"No," he protested, "I'm still following the guy I told you about."

Vladi ignored him.

"Goren, we have a problem. Where are you right now?"

Goren lied and said he was at an address on the east side of the city.

"What's the problem?" he asked.

"That bitch Sonja," said Vladi, his voice shaking. "I sent her out to get me some cigarettes and beer and she has not returned. I am afraid she has decided to leave us."

Vladi explained that he'd been on the phone with Stephan Corolev when he sent Sonja out on an errand. When he got off the phone he realized she'd taken some of his money.

"That asshole kept me on the phone for twenty minutes," screamed Vladi. "I can't believe that Sonja would run away like that."

Goren suddenly had an idea.

"Why don't I look for her?" he stated emphatically.

"What about this guy you've been following?" asked Vladi.

Goren lied and said he could come back to this guy with no problem.

"Okay, I want you to find that bitch and when you do, I want you to bring her to me, understood?"

"Where could she be, Vladi?"

"I do not have any idea where she is Goren," replied Vladi, the frustration in his voice evident. "That is why I am calling you! You idiot!"

He hesitated and thought for a minute.

"Hold on," he said, "I remember Nikolai once told me that Sonja would sometimes take her tricks to the Broadview Arms Hotel. Maybe you should check there."

Goren hung up the phone and breathed a sigh of relief. He was off the hook, for now.

"Mathew Hanson, please," Chase said, as he smiled at the security guard. She was cute and working the reception desk in the front lobby.

She smiled back and blushed.

"Is Mr. Hanson expecting you?" she asked.

"He's not," Chase replied. He thought this could be a problem so he improvised. "But you know what, I'm a close friend and I'm sure he wouldn't mind me interrupting," he added.

The young woman smiled again.

"Just a moment please," she said as she dialed the extension. "Mr. Hanson, I have a Mr. ah," she hesitated, looking at Chase.

"It's Adams, Chase Adams."

"A Mr. Chase Adams here to see you," she continued. "Thank you Mr. Hanson, I'll send him up. He'll see you right away, Mr. Adams," said the young woman.

"Thank you, ah" he hesitated, and laughed.

"My name's Cynthia, Mr. Adams," and she smiled again, this time her cheeks flushing a deep red.

"Please," he extended his hand, "call me Chase."

"It's a pleasure to meet you, Chase."

She smiled and gave him a strong handshake.

"Ditto Cynthia," he said. "I hope we meet again," as he hurried down the hallway.

"Ditto for me too," she whispered as she watched him leave.

The Hocking Building was a nondescript building from the outside and was ten floors. It was about fifty years old and had received a face-lift about four years ago. When you entered the building you could see the advanced technology. Surveillance cameras in the foyer and new elevators were significant signs of improvement. It also had a security desk with a bank of television screens that covered every floor. The FBI kept a low profile here and occupied the top three floors. But for security reasons the elevator only went to the seventh floor.

Chase had been to see Matt several times in the past so he knew where he was going. He exited the elevator on the seventh floor. It opened into a secure lobby with locked doors at either end. A phone was on the far wall with a list of names and phone numbers. Chase went to the phone and punched in Matt's extension. A moment later a computerized voice told him that someone would be right there. Chase hung up the phone and waited.

Less than a minute later a familiar face popped through the door.

"Hey Chase," smiled Matt Hanson, "come on in."

"Hey Matt," Chase said, returning the smile.

He followed Matt into to a small conference room with a table and eight chairs. Along one wall was a credenza with a large coffeemaker and several mugs.

"Coffee?" offered Matt, as he poured himself a cup.

"No thanks" he said, taking a seat at the head of the table. "Listen Matt," said Chase, then hesitated for a moment and looked away. Finally, he returned his gaze toward Matt.

"Matt I need your help," he said nervously, his gaze dropping to the table top.

Matt listened intently as Chase went through the details of his day. He described the guy who had followed him while Matt took some notes and asked several questions. When he'd finished telling his tale he stood up and poured himself a coffee.

Matt stood as well and paced the room for a moment trying to think this through clearly. After a few minutes he turned to Chase.

"The guy you're describing could be a man named Goren Skolotnev," explained Matt.

He paused for a moment and sat back in his chair. As Chase looked at him he could see his face was grim and his smile had disappeared. He was visibly upset.

"Chase, I've got to tell you, this guy is bad news," continued Matt. "His boss is the main enforcer for the Russian mob in this city. His name is Vladi Cherkov. If your friend's sister is working with these people she's in a world of danger."

Matt stared out the window, thinking. His face took on an even grimmer look. After a few moments he stood up, grabbed his coffee and motioned Chase to follow him. They walked down a long corridor to a large corner office where a distinguished gentleman was sitting. His back was to the door and he was on the phone as they came to the office entrance. Matt hesitated a moment and rapped lightly on the door. The man turned in his chair, smiled and motioned for them to sit in the two chairs in front of his large mahogany desk.

"Listen, I'll call you back. Someone's just come into my office," said the distinguished gentleman as he hung up the phone.

Before sitting, Matt introduced Chase to Assistant Deputy Director Vincent J. Fontaine, who stood and shook Chase's hand.

"It's a pleasure to meet you, Mr. Adams," said Fontaine and turned to Matt Hanson.

"What's on your mind Matt," said Fontaine as he sat back down in his high back leather chair.

"Well sir, Chase has just shared an interesting story with me and I thought you should hear it."

Matt then turned to Chase, "tell him what you told me."

As Chase retold his story Fontaine interrupted several times asking questions. He wanted whatever details Chase had about the murdered girl. When Chase couldn't provide more information Fontaine became visibly frustrated.

When Chase finished, Matt and Fontaine excused themselves and spoke for several minutes, reviewing certain details and comparing the notes they'd taken.

When they returned Fontaine eyed Chase.

"I gather Matt has told you how dangerous these people are."

"Yes sir he has," he replied, exasperated, "but I'd already figured that out."

"Well then, why don't you let us help you?" said Fontaine, softly.

Chase stood up and leaned over the desk.

"With all due respect, Mr. Fontaine, I came here to get a lay of the land, if you know what I mean. What I need is a list of the players I'm up against."

Chase then moved away from the desk and faced the window.

"What I don't need are more teammates," he added rather loudly, then turned back to Fontaine. "So, can you help me? Or not?"

"I think I can do that Mr. Adams," smiled Fontaine.

"However," he paused, "you need to let me know how you're progressing."

Chase smiled.

"As often as I can," he replied.

"Okay then," said Fontaine as he turned and picked up his phone. "Matt, get Mr. Adams what he wants."

~

Chase left the Hocking Building with two opposing senses on full alert. Having a much better idea of the people he was up against gave him a strong sense of confidence. However, that same knowledge gave him a terrible sense of dread. These men were brutal murderers and would kill without warning. Matt Hanson had gone over everything he knew about the Russian mob in this city and provided some messy moments of the many crimes they had committed. At least now he had some names and faces he could look out for. And after seeing his picture, confirmed it was Goren Skolotnev who'd followed him earlier that day.

He sat in his car studying the faces and names of the Russians. Though he'd been reluctant, Matt gave him a copy of the FBI's file on the Russians. But did so only after Chase promised to update him with any progress he was making. He'd also supplied him with his cell phone number and told him he could send a message either by voice or text. Chase looked at the number, crumpled the piece of paper into a tight ball and threw it in the ashtray. He knew he wouldn't be using it, but was still suspicious. Somehow he'd managed to get everything he needed without giving up much in return and he wasn't sure why. Oh well, not to worry he thought, maybe it's just my charm.

It was time to meet with Nigel, Lisa and Julie. He turned the ignition, put the car in gear and headed out of the underground parking garage.

~

"You know Matt," Fontaine turned in his chair, "this may be just the break we've been hoping for."

"I hope so sir," replied Matt.

Both men watched the blip on the screen that represented Chase Adams and his bright red Mustang convertible. An FBI technician had attached a tracker to the undercarriage of Chase's car while he was with Matt and Fontaine. Now the FBI could track his movements.

Matt pulled out his phone and punched in a number.

"The tracker is working flawlessly at this end, how's it look at your end?" said the voice on the other end of the line.

"Good," Matt replied. "Listen McVittee, he knows how to spot a tail, so don't spook him, okay?"

Matt hung up and smiled at Fontaine. "I think this is going to work just fine."

Fontaine turned in his chair and smiled, "I have no doubt it will Matt," he said as he turned his chair and reached for his phone. "Keep me up-to-date on your progress."

~

Chase slowly pulled up to the restaurant. As he entered, he noticed a beautiful young woman sitting alone in a booth by the window. She looked frightened and turned away as he passed by. He was about to stop when he heard Lisa call to him from a large table at the back. He waved and headed toward them.

"Chase, what are you doing?" Lisa whispered frantically.

"What?" he answered, surprised by Lisa's tone of voice. "The girl looked scared. I was just going to ask her if she was alright," he explained and then looked over at Nigel and Julie. Their backs were to the girl and Julie was cowering. She was wearing a large sweater that made her look tiny and her hair was cut short. She also wore a large baseball cap that covered most of her face and, to complete the look, she sported a pair of dark sunglasses. Chase thought she looked ridiculous.

"I'll tell you what's wrong," continued Lisa, "Julie knows that girl. She's the crazy guy's girlfriend!"

Nigel spoke up.

"She came in about five minutes ago and when Julie saw her she freaked out."

"Julie says her name is Sonja," said Lisa, "and I'm sure she hasn't noticed us."

"Maybe we should get the hell outta here," said Nigel, looking around the restaurant, his gaze stopping at the young woman. "I gotta feelin' that somethin' bad is about to happen," he whispered.

Just then the door to the restaurant burst open and the young girl, named Sonja, screamed. A man rushed through the door and headed straight at her. He looked determined. When he tried to grab her she turned and slapped him in the face as hard as she could. He screamed an obscenity at her and made another lunge for her, but she eluded his grasp. His face turned when the woman slapped him and Chase got a good look at him. It took a few seconds to register what was happening but he suddenly realized this was the same guy who'd been following him earlier. He turned to Nigel and calmly told him to get the girls out of here and back to the apartment. Then he quickly moved in behind the attacker, the man he now knew as Goren Skolotnev. Goren's attention was on the young woman so he didn't see Chase as he came up behind him. This time he grabbed the woman by the hair and tried to pick her up but as he straightened, Chase threw a vicious punch to his kidneys, causing him to buckle at the knees. The man screamed in pain, his grip on the girl weakening which allowed her to scramble away. Goren struggled to his feet and as he looked up he gave Chase a look of surprised recognition. He cursed and pulled out a knife. By now, the few patrons in the restaurant had run into the street. Sonja was on the floor, conscious, but stunned by the force of Goren's blow. Goren lunged at Chase with the knife but missed. The move put the Russian in a vulnerable position and Chase took advantage. He grabbed a nearby chair and swung it, viciously, across Goren's back, knocking him to the floor. The knife skittered across the floor, and lay under a booth out of reach from either man. Chase grabbed Goren by the collar, pulled him to his feet and gave him a roundhouse to the jaw, sending him across the room where he collapsed, momentarily stunned. From a distance Chase heard sirens wailing. The cops were coming! He had to get out of there! He grabbed a dazed Sonja and hurried out the back door.

Sonja did not understand what was happening! Yet she sensed this man was someone she could trust. Someone who could help her. She looked over at him and somehow knew he was a kind and gentle soul, yet strong and unafraid.

He drove without saying a word. Once or twice he looked over at her and smiled, trying to reassure her she was safe.

She looks like a frightened child thought Chase. He wondered what her background was and how she'd gotten hooked up with these Russians. But now wasn't the time to grill her. That could wait.

They drove straight to Nigel's apartment and pulled in around the back of the small three-story building.

"Come on Sonja," Chase said as he jumped out of the car.

She gazed at him with a look of astonishment.

"How do you know my name?" she asked.

"I'll explain when we get inside," he said as he took her by the arm and led the way.

Sonja pulled her arm away and stopped in her tracks.

"I will not go any further until you tell me who you are and where you are taking me," she stated defiantly, hands on hips.

"Listen Sonja, I'm a friend. Trust me, okay?" Chase looked around to see if anyone was coming. "I'll explain everything but we've got to get inside."

Sonja just stood there and shook her head. She wasn't moving.

"Okay, Okay, my name is Chase Adams and I know one of the young women who was working for your boss, Vladi. Her name is Julie. She was at the restaurant and she recognized you."

When Sonja heard Vladi's name she became visibly shaken.

Chase gently put his hands on her shoulders.

"You're safe with us Sonja, trust me," he reassured her.

He looked around the parking lot to make sure no one had followed them.

Then took Sonja's hand and said, "come on, let's get inside and we can talk. Okay?"

Sonja nodded and followed Chase to the door of the apartment building.

Lisa was frantic. She was pacing the apartment like a cornered animal.

"What the hell happened in there?" she screamed. "Why didn't you help him?" she demanded, screaming at Nigel.

She was furious.

Nigel tried unsuccessfully to calm her down.

"Relax Lisa," Nigel stepped in front of her and gave her a stern look, "Chase knows what he's doing. He can take care of himself, don't worry."

Just then there was a knock at the door. They looked at one another expectantly. They both stared at the door for a moment, and then heard another knock. This one sounded a little more urgent.

Nigel moved toward it and whispered quietly, "who is it?"

"Nigel it's me, open the door, will ya?" said the familiar voice.

As Nigel opened the door Chase quickly pulled Sonja in behind him and shut the door.

Lisa rushed toward Chase and threw her arms around his neck.

"Thank God you're okay," she said, as she took his face in her hands, looked at him and smiled. Then she looked over at Sonja, turned back to Chase and kissed him on the lips. When their lips parted she gave Sonja another long look as if to say don't even think about it sweetheart, this one's mine.

Chase smiled at this and snuck a peak at Nigel, who shrugged his shoulders and smiled in return.

"Where's Julie?" he asked, taking on a much more serious tone.

"She's in the bedroom lying down," said Lisa, eyeing Sonja again.

Chase introduced the two women and explained that Lisa was Julie's sister. He also told Sonja they were trying to help Julie and take her somewhere safe.

Yet it seemed at that moment there was no safe place. Every time they made a move the Russians were close behind.

Sonja told them about her ordeal with Vladi and how close she'd come to getting killed. She also told them she had witnessed the other girl's murder at the hands of Vladi. Lisa watched as this young girl told her story. She felt sorry for her and realized she couldn't imagine the fear this poor girl must be living under.

Lisa got up from the sofa and asked the others if they wanted to eat.

"I think we'd all feel better if we ate," she looked over at Chase. "Don't you?"

Chase smiled and nodded.

"Sonja, why don't you go into the other room and lie down while Lisa fixes us something to eat?" he said and pointed to the bedroom down the hall. "Nigel and I need to talk."

Lisa took Sonja by the hand.

"Come on," she said, and led her to the bedroom.

Chase moved toward the balcony and motioned for Nigel to follow. He closed the sliding door behind them and filled Nigel in on what he'd learned from his friend at the FBI. He could tell it worried Nigel. Hell, it worried him too. What they needed was a plan. A plan to bring Vladi out into the open. Once they did that they were sure they could get Vladi do something criminal and arrest him for it. Something to put him in jail for a long time. They went over several alternatives and finally, after discussing it for some time, decided on a plan of action.

"We can do this buddy," smiled Chase, trying to reassure his reluctant partner. "Trust me."

Nigel just shook his head and headed straight for the fridge. He was not happy and needed a drink. He was a cop, and cops didn't do the things Chase was suggesting. The problem was, however, he owed Chase and would not let him down.

Chapter 5

He stood at the window of his luxurious office surrounded by all the trappings of wealth. Dark oak paneled walls encased a room filled with deep, soft leather sofas and chairs. The wood for the floors was imported oak, stained a rich dark brown and expensive rugs handmade in some exotic country in the Middle East adorned them. His desk was a table carved from the redwoods of Northern California. A bank of computers covered the desk, providing instant access to a vast array of organizations under his control, all of them illegal. From here he could survey acres of prime real estate, much of which he owned through numbered companies that no one could trace to him. Beyond his holdings, which extended to the waterfront, lay a scenic vista of sailboats and other pleasure craft lazily bobbing on the still blue water. Their wealthy owners enjoying the bright sunshine of a late afternoon. He smiled. He knew all, but an elite few were oblivious to the wealth and power he controlled.

However, Stephan Corolev's smile slowly turned to a frown as he considered what a serious problem Vladi Cherkov had become.

He remembered the first day Vladi had arrived. He had impressed Stephan with his firm handshake and that air of confidence. He'd been polite, not cocky when they first met. He was respectful and polite to Stephan and the colleagues Stephan introduced him to. They'd talked about Vladi's days in prison and Stephan asked many questions about his father. Vladi shared his prison experiences with Stephan and they quickly became friends. At first it was like they were family. Although their experiences were so different, they were with the same man. A man that was father to one, and to the other, even more than a father. Their bond seemed unbreakable.

But that didn't last. Vladi began to resent the authority figure that Stephan represented. He started to rebel. He started using drugs and showing himself for what he was. A simple thug.

The responsibility and stress were showing. Stephan had asked Vladi to kill for him because killing was part of the territory. He'd also always insisted the killings be neat and tidy.

"Make them look like an accident," Stephan would always say. But lately Vladi seemed out of control.

Stephan cursed his father under his breath. What the hell had his father been thinking? He knew his father had been old school and in his day a show of violence was part of the culture. But today, it was different. While the ventures weren't legitimate, he conducted business subtly and, to Stephan, Vladi was becoming a liability. Subtlety was not his style. More like a bull in a China shop. He needed to do something about him but what, he wasn't sure.

When he spoke with him an hour ago he could tell that something wasn't right. Vladi seemed preoccupied and Stephan worried that he would once again rage out of control and do something stupid. His behavior was unacceptable and it had to stop.

"Well then, let's put a stop to it," he said aloud to himself.

He reached for the phone. He was reluctant, but he had to act.

Goren sat at a table at the back of the café pressing a wet towel to the gash on his forehead, trying to stop the bleeding. With him were two cops taking his statement. He explained to them that he'd been sitting peacefully, minding his own business, when this guy grabbed him and threw him across the room.

"He was screaming at me," Goren told the cops.

"Something about his whore wife, and I better not screw her again. I didn't know what he was talking about. He was crazy, man. He must have thought I was somebody else."

There were no other witnesses because everyone left once the fight began. The cops took his statement and offered to call an ambulance. Goren refused. The two policemen told him they'd look into it and promised to follow up with him later. He thanked them and left the restaurant knowing he'd never see them again. Not because they wouldn't follow up, but because the name was fake and the address he had given was an abandoned warehouse near the river.

Goren was in deep trouble. He'd not only lost Sonja, he also let the guy he was following get away. Everything was going wrong. What he needed to do was right this sinking ship. Deciding to do just that, Goren grabbed his cell phone and punched in a number.

⁓

The business was falling apart. Julie had disappeared and now so had Sonja. And where the hell was Goren? His frustration was getting to him and it was making him angry. And now Stephan was mad at him too! Vladi sat down on the couch, lit a cigarette and sighed. This was all happening because he'd gotten angry and killed that girl. Regretting that move, he wished he could control his temper because it was getting him into serious trouble. Until now Stephan had left him alone to run his little ATM scheme. As long as he delivered the seventy percent share that Stephan demanded.

Seventy percent! He thought. *That's just crazy!* He did a quick calculation in his head and guessed that he'd paid out over three million dollars to Stephan in the last six months. *Three Million Dollars! And for what?* he thought. He'd done all the legwork, hired all the girls and taken all the risk. What had Stephan done? Nothing.

But then Vladi remembered what Stephan had said when he'd complained about this recently, sitting in the limo, making his weekly delivery of Stephan's cut. Stephan had just smiled and told him he provided protection. He did not elaborate. He merely told Vladi that, without him, his little business would be worthless.

"Vladi, if you think I am lying why don't you try not paying me my share?" he said as he looked out the window of the limousine. He slowly turned to look at Vladi, smiled and said, "let's see what happens then," in that syrupy voice of his.

Since then he had paid Stephan's share faithfully and never once uttered a complaint. He didn't need Stephan Corolev breathing down his neck. He needed to get his little business venture back on track and making money. He grabbed the phone and hit the speed dial for Goren's cell phone.

It was busy.

"Fuck!" he screamed and was about to throw the phone across the room when he realized he was losing his temper again. It had to stop. He decided it was time to use some of his pent up energy and take some action. He grabbed his car keys and headed out the door.

Racing out of the parking lot Vladi smiled to himself. He loved his new black Porsche 911 Turbo. He'd tested its power once before and had the speedometer needle just past the 180 mph mark. It was an awesome feeling!

Vladi loved three pursuits more than anything. Speed, cocaine and killing. Though not necessarily in that order! He hadn't thought about it lately but he guessed it was the danger he loved the most, and sense of power all three gave him.

As he drove, he looked out and noticed the sun sinking. He decided he'd stop and get a bite to eat before looking for that idiot Goren. Maybe he'd try some of Goren's favorite haunts and if that failed he'd go over to his apartment and wait for him there. Maybe he'd get lucky and score some coke while he was on the prowl.

He saw the exit ramp up ahead, put the pedal to the floor and roared onto the highway. He smiled and thought just maybe, if he got real lucky, he'd find that little whore Julie and kill her too! As he watched the needle skip past the 160 mark he felt a tingle run up his spine. Suddenly Vladi was feeling lucky.

"Good evening Mr. Cherkov," the waiter smiled as he approached the table. "How are you this evening?"

Without looking up from his menu, Vladi ordered a Stoli on the rocks. He sat in a dark corner of the restaurant at a table reserved for him. He had made a quick stop at one of his many drug suppliers and picked up some cocaine. So when his drink came he ordered his meal and quickly headed for the washroom for a little snort. The restaurant was busy and he waited several minutes for the men's room to clear. Once it did, he quickly locked the door, set out a small mirror and, using a razor blade, cut two lines for himself. As he was about to take in his second line there was a sharp rap at the door. The sudden noise startled him, causing him to suddenly exhale and blow his coke all over the counter. Another, louder knock followed and someone yelled. Vladi quickly put away his tools, brushed himself off and went to the door. He opened it abruptly, grabbed the man standing there and pulled him inside.

"Who the fuck do you think you are?" Vladi whispered harshly. Vladi held him by the lapels of his expensive suit, his face only inches away. The man looked to be about sixty years old with gray hair and his glasses sat halfway down his peaked nose. Soaking wet the man wouldn't have weighed more than a hundred and forty pounds and stood about six foot tall. He was a frail old man with a look of sheer terror. He suddenly realized whom he'd interrupted and he sputtered, trying desperately to apologize, but Vladi just ignored him, threw him against the nearest stall door and stormed out.

"Is everything alright, Mr. Cherkov?" asked the owner of the restaurant. He'd overheard the commotion and didn't want a scene. He knew it could be bad for business.

Vladi took a sip of his vodka and told the owner everything was fine. There was no need to worry. The owner smiled and walked away but as he did, he thought, Mr. Cherkov, my ass! More like Mr. 'Jerkoff'!

If this imbecile had not been an associate of Stephan Corolev, he would have him removed. He had a good mind to speak with Mr. Corolev but he feared that Mr. 'Jerkoff' would kill him if he found out he had.

Vladi took a deep breath and slowly settled down. He felt the buzz from both the vodka and the cocaine. And the fact he was enjoying a fine cut of prime rib with all the trimmings was beginning to mellow him out. Maybe he'd get one of those high priced whores from the escort service tonight and worry about Goren tomorrow. Then, without warning, he thought about Sonja.

What a fine piece of ass, he thought. He missed her. He knew he shouldn't have gotten so angry and lost his temper. There it was again, his temper causing him grief. He wondered if he could ever change, but deep down he knew it was impossible. Vladi just smiled and took a sip of his iced vodka.

Change did not come easy for Vladi Cherkov. Besides, he enjoyed feeling the sense of power he got from seeing the fear his tirades produced. He shook off the regret he felt and decided it was time to find Goren. He had tried him several times on his cell phone but he kept hearing a recording that said the customer he was trying to reach was not available. He tried once more and got the same result.

"Damn," he whispered. "Where the hell is he?"

Once Goren had made his call he turned off his phone. He had to avoid Vladi at all costs. He also knew he could not watch both the addresses he had for this guy without help and help had arrived in the form of his good friend Vasily Adneyev.

"What the hell happened to you?" asked Vasily, as he arrived at the bar.

"Don't ask." He had a bandage covering the cut on his forehead and a large bruise was forming under his right eye. And the scar on his cheek was blood red. He looked like hell.

"Listen Vas, like I said on the phone, I need your help."

Vasily smiled.

"Goren, plastic surgery is not my specialty," he said, and laughed, "but I'll do what I can."

Goren was not in the mood. He grabbed him by the arm and pulled him toward a booth away from the bar. Vasily protested but Goren put a hand over his mouth and forced him to sit.

"Listen to me Vas," as he sat down across from him. "This is not funny. I'm in deep shit here. If Vladi finds out I've lost Sonja and this guy I've been following he is going to kill me, do you understand?"

Vasily nodded, getting serious now. The mere mention of Vladi Cherkov's name frightened him.

"Okay Goren. I get it."

"Good," said Goren, relieved.

When he'd called, Goren had asked Vasily to bring two of the throw away phones they used for the ATM couriers. This would allow them to communicate without using Goren's regular cell phone. He briefed him on all the details including descriptions and told him to call the minute he saw anything. The plan was for Vasily to stake out the first building and Goren would watch the other.

All he had to do now was avoid Vladi and find this guy as soon as he could. He was sure that if he found him, he would find Sonja too. The only problem with his plan was time. He had to arrange for the delivery of the bankcards for the ATM scam early the next morning and it meant he couldn't avoid Vladi for much longer. Since Vladi had killed one girl and another two had skipped he was down to five. He'd have to add a few cards to each of the girl's quota. Though Vladi was smart enough to keep himself out of the chain of command, he knew where they kept the phones and cards. He was sure if Vladi didn't hear from him by morning he would be at the warehouse, waiting for him. For now all he could do was hope he had something positive to report by then.

Chapter 6

Fontaine placed the phone in its cradle and thought a moment. He graduated with a law degree and a PHD in criminology from UCLA and joined the Bureau right out of college. In Quantico they identified him as a leader and put him on the fast track. He began his career in a small outpost in New Mexico but after only two years was the Special Agent-in-Charge of the Denver Office. Now, at forty-five, he was next in line to become DDO, Deputy Director of Operations. The youngest man to reach such a lofty position until now had been fifty-six and Fontaine was sure he'd be there before his fiftieth birthday. Throughout his tenure he had often cut corners but his superiors had always looked the other way. His motto was similar to that of a Canadian Mountie. He always got his man. His arrest record was spotless and he had one of the highest conviction rates in the Bureau.

He stood and walked to the window. At six foot four he towered over those he worked with. He liked looking down on people. His body was muscular and lean from the workout he put in four times a week in the basement gym. His hair, like most in his environment, was cut short. What bothered him was it was showing some gray among the jet-black that was his natural color. He would have to look into that hair colouring for men product he'd seen advertised on television recently.

As he peered out he could see the bay in the distance, its calm waters glistening in the late afternoon sun. Some small specks, that he guessed were sailboats or other watercraft, were swaying on the orange tinted water. He wondered what it would be like to have the time to enjoy such trivial pursuits.

As the Assistant Deputy Director he was directly responsible for three regional offices of the Bureau and had an Elite Task Force under his command. This group was responsible for overseeing the comings and goings of the Russian Mafia on the entire north eastern seaboard.

Initially, the Task Force put together some credible information. However the past few months had been frustrating due to a lack of good intelligence. Several recent wiretaps had provided little in the form of hard evidence. What showed promise was the meeting he'd had this afternoon. He hoped this amateur PI might bring them a little closer to an arrest. Matt Hanson had praised his friend and felt he could be helpful. They decided that, for now, they would keep Adams out of the loop, but keep track of him and use him to get closer to Vladi Cherkov. No sense giving Adams too much information. The less he knew, the better. It would be easier to manipulate him this way.

Two floors below Matt Hanson was busy in the tiny cubicle his superiors had the nerve to call an office. He'd just spoken to the agents assigned to follow

Adams and they provided all the details of the fight in the restaurant. Now the agents were outside an apartment building on Austin Ave. where Adams was somewhere inside. According to the two men, Adams had fled the restaurant with a dark haired woman fitting the description of Vladimir Cherkov's girlfriend Sonja. Matt directed them to keep an eye on Adams and to report any movement.

His phone rang.

"Hello?" he asked tentatively. He was not expecting any calls.

When he heard the voice on the other end his face flushed and he jerked his head around to see if anyone was close by.

"I told you never to call me here!" he whispered harshly. He slumped down in his chair and brought the phone in close. "They can trace calls in this building," he explained, "and if they do, you will have put me in a difficult position. Do you understand?"

The voice on the other end was calm and soothing.

"Do not worry, young Mathew," said the caller. "As for any trace. It will show this call came from your lovely wife Amanda."

"Are you with her?" he asked urgently, suddenly concerned.

"Does that frighten you, young Mathew?" said the voice calmly. "Please do not be afraid. I am not with your wife. I am not at your home. But believe me, I have many ways of doing what I need to do, my young friend."

The man laughed.

"What do want?" asked Matt.

The caller told him they needed to meet this evening. He told Matt to be at their regular meeting place at midnight.

"And don't be late Mathew. You know how I hate tardiness."

Mathew was about to ask what the meeting was about when the phone went dead.

Something was wrong and Matt didn't like it.

Stephan Corolev had never called him at the office, ever. To take such as risk meant that whatever was going on was important.

He immediately called home and when Amanda answered he grilled her about what she'd been doing and whom she'd seen. Had anyone been at the house? Were there any strangers hanging around outside? Amanda became irritated at the barrage of questions and asked him what was wrong. Matt said nothing and hung up.

He breathed a sigh of relief, remembering what had happened last year when Stephan showed just how easy it would be for an accident to befall Matt's lovely wife and their six year old son.

⁓

"Hi honey," said Amanda as she walked in from the garage entrance into the kitchen.

"Hey," said Matt, deep in concentration. He was trying to solve the daily crossword.

"Something strange happened today."

She paused, and gave Matt a peck on the cheek.

"What?" asked Matt. He was paying little attention to Amanda, choosing instead to work on his crossword.

"Well, a man came up to me at the grocery store and showed me this headline from one of those tabloid magazines."

That got his attention. Matt put his pencil down and listened.

As Amanda continued the story she explained the news article was about a terrible accident that killed a mother and her child. It said the brakes in their car had failed. And because of the failure they ran a red light and died instantly when a transport truck plowed into them.

"What was strange, though," continued Amanda, "was that he told me I should insist you take a look at my car and make sure there was nothing wrong with the brake lines. He was very persuasive and insisted I promise to tell you. And he had a Russian accent."

Matt's gaze intensified.

"He had a what?"

"A Russian accent," she repeated. "He was good-looking and distinguished."

Matt hurried into the garage. Amanda's Toyota was in its usual spot. Matt moved around to the passenger side and got to his knees. He couldn't believe what he was seeing! There on the garage floor was a tiny puddle of fluid just inside the right rear wheel and as he gazed at the brake line he could see three small nicks. It was obvious someone had tampered with the car. And he knew exactly who it was!

He cleaned the spill and quickly taped the cut in the line as a temporary measure.

His heart was racing.

"There's nothing wrong with your car Amanda," said Matt, as he came back into the kitchen.

"But you know what? I think I'll take the car in for a checkup at the garage, anyway. You can use my car tomorrow, okay?"

"Sure honey," replied Amanda. "Matt, can you go and pick up Jeremy? I left him over at Evan's house so they could play. I told Jenny I'd pick him up before dinner."

Matt grabbed his coat and headed for the garage once again. His hands were shaking and sweat dripped down his neck making his collar damp.

He hopped into the car and immediately dialed a number on his cell phone. He was both furious, and frightened. He let it ring five times and then heard an answering machine kick in. He cursed and shut his phone off. As he pulled around the corner another car pulled up and the driver motioned for him to stop. He recognized the driver. It was Goren Skolotnev, one of Corolev's henchmen.

"What the hell do you think you're doing?" screamed Matt, as he got out and approached the driver's side of the car.

"You got the message?" asked Goren, as he smiled at him. "You know I can't believe how easy it is for an accident to happen. Don't you agree?"

Matt was seething.

"You tell Corolev to leave my family alone," he yelled, his fists clenched.

"Listen Mathew, just do as you're told and every-one will be fine. You got that?"

Goren put his car in gear and slowly moved away, leaving Matt standing in the street.

Matt was in way over his head and he knew it. But he could do nothing. His indiscretions had gotten him in this mess and at this point there was no way out. He had to follow Corolev's orders or risk losing everything. He would meet him tonight and find out what this was all about. Whatever it was, it must be urgent for him to call his office. No matter how careful you were, calling an FBI office was risky. Especially for a man like Stephan Corolev.

What he needed right now was a drink. He called his wife and told her he'd just received a call from his boss and had to get back to the office. He told her he couldn't pick up Jeremy and would be late for dinner. When Amanda asked what was going on, he just said what he always said.

"I can't talk about it honey, it's just business. Trust me, okay?"

Matt sat at the bar nursing a scotch and soda. How had he gotten in so deep? He could remember the day that videotape arrived at his office like it was yesterday. How could he have been so foolish?

He remembered how his heart had jumped into his throat when he saw himself, sitting on the edge of the bed, naked, holding that mirror between his legs. The young girl, *"what was her name again?"* he thought, *"Oh yeah, Sonja."*

Sonja had snorted the line of coke on the mirror and then ran her tongue slowly along his inner thigh, looked up at him, and smiled. She was high and would do whatever he asked. It was an exhilarating night and she was insatiable.

He'd watched the video twice in the hotel room he'd rented, cursing to himself. How could he have been so stupid? But what he couldn't believe was that he'd gotten an erection each time he watched.

The next morning the call came. He'd been expecting it. He knew how this worked and knew blackmail was certain. Amanda looked at him as he listened to the call, his face growing ashen. To cover up, he said there was an emergency at work. He had to go.

Now he was in bed with the Russian mob.

He sipped on his drink, feeling sorry for himself, wishing he could get out of this mess.

He wondered if his friend Chase Adams could help. He needed to tell someone or he would explode. But could he trust Adams?

Chapter 7

Chase sat quietly on the balcony, looking out at the neighborhood below. He could see people coming home at the end of their working day, oblivious to the crime and corruption that is the underbelly of this city. As the sun set, he felt a shiver run through him. Not because he was cold, but because he knew that as night fell the landscape of the city would change. Like in the jungle, the night creatures would come out and prey on the weak, satisfying their hungers and making the weak ones suffer. Addicts would use the cover of darkness to ply their trades. Trades that would allow them to feed their need for one more day, keeping the cycle of their abysmal lives turning. Then there were the dealers, using the night to sell their wares in dark alleys and corners, in crowded bars and after hour's clubs. This was when the hard-core came out to play. Not the preppy white boy or the tattooed party girl looking for a little action. Not the rich young couple in their BMW looking for their weekend supply of cocaine. These were people who would kill to feed their habit and wouldn't remember it the next day. They would feel no remorse. These people only valued their next fix. Nothing else mattered. Chase had seen people from this world and could tell just by looking into their eyes. What disturbed him, now, was that Sonja and Julie had come from that world and their eyes told their story. Eyes, void of feeling. Eyes, that stared right through you, into a world only they knew. A world filled with fear and loathing. A world filled with pleasure and danger, a world he knew. A world that took his sister. A world that chewed her up and spit her out.

Lisa came up behind him and put her arms around his neck.

"Are you okay?" she asked, as she moved around and sat on a chair beside him.

"Hi Lisa".

He looked at her and smiled. *Here was a kind-hearted soul,* he thought. Someone, with a certain innocence, who knew nothing of the world he'd just been thinking about. And that innocence appealed to him. There was a sexual energy between them that was just below the surface. He could feel it.

"You look sad, Chase," she said and turned herself to face him.

"I was just thinking about Julie and Sonja. They remind me of someone I once knew," Chase said softly.

Lisa sat quietly, took Chase's hand and held it, rubbing it gently with her fingertips.

It wasn't long before he began to tell his story. Lisa sat quietly and listened.

He told her about his hockey career and how the frustrations of broken dreams had taken a toll on his family. He was a high school star and all signs were the National Hockey League would be his playground. When he was a kid, his father had pushed him hard. He never had time for friends to just play around with. Everything was work and, over time, he resented it. But he couldn't disappoint his father. He wanted to make him proud. And to hear the pride in his father's voice whenever he spoke about him. That was his fix.

"I never realized the pain I caused my little sister," said Chase, looking over at Lisa.

She looked at him, puzzled, not getting the connection just yet.

He went fourth overall in his draft year. He was so happy! But his father was angry that he hadn't worked harder. He could have gone first overall, "*if you hadn't goofed off,*" was how his father put it. His dad did not understand how hard it was. His father was so disappointed when he didn't make the team his first year and went back to the minors to get more play. He was only nineteen years old and he was making more money in a year than his father made his entire life. And still, he couldn't satisfy him.

"That was all I wanted," said Chase, sadly. "I just wanted him to say he was proud of me. The way he did when I was growing up."

"What happened to your sister?" asked Lisa.

Chase ignored the question and continued his story. He still remembered the hit that ended his career. It happened during the second period of his fourth and final game in the NHL. He worked hard at the minor league level and people at the top noticed. Two goals in his first three games had turned some heads. He would be a force, according to the talking heads at all the sports channels. Then it happened.

The hit was one of those knee-on-knee types you hear about. The other guy got a four-minute penalty and a two game suspension. Chase got a year of rehab and an insurance payout. He tried several times to come back but the knee just couldn't take the punishment. The talking heads never mentioned his name again.

His hockey career over, he packed his bags and went back home. The problem was he'd been away for five years and the home he returned to wasn't the same. His dad had always been a drinker but now he drank himself to sleep every night. He was on the verge of losing his job at the plant because he was often too hung over to go to work. His mother had been his biggest supporter, but she was a bitter woman trapped in a loveless marriage. She smoked too much and spent most of her days in the local casino playing the one-armed bandits for a dollar a pop. Chase had been generous with his money, sending a care package home every month. His parents had made many sacrifices so he could play hockey. They deserved something in return.

His younger sister, Joanne, had just turned fourteen when he'd left home. Though she remained silent she felt abandoned by her big brother. He'd always been there to protect her and when he left, she felt lost. He remembered how she cried when he left for the airport. How she begged him not to go. At the time he couldn't understand why she'd been so upset. Not until years later did he learn the truth.

Chase didn't know their father had abused Joanne when she turned twelve. In the beginning he would only touch her in ways that didn't feel right. It wasn't until after Chase went away that it developed into a routine of weekly visits for sex between Joanne and her father. She'd known it would only get worse, she would tell him later, and that was why she'd begged him not to go.

During his years in hockey he'd come home regularly, but never for long stretches at a time. His off-season training regimen kept him busy and sponsor commitments also kept him away. It was usually only a weekend visit. Frankly, that was about all he could take himself. Often, Joanne would be out partying with friends in the big city. Chase just never took notice. She was a teenager and had a life of her own. To him it all seemed so normal.

But when he came home for good, he saw the changes in her. She was moody and sullen and would talk back to their mother, showing her little respect. And he could see she feared their father. She spent much of her time in her room, avoiding him. But when he called, she would show little resistance and would do whatever he told her to do. Chase blamed himself for not seeing the signs. If he had, perhaps he could have made a difference.

"She was just a kid," said Chase, wiping a tear from his eye.

"What happened?" pressed Lisa. "Where is she?"

"She's dead," he whispered. Then he suddenly broke down and sobbed.

"Oh, Chase I'm so sorry," said Lisa, as she moved closer and put her arms around him.

Chase put his head on her chest and wept openly.

After a few minutes Chase composed himself.

He stood and walked to the edge of the balcony and looked out into the darkening sky, cursing it.

The lures of the night had gathered Joanne into their trap. The trap of satisfying her addiction. She'd tried many drugs so she could join the in-crowd. What was different for Joanne was the consistent abuse she endured at the hands of her father. And it caused her to develop an addiction she could not satisfy. She needed to numb herself constantly and this need led her to harder and harder drugs, and a life of petty crime and prostitution. The crimes often committed by addicts. It paid for their drugs. When she was nineteen she had to move to the city, a place where she could blend in and preserve her anonymity. That summer she disappeared into its underbelly. Living with the people of the streets, going from shelter to shelter and staying wherever she could, Joanne soon developed a network and was plying her trade with regularity. Like many children of the night she was "helped" by those who preyed on the needy and unsophisticated. People who took their pound of flesh and made sure the cycle became a never-ending story of abuse and addiction. Joanne took on a new identity, a street name of "Luna" which was a reference to the moon and her life as a night owl. She even got a tattoo of a quarter moon on the small of her back. The name "LUNA" was tattooed below it. The police knew her pimp and knew he kept his girls on a short leash. He was a violent man and often beat his girls. The rumor was he'd once beaten a girl to death. But he kept his girls in good supply of any drug they wanted and they appreciated that. Joanne had used them all.

When Chase saw her on that cold slab he hardly recognized her. Her dead eyes sunk into deep, dark sockets and her skin was as white as that of a ghost. She'd been dead for less than four hours but it looked more like four days. An overdose of heroine killed her. She'd left home just 3 months ago and now she was dead. Chase's search for his sister was over.

At first, he'd gone to his friend Nigel and begged him to help. But help was difficult. Nigel explained there were over twenty thousand street kids in the city and they lived in a wide variety of places from the local homeless shelters to cardboard boxes under bridges and back alleys. He promised to keep an eye out but there was little else he could do. The police just didn't have the money or the time. So Chase taught himself about the streets. He sought out the kids in bus stations, train stations. He checked the shelters and the youth centers for any clues about his sister. He carried her picture and showed it to anyone who would look. But nobody knew her, or if they did they weren't telling him.

Chase couldn't believe what he saw. The filth and squalor he witnessed just blew him away. He had no idea how bad it had become. Sure, he'd seen the news stories on 60 minutes or CNN, but it hadn't touched him in the same way. Not until he saw it up close and personal. About two weeks before he got the call telling him they had found his sister's body he'd been so close to finding her. A girl named Mandy recognized her picture. She told Chase she worked for a pimp named Darrell. Or was it Derek? She couldn't be sure. No, it was Darrell. Unfortunately, Mandy hadn't been sure about too much since she was high on crack most of the time. It was a lead and Chase felt a surge of adrenaline. But for the next two weeks he kept running into dead end after dead end. He met several more people who'd seen her, and Nigel had a line on a pimp named Darrell. So one night they went to see him. He was a piece of work and it became clear he would not cooperate. Chase was ready to kill the bastard but Nigel pulled him aside and reminded him that a dead Darrel would be of no value.

"Besides," said Nigel, "you don't want to sacrifice your future on a scumbag like this."

They left empty handed.

~

"When I saw her on that cold slab I vowed to do everything I could to stop this from happening again," Chase said turning away from the darkened sky and looking at Lisa.

He sighed.

"But you know what? This past year has been frustrating. I feel like what I've done has been like tossing a pebble into a vast ocean."

He turned to her his eyes searching hers.

"You know what I mean?" he asked. "I've made a ripple, but it's so small that no one even feels it."

Lisa stood and moved to him.

"That's not true," protested Lisa. "Someone told me you'd help. That you could make a difference, Chase. And you're helping me and my sister."

Lisa took his hand in hers and looked into his eyes.

"You know Chase," she said and took his hand, "I'm sorry I deceived you in the beginning. I want you to know that I care about you. I didn't know about your sister and I'm sorry. I'm sure you did all you could."

Lisa took his handsome face in her hands and kissed him gently on the lips.

"You're a good man Chase," she said, as she took his hand. "Why don't you come and have something to eat?"

The others were already at the table and halfway through their meal when they joined them. Both Sonja and Julie picked at the food on their plates and eyed each other suspiciously. Lisa tried to lighten the mood by making conversation while Nigel ignored them all and concentrated on the food and drink laid out before him. He hadn't eaten all day.

Chase sat quietly and looked at them as he ate. He needed each to play a critical role in the scheme he and Nigel devised and the more he watched, the less confident he was in their ability to pull this off.

They were all tired and cranky after their meal, so Chase suggested they get some sleep. Tomorrow would be a busy day. The girls shared Nigel's spare bedroom and Chase said he would sleep on the couch. He sat and watched as Nigel left for his room and all became quiet. He waited twenty minutes and when he was sure that everyone had fallen asleep he grabbed his coat and headed out the door. He needed to do some prep work for the day ahead. He knew how dangerous this would be and the more he prepared the greater their chance of success.

Lisa lay in her bed, not able to sleep, and stared at a spot on the ceiling. Then heard the door to the apartment click shut. A few minutes later she heard the distinct rumble of the Mustang's engine. She closed her eyes and prayed.

Chapter 8

"I need him dead, Mathew!" he screamed. "And I need the FBI to kill him. Do you understand?"

They sat across from each other inside the stretch limousine in complete privacy. Soft music was playing and the aroma of leather wafted through the cabin. It created a dichotomy for the senses, between the luxurious surroundings and the tension that enveloped the two occupants.

"No I don't," replied Matt Hanson. "Just connect him to a crime. Then we can arrest him. That way we look good and he's out of your way."

Stephan Corolev sighed heavily.

"Mathew, Mathew, Mathew. You don't understand. I cannot have Vladi Cherkov in jail. He knows too much. And he has a big mouth. And Mathew, I don't care how good the FBI looks."

Stephan leaned over and put his face inches from Matt's.

"Don't make me remind you of what I can do to your career, Mathew," he said as he grinned. "You know, I still get much pleasure in watching you and Sonja. She's got talents, doesn't she Mathew? Do you think your boss Mr. Fontaine would appreciate the talents of a woman like Sonja? How do you think your wife Amanda would react if she witnessed Sonja's talents?"

Stephan leaned back in his chair, looking smug.

"Well, never mind all that. I'm sure that neither your boss nor your wife will ever become aware of Sonja, will they Mathew?"

Matt smiled back and tried to remain calm. He put on a brave face but he was seething inside.

For the past three and a half hours Matt had been sitting at the bar debating whether he should tell Stephan about Chase Adams. Should he tell him about the tail? Or the fact Goren had been following Adams for the last two days. Or should he keep it to himself and use the information later. It was pure speculation, but, from the description he'd received, he guessed that one of the women with Adams was Sonja.

Maybe he could kill two birds with one stone, as the old saying went.

"Listen Stephan, I have some important news," hissed Matt. "Did you know that one of Vladi's girls skipped on him earlier this week? A young girl named Julie."

Matt gave Stephan some of the information. The rest he would keep to himself.

Stephan sat up straight in his seat and asked Matt how he knew this. Matt then told him about the day's events. When he finished telling him about his meeting with Adams and the report he received from his field agents, Stephan asked him several questions. Who was this Adams? Was he sure that Julie worked for Vladi?

Was she talking to the Feds? Who were the others involved?

Matt didn't tell Stephan he thought one of the others was Sonja. He wanted to keep that little tidbit to himself, at least for now.

Stephan sat thinking it over. Finally he turned to Matt.

"I think that we should arrange for Mr. Adams and Vladi to meet," smiled Stephan. "Don't you Mathew?"

"I would agree with you Stephan," said Matt, as an idea flashed into his brain. "And I think I have plan that will make that happen."

As Matt elaborated Stephan nodded and the tension in the limousine faded. A partnership in crime was forming rapidly and FBI agent Matt Hanson would soon be enjoying the trappings of wealth this partnership promised.

~

The young girl giggled, her ample breasts swaying softly beneath her satin top. Her long black hair cascaded over her shoulder creating a harsh contrast to the white satin and her milky skin. She wore just the night shirt which allowed her to show off her long, milky white legs and just a hint of her tight, round bottom. Vladi had been with this young woman before but didn't know her name and didn't care. There was also something vaguely familiar about her. Something in his past that he couldn't put his finger on.

He spent over two hours looking for that asshole Goren and had finally decided he'd had enough. He knew he could find him in the morning so he called the escort service he and Stephan financed and had that one girl he liked sent to the hotel room he kept downtown. She was there when he arrived.

They spent their first hour getting high on the coke Vladi bought earlier. And the two bottles of champagne he'd ordered. He loved the sex when he was high on cocaine. It was just so intense! And he could tell this young beauty did too.

Right now she was laughing at Vladi, who was standing by the desk with a telephone in his hand. He was looking both serious and ridiculous.

"It's just a friend Stephan," he said into the phone, looking at her rather sternly.

"Yes, I can arrange that Stephan. For what time again?" he asked. "Three o'clock will be fine."

Once again he frowned at the young girl as he shut the cell phone down.

"What is so fucking funny?" he asked moving toward her.

"Well," she laughed, "you look funny standing there with a phone in your hand and that huge hard-on."

The girl crawled toward him, giving him a sexy look. Her breasts swayed under the sheer white top as she moved toward him.

"Would you like me to take care of that for you?" she asked seductively.

"Yeah, why don't you do that, little girl," he said, as he turned toward her, waiting.

She reached out to him but he grabbed her by the hair and slapped her face. He did so with a force that propelled her across the bed, stopping when her shoulder slammed into the headboard. She screamed and began to cry. He had cut her lip and blood spilled on the bedsheets and her pajama top. Vladi gave her a look of disgust. He was furious and once again his temper was getting the best of him. He needed to get out of there before he did something he would regret. He stomped into the bathroom, shaking.

"*Who did this little bitch think she was?*" he thought and more importantly, "*why was Stephan Corolev calling at this hour?*" *For Christ sake it was after midnight!*

His mind was racing. He took a couple of deep breaths and tried to calm down. He could hear the young woman's sobs as he looked at himself in the mirror. He felt no remorse, only anger at his inability to control his rage. Once again he had made a mess that someone else would have to clean up. He splashed cold water on his face and returned to put his clothes on.

He looked at the girl. She was still sobbing and he realized he'd hit her hard. Aside from the cut on her lip, a bruise was forming on her left cheek. He guessed that he had probably broken her cheek bone. He moved to the bed and, as he sat on the edge of it, she cowered and moved away.

"I am sorry," he said and moved in to get a closer look. "I did not mean to hurt you."

She nodded but kept her distance. He told her he had to leave but he would send someone to pick her up and get her medical attention. Vladi then got up from the bed, quickly dressed and made a call to the owner of the escort service. He tried to explain what happened but the owner wouldn't listen. She was furious and told him he was no longer welcome to use her girls for his pleasure. He laughed at the woman and told her he would use her girls anytime he wanted and hung up the phone. He cursed under his breath and took a moment to admire the view from the large picture window, when out of nowhere a blood curdling scream came from behind him. It was the girl and her sudden scream startled him, catching him flat footed and off guard. As he turned around to see what was happening he saw the girl, inches from him, with a look of primal rage on her face. There was a blur of movement to his left and suddenly he felt a searing pain to his temple. The force of the blow was enough to daze him and he fell to the floor. The girl jumped on top of him and hit him again with the table lamp, continuously whispering obscenities. Vladi lost consciousness after the second blow and lay there bleeding from a deep gash to the back of his head.

Twenty minutes later the owner of the escort service found the young girl lying next to Vladi Cherkov's lifeless body. Still holding the lamp and lying in a pool of blood.

"What in God's name have you done?" she screamed as she ran toward them. At first she thought both were dead. It was only when the young woman moaned she realized she was alive. She looked around, then gathered any evidence she could find. As far as the police would know she was never there. She took Vladi's wallet, careful not to step in the pool of blood surrounding him. She took the lamp from the girl and put it in a dry cleaning bag she found in the closet. Satisfied the room was clear of the girl's belongings and anything identifying Vladi, she wrapped the young girl in a coat. Then took her back to the house, leaving Vladi for dead. The girls injuries weren't serious but she would need medical attention.

At three-thirty that morning the police received an anonymous call. Someone attacked a man at the Colony Hotel, Room 2003. When the detectives and an ambulance arrived they discovered a pool of blood in the room. The bed was unmade and the evidence they saw confirmed the attack. But there was no one there. When they interviewed the desk clerk he had no record of who may have been in that room. The police found no immediate evidence that might lead them to who was responsible. But there were obvious signs telling them there were injuries to at least two people. There was blood in several places, including the bed, the bathroom and a large pool on the carpet in the bedroom. The detectives ordered blood work to find out if all the blood at the scene was the victim's. They would run a match through their DNA data base and try to identify the victim and his attacker.

~

"What were you thinking?" howled Anya Senkin, the owner of the escort service, now back in the confines of their home and relative safety. She was trying to clean the blood off the young girl.

"He was a pig!" she screamed.

Anya looked at the girl and calmly spoke to her.

"He was a member of the Russian mob my dear, and if they find out you killed him you will be a dead girl, do you understand?"

The young girl, who name was Melanie, looked up and cried.

"I don't care," she said. "That pig killed my sister!" and she sobbed uncontrollably.

"What?" Anya replied. She didn't know that Melanie even had a sister. She'd only worked for her a little over a month and quickly became one of her most popular girls. When she started, she was willing to work with the Russian clientele. Something many of the girls were reluctant to do. The Russians had a reputation for getting violent with their women and many girls feared them. Some refused to have anything to do with them so Melanie was a busy girl.

At the time it did seem odd to Anya. But after hearing Melanie's confession, she understood why this young woman had been so interested in Russian men. She finished cleaning the girl up and led her down the hall to a bedroom where she could sleep until morning. Anya was afraid there would be retribution for Vladi's killing but she'd worry about that later.

The older woman smiled, looking down at this young girl, already in a deep sleep. She looked so innocent lying there. In the end the bastard had met his match. He'd been terrorizing her girls for the past three years and this end was a fitting one.

~

The sound of his cell phone startled Matt. Who would be calling him at this late hour? He had just left Stephan a few minutes ago and was on his way home, thinking of a way to get Adams to meet with him tomorrow. It was crucial to the plan they devised to get

Vladi and Chase in the same place. For a confrontation that would result in the death of one Vladi Cherkov. At least, that's what they hoped. It didn't matter because Matt would be there to make sure the result they hoped for would be a reality.

"Hello?" he said, as he listened to the voice on the other end of the line. "He what?" cried Matt.

He pulled to the side of the road so he could concentrate on the call. It was one of the agents assigned to Adams and he reported that Adams had left the apartment on his own and was heading downtown. He glanced at his watch. It was well past midnight. What was Adams up to? The agents weren't sure and according to them he'd been in the apartment all evening, only coming out to the balcony for about a half hour. At this point they weren't sure how many were in there but they did see a man join Adams on the balcony for a short time and soon after that, a woman came out and spent some time with him as well.

"Do you think he's figured out he has a tail?" he asked.

"Maybe he's taking a joy ride to see if any one's following him," Matt said, thinking. "It's a possibility so be extra cautious, okay?"

The agent assured him they were being cautious. There was no way he could have picked up the tail. They'd stayed well back, using the tracker on the car to tail him. Matt told them to keep him posted on Chase's movements and to call in the morning with a full report. Matt had to get his ducks in a row if he was going to have a chance at the pot of gold at the end of this Russian rainbow.

Chapter 9

Goren was feeling the heat. There had been no sign of Sonja or the guy she'd left the restaurant with. The guy he'd been following. He'd been in touch with Vasily several times. Neither had seen anyone come in or out of the apartment buildings that looked like the people they were looking for. He was beginning to worry. He knew that Vladi would go crazy if he showed up in the morning with no Sonja, plus the fact he'd lost track of the other guy. Goren knew a crazy Vladi was a dangerous Vladi.

Goren needed to take some action so he decided to have a look around. He wanted to see if he could get into the apartment and check it out. There was no red Mustang in sight so chances were the place was empty. He felt it was worth the risk. He figured that if he looked he could decide whether it was the guy's apartment or somebody else's. Surely there would be some pictures or other personal items that might give him a clue.

"Dam it," he cursed, as he tried the front door. It was locked and he knew he would need someone to let him in. He thought for a moment and then smiled. An idea came to him and he pushed a button for an apartment on the third floor.

"Hello?" said the voice from the intercom.

"Yes, Mr. Sullivan?" asked Goren in his politest voice.

"Yes, this is Mr. Sullivan," came the response.

"Mr. Sullivan, this is the meter reader and I need to get into the basement. Could you please let me in?" he asked.

Mr. Sullivan hesitated a moment.

"I think you should buzz the super," he said. "He's in 101.

Goren, anticipating this response told the man he'd already buzzed the superintendent of the building. He wasn't in.

"Listen, Mr. Sullivan, if you'd like to come down and check me out you can," he offered politely. He knew the building had no elevator and hoped that Mr. Sullivan was like most Americans, lazy. He waited and crossed his fingers.

Again Mr. Sullivan hesitated.

"Well, I guess it would be okay, come on in."

Goren heard the buzzer and quickly let himself in, pumping his fist in victory.

"Thank you," he hollered back as he scurried up the stairs to the second floor. He quickly scanned the numbers and followed them to 208. This was the apartment. He knocked on the door and waited. No answer. He knocked again and looked down the hall to see if there was anyone around. Seeing no one he took out his lock pick and deftly picked the lock. Again, he took a quick look down the hall then grabbed the knob of the door and let himself into the darkened apartment. As he closed the door he flipped the switch on a small pen light and started down a short hallway. It led to a small kitchen and, from there he could see the rest of the apartment. All but the bedroom which was off to the left through an open door.

He carefully made his way to the window and shut the blinds. Once shut, Goren turned on a table lamp that stood beside a leather Lazy-Boy recliner. It faced the biggest flat-screen TV he had ever seen. It took up the whole room.

"What a mess," he whispered, as he surveyed the living room. There were clothes and dirty dishes, even a few beer bottles, lying around the apartment. As he looked around Goren noticed a shelving unit at the end of the kitchen that acted as a divider to the two rooms. There were some photographs on it and he walked over to take a look. He smiled as he gazed at the pictures. There he was! In the picture he was younger and he was wearing a hockey uniform, but it was the guy. On a lower shelf there were several trophies with tiny bronze skaters, holding hockey sticks. Each trophy had a plaque identifying the recipient, Chase Adams.

Finally, a little luck!

Goren pulled out his phone and called his buddy. He gave Vasily the news about his change of luck and told him to hurry over to the apartment. When he hung up the phone he smiled and took a closer look around.

~

Chase had gone out alone for two reasons. He needed some time to think and he needed to take a swing by his place to pick up some personal belongings. He hadn't been home for two days and there were some items he wanted. The most important being the gun he kept in a box in his closet. He thought about his plan and how it might play out. He wondered if he should ask for some help from Matt Hanson, his FBI buddy. What was making him hesitate was that he just wasn't sure he could trust Hanson's boss, Fontaine. Chase's impression was he was a slime-ball. He seemed prepared to use Chase and the others for his own ends no matter the risk. He needed to stew on it for a while and decided he'd wait until the morning to make that call. He'd been driving for the past forty minutes, aimlessly. It was time to go to the apartment and pick up his belongings. Chase Adams made a U-turn and made his way toward home. What he saw caused him to do a double take. Coming toward him about a block and a half away was a black sedan with two guys in it. Normally, he would have thought nothing of it but it was almost one in the morning and what he saw was not normal. Going by what had transpired over the past twenty-four hours, he thought this could be another tail. He had to be more careful. He didn't want anybody to catch him off guard again.

Let's just get back to the safety of my apartment for an hour or so, he thought, looking in the rear view mirror as the black sedan disappeared into the night. He memorized the license plate and continued home.

~

Goren was leafing through some papers in the kitchen when heard a knock at the door. He turned, pulled out his gun and quietly made for the door.

Shit, he thought, standing by the thick wooden door. There was no peep hole so he couldn't see who was out there. He hesitated for a second then whispered quietly.

"Who's there?"

"It's me, you idiot!" Vasily whispered harshly. He was shaking his head as he walked past Goren. He stopped in the center of the room, turned and looked at him, still shaking his head. "Who'd you think it would be?" he asked, with a look of disbelief on his face.

"How the fuck would I know?" said Goren, getting a little pissed off at his mouthy friend.

Vasily, sensing this, dropped it and asked him what he was doing in this guy's apartment.

"This is the guy I've been looking for and I want to know as much as possible about him," explained Goren. He told Vasily to look for anything that could help them find this guy. Where he worked? Who his friends were? "Check out the bathroom," he told Vasily. "Look for items like prescription drugs, anything that might give us a clue," he said.

So far, he'd learned that he was an ex-hockey player and his name was Chase Adams. After listening to his phone messages he'd also learned he had a buddy named Nigel and that a woman named Cynthia wanted him to call. According to the message, she worked at the Hocking Building and they'd met earlier that afternoon.

"Wait a minute," he said aloud, talking to himself. The Hocking Building sounded familiar to him. "Why do I know that building?" he asked himself. He was about to chastise himself for talking out loud when he suddenly remembered he had driven by the Hocking Building earlier that day. It was while following this Adams character. Was it a coincidence? Or was there something else? In the back of his mind he felt there was. He just knew it. But what could the connection be? He racked his brain. What the hell was it?

"Matt Hanson!" he screamed out loud.

"What the hell is going on?" yelled Vasily, as he ran in from the other room. "And why are you talking to yourself?"

"I figured out the connection," he explained.

He told him about the FBI agent, how they had him in their pocket and about following Chase Adams earlier that day. He'd gone right past the Hocking Building. It wasn't until Goren told him about the message from Cynthia that he convinced Vasily.

"So do you think this guy might be FBI?" asked Vasily.

"Maybe," answered Goren, still trying to connect all the dots. "Except that he doesn't have any suits in his closet and I think that most of those guys in the FBI wear suits. At least Matt Hanson always does. Let's keep looking."

Goren walked back to the bedroom to look closely at Adam's wardrobe. It was sparse. There were several pair of designer jeans and two pair of wrinkle free khaki pants. He had a bunch of golf shirts and some button down oxfords. From what he saw Goren thought this guy's world was casual. He didn't think he was FBI. He didn't fit the profile. He looked at the shelf and noticed some sweaters and a box. As he went to grab the box he realized it was out of reach so he went for a chair. He brought the chair over to the closet and climbed aboard. As he reached above his head to get the box, his heart stopped.

Outside the window, just below him he heard the revving of a powerful engine. Through the bedroom window he could see the beam of headlights shining on the hedge that bordered the parking lot. He jumped from the chair and looked out the window. Right below him was a car he recognized. It was the shiny red Mustang of Chase Adams.

Chapter 10

Lisa lay in the dark thinking. Her eyes getting used to the darkness, she tried to focus on a spot on the ceiling. She'd heard a door close and was frightened. Chase had left the apartment. She was sure of it. Her fears were realized when she heard the rumble of the Mustang's engine. He'd been gone almost an hour now, and she was starting to worry. What could he possibly be doing?

Thinking about him made her smile as her mind drifted back to the night she'd first met Chase. She'd watched as the group came into the bar. They deferred to him. You could tell they worshiped him, hanging on his every word, his every gesture. She'd waited until they were well into the booze before sauntering over. She'd moved to the bar and gave Chase a look that said 'come join me'. He had taken the bait and sauntered over to her at the bar, his buddies chuckling at his bravado.

"Hi there," he said, as he sat on a bar stool next to her. He introduced himself and asked her if she'd like a drink.

She smiled and nodded, saying she was drinking vodka tonic. She extended her hand and told him her name.

"Your friends look like they're having a good time," she said.

"Yeah, well, that's what they do, I guess," he said. "Don't mind them, they're a good group of guys. Why don't you join us Lisa?"

"I'd love to," she replied as she followed him to the table.

She couldn't believe how much these guys could drink, especially Chase. She hadn't counted but she was almost sure he had consumed six beers and an equal number of whiskey chasers. Lisa figured most men would be falling down drunk if they drank that much and couldn't believe he could still walk. She'd taken him to her place and had a plan for the morning she thought would work. When they got to her place he tried heroically in the bedroom but she was glad nothing had happened.

Her mind continued to wander as she stared at the ceiling. She thought about her poor sister Julie. What had her life been like these past few months? Lisa could only guess. Listening to Chase tell his sister's story had made her heart ache. What it must have been like for Sonja and Julie was something she could only imagine. She wondered why this life on the street, a life of drugs and crime, filled with danger, was the one they had chosen. She thought about her own life and the path she'd taken. Then she realized these lives weren't a choice. She realized it was fate that led them to the places they now found themselves. That at some point their paths brought them to a place where, in their minds, they saw no choice but the road ahead. If only they'd had a choice, a fork in the road that would have taken them toward a life of happiness. They'd have a sense of worth. Of promise and pride, not despair and degradation. She silently vowed to help these women. She could help others too. She remembered someone helping her. Years ago.

~

"Well Lisa," she heard a voice say.

Lisa looked up and saw her teacher standing there, hands on hips, waiting for an answer. She had partied the night before and was in no mood for this teacher's bullshit. Not today, anyway. Being a popular girl in school allowed her to get by with many teachers, especially the male variety, but this bitch had been riding her all semester. She gave her a look of disgust and told her she didn't know the answer. The teacher pressed her some more, then made a remark about Lisa's lack of intelligence. Then turned to another student who provided the answer. The class laughed as the teacher continued to embarrass Lisa. Lisa was angry, so she walked up to the teacher and screamed at her. Her classmates were in shock as she picked up her books and stormed out.

She remembered that day like it was yesterday and the feelings of worthlessness welled up in her as she lay there staring at the ceiling.

She'd been crying as she ran down the hall toward an exit, intending to seek refuge by getting high on some dope she had stashed in her dresser drawer at home. She had never been a serious user of drugs but, she'd been drifting toward them as a way of dulling the pain. She was living a lie. A popular girl who had it all.

But deep inside she was a scared little girl, sensitive to the criticisms of her peers and feeling the pressure to fit in.

She also remembered how surprised she'd been when she heard the voice behind her, begging her to stop. At first it made her even angrier. What was this bitch thinking? So she kept on walking, trying desperately to get away.

"Leave me alone," she'd cried.

"Lisa wait!" the teacher pleaded. Her name was Martha Johansen. She'd been teaching at the school for only a few years and had come here directly from college. She was the school's Grade 11 English teacher and one of two guidance counselors the school had on staff. One was male. She was the female. For the past few months life had been hectic for Martha. She recently married a man who brought two young children into their marriage, aged eight and five. They were both girls. Her new husband's first wife had died tragically almost four years ago in a plane crash. Martha became a mother too quickly, she explained. And even though the children accepted her, she felt an enormous amount of pressure. She had to be the perfect mom. But because Martha had no training, life at home was difficult.

She knew she had made a mistake dealing with Lisa in the classroom that way and wanted to correct it.

"I am so sorry," Martha said, standing in the doorway, blocking Lisa from leaving the school. "I should not have embarrassed you like that, Lisa," said Martha.

Lisa stood there looking down at the floor. Martha placed her hands on Lisa's shoulders and begged her to listen.

"Look at me Lisa," she pleaded. "Lisa, we need to talk."

Lisa looked up and saw that Mrs. Johansen was on the verge of tears. She too started to well up and a tear rolled down her cheek. Seeing this, Martha put her arms around her and held her. This act of kindness made Lisa break down and she wept uncontrollably as Martha Johansen held her. Without saying a word Martha took her by the hand and led her down the hall to her office. She knew her English class was almost over so she forgot about the students. In a few minutes they would move on to their next period happy they had gotten a break and excited they'd have something to gossip about for the next few days. Martha sat Lisa down in a comfortable chair and moved her chair from behind her desk. She sat quietly and waited for Lisa to compose herself.

For the next two hours they sat and talked. They talked about boys and about girl stuff. They talked about sex and drugs, about moms and dads and stupid friends. At first Martha did more listening than talking but it wasn't too long before they were laughing and Martha was sharing her frustrations about marriage and kids. When they parted that afternoon they hugged and arranged to meet again the next day.

Over the next several weeks a friendship blossomed. Lisa had found someone she could talk to, someone who would not only listen but cared about what she thought. Martha respected her opinion. The change in Lisa was gradual, but even her classmates noticed the difference in her. No longer was she that sullen, unhappy girl. Instead, she was a smiling, excited girl, happy to be around her friends. She even auditioned for the lead role in 'Grease'. And when she didn't get the lead role, she took it in stride and accepted the understudy role.

She smiled as she lay in the dark, thinking about Martha and that stupid play. She did play the lead role in the end anyway. Amy, the girl who had won the part, got sick and had been off for several days during the play's run. The school paper gave Lisa rave reviews and though she never went on to a career in acting, she was proud of her accomplishment. Martha had been a positive influence in her life. She had shown Lisa there was a choice, something that Julie and Sonja hadn't seen. At least not so far. But Lisa vowed to change all that.

Lisa heard a door open somewhere in the apartment and looked at the clock on the night stand. According to the bright green numbers it was 2:30 a.m. She got up to see who was out there. As she opened the door she saw Nigel's face glowing from the light of the television screen. He was sitting on the couch flipping through his one hundred and twenty stations at a pace that made it look like there was a strobe light in the apartment. She stood in the doorway for a moment, watching. She didn't know why but she had little confidence in Nigel. She could tell he and Chase were close, but she just couldn't bring herself to feel comfortable with him.

"Hi Nigel, can't sleep?" she asked.

"I'm worried," he said, putting the remote down.

"Chase left over an hour ago and he didn't tell me where he was going. Did he say anything to you?"

"No," she said, curtly.

Nigel looked at her, surprised.

"What's your problem Lisa?"

"I guess I'm worried too," she said as she sat down in a chair next to Nigel. "That scene at the restaurant was intense, Nigel. I don't think we should have left him like that."

Nigel turned in his seat and looked at Lisa sternly.

"Listen Lisa, I know you have feelings for Chase. You've made that clear, but you have to understand. Chase and I have known each other for a while and we've developed a sixth sense between us. I trust him and he trusts me. I also know that you don't think much of me but I can assure you I can take care of you and the others."

He got up off the couch frustrated and turned to look at her.

"You need to trust me Lisa."

Lisa was in no mood for a lecture but she also didn't want to get into an argument with him, so she just shrugged and apologized.

Nigel looked at her suspiciously and smiled to himself. He hadn't convinced her with his speech. At some point he would have to prove himself. Then Lisa might take him seriously.

"What should we do, Nigel?"

"We just have to wait," he said. Then in a more confident voice said, "And listen Lisa, Chase will be fine, don't worry."

⁓

As he exited the car Chase looked around to see if anyone had followed him. There was no one in sight so he made his way to the back of the building and entered. He climbed the stairs quietly so he wouldn't disturb his neighbors and headed down the hallway. As he went to insert his key he instinctively glanced at the top of the doorjamb, and stopped. He was expecting to see the tiny piece of clear tape he had stuck there when he'd left the apartment. Instead it was dangling from the frame like a tiny red flag! Somebody was in the apartment! He quickly pulled the key back and took his hand away from the door. He scanned the bottom of the doorway but saw no light coming into the hallway. Chase saw only two possible reasons for that. Either the trespasser had been and gone or they were lying in wait for his arrival. He retreated to the end of the hall and called Nigel.

⁓

Goren waited in a room so dark he couldn't see his partner Vasily at other end of the living room. He looked at his watch and wondered what was taking this guy so long. They'd been waiting for over five minutes. He moved to the window and saw the Mustang still in its space. He must be on his way.

But why was he taking so fucking long? he thought. All he could do was wait. He cursed, knowing he was blind to the movements of his opponent and that this put him at a definite disadvantage. He tried to get Vasily's attention but in the darkness there was no way he could signal him. They'd worked out a plan to subdue the guy by catching him off guard. But after this long, Goren was certain surprising him wouldn't work. They waited.

Vasily sat in the dark wondering what he'd gotten himself into. They'd been waiting for over five minutes and saw no sign of the guy who lived here. And this Goren was a piece of work. They were sitting in the dark with no way of communicating, waiting for a guy they knew nothing about. Goren had the only weapon between the two. Well, except for the bat Vasily had taken from the hall closet when they'd first walked in. Goren had a gun but the last time Vasily had seen Goren use a gun was at the carnival. It was the middle of the day and Goren spent over an hour, and a hundred dollars trying to win a stuffed animal. He walked away empty-handed. He shuddered to think what would happen in this dark apartment. This could be a disaster. He waited.

Chapter 11

They were in the kitchen making tea when the phone rang, causing Lisa to jump from the sudden noise. Nigel, not wanting to wake the others, hurried to grab the phone on the first ring. Lisa looked on while Nigel nodded and listened.

"Who is it?" she asked insistently. "Is it Chase?"

Nigel shooed her away. He didn't want to miss anything Chase was saying on the other end of the line. A frustrated Lisa sat impatiently, hearing only the occasional okay, as Nigel made notes.

Lisa was sure something was happening. Nigel's face took on a serious look of concern as he listened intently to whoever it was on the other end of the line. She was sure it was Chase.

Finally, Nigel hung up the phone. Lisa was about to question him but he was heading for the door, his jacket almost on. She ran after him and grabbed him by the arm.

"Who was that, Nigel?" she asked.

He turned and looked at her. She could see the worried look on his face.

"It was Chase," he said. "I have to go Lisa. There may be trouble."

Lisa stood in the doorway, barring Nigel's exit.

"I'm coming with you," she insisted.

Nigel looked at her, incredulously.

"I don't think so," he said, laughing.

Lisa took hold of Nigel's arms and looked into his eyes, pleading with him.

"Nigel, if Chase is in trouble I have to help. I can't just sit here waiting. I'll go crazy. You have to take me with you," she insisted.

Nigel looked at her and shook his head slowly.

"No way, Lisa." Nigel would not budge on this one. "I have no idea what's gonna happen over there. It's just too dangerous."

She placed her hands on her hips and stood there. She wasn't moving.

"Nigel, I won't take no for an answer. You have to take me," she pleaded. "Please!" she screamed.

Nigel could see she would not give up. And she would wake the others if he didn't shut her up. He couldn't believe he was about to let her come along. He simply sighed and told her to put some clothes on, and fast. They were already late and had to hurry. She smiled and ran to the bedroom.

As she was leaving the room her sister stirred, opened her eyes and looked up at Lisa.

"Where are you going?" she asked, sleepily.

"Go back to sleep Julie. Nigel and I are just going to pick up Chase, okay?" she replied, her voice sounding much calmer than she felt. Her heart was racing, her hands sweaty and shaking.

"What time is it?" Julie asked.

"It's late, Julie. Go back to sleep," she said softly and left the room.

Nigel was at the door waiting and they hurried out to his car. Both were in their own worlds as they drove toward Chase's apartment, neither saying a word.

Lisa looked over at Nigel. She could tell he was angry but she didn't care. She was going to see Chase and it excited her. She couldn't believe that she missed him. He'd only been gone an hour. And yet, she was afraid. Afraid of what was coming, of what would happen next. Who was in his apartment? Was it the Russians? If so, how had they found him so quickly? And what were they doing there? Everything was happening so fast. She needed to feel Chase's touch, the comfort of his presence.

As they approached the apartment building, still several blocks away, Lisa noticed something unusual. Two men sitting in a car parked at the side of the road. Normally she'd've thought nothing of it but it was almost three in the morning and right now she was hypersensitive to her surroundings.

She told Nigel and he looked in the rear view mirror and saw them too. He stored the information and told Lisa not to worry. But he silently cursed himself under his breath. How could he have missed that? He felt he wasn't at the top of his game and that scared him a little. As a cop he knew it was important to be mentally and physically ready. That was especially true if there was any possibility you'd be confronting bad guys. He knew from his training that all too often a cop died because he wasn't mentally sharp. Being aware of your surroundings was necessary if you planned to survive.

Chase told them to meet at the park. It was a block from his apartment but Nigel wanted to get an idea of what they'd be up against so he drove by the building. He slowed the car as they passed but not too much. He did not want to alert anyone who might be watching as he had a quick look around. Unfortunately, there was nothing to see so he continued toward the park.

"What the hell are you doing?" he demanded, as he saw Lisa standing beside the car with Nigel.

"I came to help, Chase," she said sheepishly, knowing from the tone of his voice he was angry. "Besides, I just couldn't sit in the apartment waiting."

He turned to Nigel.

"I can't believe you would bring her here. Are you out of your mind?"

"I'm sorry Chase. But have you any idea how persuasive she is?" he said and smiled at him.

He didn't answer but he sure understood. He turned back to Lisa and told her she would have to stay with the car. He told them how he discovered the tape but had no idea whether there was somebody in the apartment or not.

Before he could finish Nigel interrupted him.

"Listen, Chase, there were a couple of guys sitting in a car about five or six blocks back. Lisa noticed them before I did so I only got a look at them from the rear view mirror. Is there any possibility that these guys had been in your apartment and were waiting for you?"

Chase thought for a moment then asked Nigel to describe the car.

"Nigel, that sounds like the same car I passed as I was coming out here tonight," he said, feeling agitated. "But they were a long way from the apartment," he said out loud, but it was as though he were talking to himself.

"What do you mean?" Lisa asked, confused.

He explained that normally, when following someone, you had to be in sight of them, otherwise there was always a risk of losing them. But these guys had been several blocks away and out of sight on both occasions, yet still managed to follow him. Chase told them he had been extra vigilant on the way over here after seeing them. There was no way he could have missed them if they'd been on his tail. Something was fishy. He wasn't sure what, but for now there were other fish he had to fry.

He turned to Nigel.

"I don't know what those two guys are up to, but I think we should assume there's someone else in my apartment."

He had a feeling it was that Russian he'd tangled with at the restaurant earlier. He wasn't sure why but the feeling was strong. Somehow they were always one step ahead of him. His mind was racing. What should they do? Wait them out or storm into the apartment. He was cursing himself for not noticing whether any lights were on as he'd driven up to the apartment. Once he'd realized there was a trespasser he'd checked out the apartment from the street and saw no light emanating from the apartment. Still, he couldn't be sure. They could have seen or heard him as he drove into the parking lot and turned off the lights. They could have been there hours ago. There was just no way to know. If they sat and waited until daylight they were wasting valuable time. He smiled. Once again an idea popped into his head.

In the apartment Goren was sweating bullets. Where the fuck was this guy? They'd been waiting almost thirty minutes. Had he made them? Were they in the right apartment? They had to be, there were pictures of this guy everywhere. What the hell was happening? Something was wrong.

Twice, Vasily had threatened to get up and leave, and it had taken all of Goren's strength not to take out his gun and just shoot the idiot. Why had he brought this jerk into this? His plan was not going well and Goren was wishing he could just go home to Russia, get that prick Vladi out of his life, and start over. He just knew if he screwed this up Vladi would kill him.

Then he heard the car. There was no mistaking the sound of that engine. It was the red Mustang. He scurried to the window and as he peered over the sill he saw the car leaving the parking lot. It didn't make sense but it was headed back down the street the same way it had come.

He breathed a sigh of relief, got up and went to the door switching on the light as he moved back to the living room.

"What the hell are you doing?" screamed Vasily, as Goren turned on the floor lamp in the living room.

"Don't worry," Goren said calmly. "He's gone. I just saw the Mustang drive away."

"Are you sure?" asked Vasily.

"I'm sure," he insisted. "Let's get back to work."

Vasily got up from his crouched position and put the bat down on the floor. As he moved into the hallway, there was a loud bang at the front door of the apartment. Without warning the door crashed open and two men rushed in.

Vasily stood there stunned. He turned to see where Goren was and felt the rush of air as the men entered the apartment. Then they split up and dove to the floor. Vasily heard a thunderous boom, but before he could grasp the origin of the blast, his world went black. Vasily was dead! His body flew through the doorway and landed in the hallway. Thankfully, Vasily didn't know that half his head and most of his face were spread over the wall, some ten feet away.

~

Lisa turned into the park and was heading for the parking lot when her heart sank. She stopped the car. Just ahead she saw two men standing beside Nigel's car and then she heard gunshots. She thought the two men were shooting at her, so to protect herself she crouched behind the dashboard. Then she realized the shots were coming from the apartment.

"Oh my God," she screamed. She was frantic. Suddenly the two men were banging on her window, screaming at her to stop. She panicked, threw the car in reverse and gunned the engine. The car jerked back abruptly and the powerful engine revved, causing Lisa to lose control of the car. She tried desperately to regain control but it was too late. The torque of the steering wheel pulled her hand with such force, it broke her wrist, causing her to let go of the wheel. The car swerved and hit a huge oak tree at the edge of the park stopping with gut wrenching force. Inside the car, Lisa flew around the cabin like a rag doll. The force of the crash knocked her unconscious when her head hit the window. Lisa was thankfully unaware the car had come to rest on the edge of a deep ravine. The oak tree had prevented the car from careening more than a hundred feet to the bottom.

Chapter 12

Vladi groaned as he regained consciousness. For several seconds he had no idea where he was or what had happened. As he sat up he felt a dull ache at the back of his head and instinctively put his hand up. It was then he realized something was seriously wrong. He pulled his hand away when he felt the thick warm fluid oozing through his fingers and to his horror saw his hand covered in blood. Seeing the blood, he panicked and tried to get up. But when he got to his feet he became dizzy and staggered across the room, falling on the bed. As he lay there stunned he heard sirens coming toward the building and knew he had to get out of there. Shaking the cobwebs from his head, he grabbed a towel from the bathroom. He held it over the gash in his head, trying unsuccessfully to stem the bleeding, and headed for the door. He knew the hotel like the back of his hand and quickly made his way to the service elevator. In less than two minutes he found his car and was heading for the exit to the hotel's parking garage. As he pulled into the street he saw a police car and an ambulance pull up to the front entrance. His head pounded and his vision was blurry. As he pulled the towel away from his head he could see the blood. He needed medical attention and quickly. Luckily for him he knew just the man to see.

~

In the confusion, Goren had fired two more shots wildly as he ran out of the apartment and escaped down the hall. As he passed the first apartment an older woman stuck her head out of her apartment. She turned and saw a man running away but when she turned back and saw the bloody mess oozing down the wall she screamed! Goren ignored the old lady and within seconds he was on the main floor, heading for the exit. In the distance sirens were wailing so he crossed the parking lot and clamored down a slope leading to a wide ravine that ran along the edge of the park. He hid in the bushes and waited for his chance to escape.

~

Nigel landed hard on his shoulder and it disoriented him. Chase got up quickly and was going to give first aid to the shooting victim when he saw the damage. He could do nothing for this guy. He looked across the hallway and saw the blood and brain matter oozing down the wall.

As they were about to take stock of the apartment they heard the Mustang's engine roar. Then heard the crunch of metal and shattering glass. It was Lisa! Chase ran to the stairs and took them three at a time. He was on the first floor in seconds. But when he got to the rear exit he hesitated. About thirty yards away he saw two men running towards him. And they had guns! He turned and called out to his buddy.

"Nigel!" he screamed. "There's someone coming! And they've got guns!"

He told him to hurry and ran down the hallway. As Chase hurried to the front entrance Nigel moved in right behind him and they left out the front door, moving around to the side of the building. They stood and watched as the two men sprinted toward the rear entrance. When they got to the door one man took aim at the lock on the door and fired. He kicked at the door and it held for just a moment before giving way to their assault. As soon as the two men rushed through the door Chase and Nigel made a beeline to Chase's cherry red Mustang.

Matt Hanson looked at his watch. It was two in the morning and he wondered who was calling at this late hour. Then it dawned on him and he scampered to the den and snatched up the phone.

"Hello?"

"Yeah, Mr. Hanson, it's agent McVittee. We've got a problem and I think you better get out here."

"What the hell's the problem McVittee?" asked Matt, with a slight note of impatience in his voice. He was suddenly anxious. He knew McVittee and his partner had been following Chase Adams.

"Well sir, there's been some gunfire and we've got a dead body."

Matt sat straight up in his chair.

"Who is it?" Matt asked. "Is it Adams?"

He was frantic.

"Well sir, that's just it. We can't tell because half his face is gone."

He was about to continue when Matt interrupted.

"What the hell happened?" he demanded.

"Well sir, we're not sure. It seems once the shooting stopped everyone involved boogied," explained the agent. "And when we entered the apartment we found this dead guy. We've secured the building and called off the local cops," he explained, adding the superintendent of the building had called the police and was being belligerent.

"Where are you?" asked Hanson.

"Well sir, we're at Chase Adams place. It's located at…."

McVittee was getting on Matt's nerves so he dismissed him impatiently, saying he knew where the apartment was.

"I'll be right there," he said and he hung up the phone. He hurried to the bedroom to put some clothes on.

~

"Nigel!" Chase cried, as he pointed to the large oak tree at the far end of the park. Running flat-out, Chase got to the car first. He was frantic, desperately trying to open the passenger door of the demolished Mustang. Nigel could see the car wrapped around the oak tree like a big red ribbon. He watched Chase struggling with the door and ran over to help. They both pulled on the door and it slowly gave way, the metal screeching as it opened. Chase scrambled inside and felt relief as he touched her neck and detected a faint pulse. She had a deep gash near her temple, oozing blood. It didn't appear too serious. What did appear serious was the bone protruding through the skin of her forearm. The break had obviously severed an artery and she was bleeding heavily from that wound. It was clear she was losing blood rapidly. They needed to stop the bleeding and get her to a hospital, fast.

"Nigel, go get your first aid kit from the car. She's bleeding badly. Please hurry!" he yelled over his shoulder. Knowing he needed to act quickly Chase dragged Lisa from the car and laid her on the grass. Nigel came back with the kit and quickly applied a pressure bandage to the wound. As Chase gave Lisa first aid Nigel ran back to his car and parked it beside Chase and Lisa.

"Let's get her to a hospital Nigel," Chase shouted. "Quickly," he pleaded, hoping they got to her in time.

Chase sat in the backseat cradling Lisa in his arms. She was still unconscious and her breathing was shallow. She looked so tiny and frail lying in his arms and for the first time in his life, Chase was afraid. At that moment another first occurred. Chase Adams prayed. He prayed God would spare the life of this beautiful young woman. He pleaded with this entity, one he'd given no thought to, and promised, that if God spared her life, he would devote his life to her.

"Chase, we're here," Nigel said as he pulled up at the emergency entrance. He ran in to get an orderly, explaining they had a seriously injured woman in the car. They hurried out with a gurney and rushed Lisa into an emergency room. There, a team of doctors and nurses began their work. Through the glass doors Chase could see them working feverishly to save Lisa's life. He closed his eyes and made a final plea.

~

"What happened?" he screamed, looking down at the dead man with half a face.

"Well sir, we not sure," Agent McVittee said, feeling a little apprehensive.

"What do you mean you're not sure?" Matt Hanson was at the end of his rope and was about to snap.

"Well sir,"

Matt put his hands up, causing the agent to stop talking.

"Listen McVittee, if you say 'Well sir' to me one more time I'm going to blow half *your* face off. You got that?"

"Yes sir," replied McVittee, now more than a little worried. His boss was acting very strange at this point and he decided to tread lightly. He was about to say 'Well sir', out of habit, when he bit his tongue and told Matt how he and his partner had followed Adams back to his apartment. Since the tracker was on the Mustang, they'd stayed out of sight. Their position was several blocks away. Shortly after settling in, he guessed about forty minutes, they saw a guy and a girl drive by heading toward the apartment. It was then they moved to a position closer to the apartment remaining undetected. At this point they were about a fifty yards from the building. Once they were in their new location they noticed Adam's Mustang leaving the parking lot and they followed it. They watched as the car drove into the park and stopped next to another car. It was the one they had seen drive by earlier. They got out of their car and were slowly approaching the Mustang when they heard gunshots. Not knowing what was happening, they ran from the gunfire toward the parked cars looking for cover. As they moved closer they saw a woman sitting in the driver's seat of the Mustang. A look of panic came across her face and she abruptly jammed the car into reverse, gunning the engine. The two detectives watched, horrified, as the car lurched across the grass. The driver lost control and slammed it into a tree. They were moving toward the Mustang when suddenly, they heard more gunshots and a bone chilling scream. It was coming from the apartment building.

"Sir, at that point we decided to head toward the gunshots and the scream," explained McVittee. "We thought there might be innocent lives in danger."

When they got to the apartment the gunfire had stopped and everything was quiet. Still, they approached the apartment with caution, unsure whether anyone was still inside. As they made their way down the hallway they saw the apartment door wide open and could smell gunpowder in the air. There was also a huge hole in the wall across from the open door with blood and brain matter dripping down the wall. Then someone looked out from behind an apartment door and McVittee almost shot before realizing it was an old lady. The woman almost let her curiosity do to her what it does to a cat. He quickly motioned for her to get back inside and the two agents made their way slowly toward the apartment. Just inside the entrance lay the body they were now standing over.

"We've checked through the entire apartment and it's empty," explained McVittee.

Hanson stood there thinking. Who the hell was this person on the floor? He was sure it wasn't Adams. The build was all wrong. So was the hair color. Could he be one of the Russians? With just half a face to go by he just couldn't be sure.

"Alright," he said. "Let's get this guy to the morgue and try and figure out who the hell he is."

He glanced around the room.

"I want the entire apartment fingerprinted and I want to know who, besides Chase Adams, has been here. You got that?"

He glared at McVittee as he said this and then left the apartment.

"Sir, Sir!" yelled McVittee as he ran after Matt, who stopped abruptly causing McVittee to bump into the back of him.

"What is it, McVittee?" he asked impatiently.

"Sorry sir," he apologized. "What do you want us to do about the building super, sir? He's been threatening to call the papers since we called off the cops. He doesn't believe we're the FBI, sir."

"I'll have a talk with him. Where is he?"

McVittee told him he was in 101 and went back to his duties.

Matt stood there staring at the numbers on the door. His blood was boiling. He took a deep breath and counted to ten. With a heavy sigh he rapped on the door and waited. No answer. He waited patiently and then knocked a second time. Through the door he could hear footsteps and someone mumbling something about keeping his shirt on.

The door opened with a rush and a gruff looking fat man stood in the doorway wearing a torn t-shirt and a pair of baggy jeans.

"Who the hell are you?" he demanded.

Matt was about to say 'Well, sir' when he caught himself and cursed under his breath.

Instead he pulled out his I.D. and showed it to him.

"I'm Matt Hanson of the FBI, sir. Who are you?"

The fat man looked at his badge and then at him, his head cocked to one side.

"None of your business," he said. "It's late and I'm tired."

He was about to close the door when Matt stuck his foot out, grabbed him by his dirty, torn tee and shoved him into the apartment. The man became angry and protested. He went to grab Matt's arm but in one swift motion Matt grabbed the man with one hand and shoved him against the wall. Simultaneously he pulled out his gun with the other and roughly placed the barrel under the man's chin.

"Now listen closely, mister, because I'm not going to ask again" said Matt, fed up with this prick. "Who, in the hell, are you?" and shoved the gun a little further into his chin.

The man grimaced, the look of defiance leaving his face altogether. The look now was one of fear.

"I'm the building superintendent," he spat. "My name is Dolinski, Gus Dolinski"

Matt relaxed his grip slightly.

"Well Gus, I understand you've been threatening to call the newspaper about what's happened here tonight, is that right?" asked Matt.

Gus was a little less frightened now and a lot less defiant.

"No sir, I ain't gonna say nothin' to nobody," Gus promised.

"Well that's good Gus, because I want you to understand something, okay?"

Gus tried to nod but the gun at his chin prevented him from doing so.

"This is an official FBI investigation Mr. Dolinski and I want no interference from you or anyone else."

Matt released the man and shoved him into a nearby chair.

"Do you understand?"

Mr. Dolinski nodded his head vigorously, assuring Matt he would keep quiet.

"Good. Now I suggest you get some sleep. It's getting late" said Matt as he turned and left the apartment.

Walking to his car Matt was deep in thought. He'd lost the two men he wanted to have in the same place at the same time. Vladi Cherkov, who had disappeared off the face of the earth and Chase Adams. And while he was sure the dead man found in the apartment was not Chase Adams, he had disappeared too. Stephan would not be happy, and an unhappy Stephan was a dangerous Stephan. Matt felt he needed to act, so as he opened the car door he pulled out his cell phone and dialed the number Chase had given him. He closed his eyes and crossed his fingers, hoping Adams would answer.

~

The shrill tone of his cell phone startled him as he sat there waiting for word on Lisa's condition. It took a moment to figure out where the harsh noise was coming from but when he realized, he pulled out the phone and stared at the call display. It was a number he didn't recognize. He was about to answer when a stocky black nurse snatched the phone from his hand.

"Mister, ain't no cell phones allowed in here, understood?" she said as she turned it off and pocketed the phone.

"Excuse me miss, but that's my phone," said a surprised Adams. "Could I please have it back?"

"No sir, you may not," the nurse replied.

As she walked away she called over her shoulder.

"When you're ready to leave, sir, y'all just ask for me. My name is Swanson. I'll give you back your phone then, got that?"

"Yes ma'am," he replied, with just a hint of sarcasm. Chase sighed heavily. He was in no mood to fight with anyone, least of all some crazy militant nurse. He glanced at his watch again. The sun would be coming up in less than an hour. The doctors had been working on Lisa for a long time. A nurse, not the crazy black one, came up to Chase and asked him to follow her. He fell in silently behind her as she led him to a large corner office. Sitting behind a desk was an older gentleman that Chase assumed was a doctor. The man motioned for him to take a seat in a chair in front of a large steel desk. Chase took little notice of the drab surroundings he now found himself in. The gray walls were bare, except for a diploma hanging above the doctor's head. There was one small window in the room but the thick steel blue curtains kept the light that shined on the outside world from coming in. The floor was cold, making the room feel like it was part of the hospital morgue, but he was oblivious. He sat there staring at the man with the grave look on his face. The man introduced himself as Dr. Morrison. He told Chase that Lisa had lost a lot of blood and suffered a severe head injury. He told Chase the team had done all they could and was about to continue when Chase dropped his head. He put his face in his hands and sobbed. The doctor suddenly realized what he'd done and quickly continued.

"Mr. Adams, Mr. Adams!" the doctor raising his voice to gain his attention. "Lisa is still alive Mr. Adams! Do you hear me, Lisa is alive."

Chase lifted his head, staring into the doctor's eyes with a look of relief. He stood up and began pacing the room. Once the doctor had his attention, he elaborated on Lisa's condition.

"She is, however, in critical condition and not out of the woods yet."

He paused, and took a deep breath.

"Please Mr. Adams, take a seat. Let me explain."

Chase too, took a deep breath and sighed. He suddenly felt euphoric.

"May I see her," he asked, his heart racing.

The doctor told Chase there were no visitors allowed while she was in intensive care and she was under sedation.

"We are doing everything we can to ensure a full recovery, Mr. Adams," assured the doctor. The doctor explained there was swelling on Lisa's brain due to a severe blow. Coupled with the blood loss, Lisa had experienced significant blood depletion to the brain. The effect of this meant there was a chance of brain damage.

"What does that mean?" he asked, his fists clenching and his heart still beating rapidly.

The doctor explained the tests showed the brain functioning fine but until she awoke they couldn't be sure.

"There is not much you can test for when a patient is unconscious," he explained. "So for us to be sure we need to have her awake."

"When will that be?" Chase asked anxiously.

"Because of the severe swelling, we've put Lisa into an induced comatose state and it's going be at least twenty four hours before we can safely take her off life support and revive her. It is a tricky procedure and I need to be honest with you Mr. Adams, it's also dangerous. Unfortunately it was the only alternative that gave us a chance at saving her."

The doctor's phone rang. He held up a finger to Chase, which he took as a signal to sit tight. He watched as the doctor listened intently to the voice on the other end of the line. After a few minutes the doctor hung up and looked at Chase suspiciously. He stood up and walked to the door. As he opened it Chase turned and looked to see who was there. As the figure moved out of the shadows cast by the doorframe he couldn't believe his eyes. This was the last person he expected to see.

"Hello Chase," said the voice at the door.

"Hello," he replied. "What the hell are you doing here?"

"We need to talk, Mr. Adams," said the voice. Standing in the doorway was Vincent J. Fontaine, Assistant Deputy Director of the FBI.

Chapter 13

Sweat dripped from his brow causing his eyes to sting, his breath coming in great gasps. His hands were shaking and his heart pounded. He couldn't believe what had just happened. He'd just blown his friend's head off with the gun he held in his hands. Not that Goren felt sorry he'd killed him. He didn't like Vasily anyway. He was just so shocked at how fast everything happened and at how stupid that idiot had been. Why had he jumped up at that moment? Goren had that P.I. in his sights and was about to blow him away when suddenly Vasily's head appeared. Then half of his head disappeared! All that brain matter flying everywhere. Goren shuddered at the memory.

Goren stood near the bottom of the ravine running along the parking lot next to the building where his friend lay dead. From his vantage he could see two dark blue sedans with their lights flashing. How had they arrived at the building so quickly? Just minutes after the shooting stopped. He caught his breath and the pounding in his chest subsided. Goren climbed the rise and looked around. He could see his car but he couldn't get to it. The police had surrounded the lot with yellow tape and an SUV was covering the exit.

"Shit," he muttered under his breath. The car could be traced back to him. He needed to plausibly explain how the car got there. Goren pulled out his cell phone and called 911.

When the operator answered Goren told a tale he hoped would get him out of this mess.

"Yes, I wish to report my car stolen," he said to the operator.

"Is this an emergency, sir?" asked the female voice on the other end of the line.

"Well no, I guess not, but I was not sure who to call," explained Goren. "I want to report a theft of a car."

"Sir, you need to call your district's precinct. Where was the car stolen?" she asked.

Goren gave her the address and she gave him the number of the precinct that would handle his complaint. He thanked her, hung up and dialed the number. He told the officer who answered what had happened. When the officer asked, Goren said he parked his car several hours before. He was at a friend's birthday party and couldn't remember the last time he saw the car. He only discovered it missing a few minutes ago, when he was ready to go home.

"That is why I am calling now, officer," explained Goren.

The officer sounded bored but took the information from Goren and told him that his car would be on the watch list today. He also told Goren not to hold his breath and to contact his insurance company in the morning.

"Most of the time they just take the parts from a car like yours," explained the cop. "So it's rare we recover 'em. I'm sorry sir but we'll do our best," he assured Goren.

"That is all I can ask, officer," he said, hanging up and feeling smug. He thought his story would be good enough to fool the cops and he knew he could always use a fallback position. If the police questioned why there was no evidence of forced entry he would just explain he'd forgotten his buddy Vasily borrowed the car. After all, Goren had been drinking heavily that night.

Now that Goren had taken care of that problem he headed back down into the ravine and followed the path leading away from the parking lot. He wasn't sure of the direction it was taking him, he only knew it was away from the cops and for now that was good enough. After traveling along the ravine's path for several minutes he noticed a car above him. From where he was it looked to be hanging over the edge of the steep ridge. He glanced around to see if there was anybody nearby. Seeing no one, he scrambled up the steep slope to take a look. As he got closer he recognized the car. It was the red Mustang owned by that private eye, Chase Adams. He wondered what the hell had happened. Struggling the last few feet up the slope, he pulled himself up by some thick roots dangling from the large oak tree just above him. When he reached the top he took another look around. There was no one there so he approached the car. From this angle he could see the damage to the car so he peeked inside. The Mustang was empty but there was blood on the seat and floor. It was obvious someone had suffered severe blood loss. Had he hit one of those jerks after all? He couldn't be certain. Then he remembered it had been someone else driving the Mustang away.

Who he wondered.

Suddenly an idea flashed into his brain. Someone bleeding that badly would need a hospital. So why not check the nearest hospital to see if he'd shot that prick Adams or his friend. He wasn't sure where the nearest hospital would be but knew a way to find out. He quickly left the park and flagged down a passing taxi.

"Take me to the nearest hospital," he said as he slid into the back of the cab. The cab driver looked back at Goren saying the nearest hospital was the Whitney Medical Center.

"Well then, what the fuck are you waiting for? Take me there, now" screamed Goren.

~

Matt stared at his phone and cursed. He tried the number again. He was positive he'd heard Chase saying hello on his first call, but before he could say a word, the phone went dead. Now all he kept hearing was that annoying recording telling him the cellular customer was not available. He desperately wanted to get in touch with Chase to find out where he was. He also had to be sure it was Chase's voice he'd heard earlier to confirm he was still alive. Matt was more than frustrated but the confirmation would wait.

He looked at his watch. It was too late to call Stephan and he'd been unable to track Vladi down. With all that had happened tonight he had to alter his plans. He told McVittee and his partner he was heading down to the park to check out the Mustang.

"Maybe I can find a clue or two there," he explained.

As he entered the park he saw a pair of taillights in the distance. Though he couldn't be sure, it appeared the car had a light on top. Was it a taxi? It had to be. He was too far away to see anyone getting in but he could see the interior light turn on and go out as the car drove away. Matt wondered who, other than himself, would be at the park this late. Was it a coincidence? He doubted it. He made a mental note to have McVittee check out taxi traffic. As he approached the car he could see it was in bad shape. He peered inside and saw all the blood caked on the seats and pooled on the floor. There was blood everywhere and Matt knew there was no way the woman could have escaped on her own. Matt thought there were two possibilities, the woman was dead or was at a nearby hospital. He immediately contacted McVittee on his cell phone.

"McVittee I want you to secure this car now and I want a crime scene unit here on the double, you got that?" he ordered. "And McVittee, I want you to find out what taxi company picked up a fare near the park in the last five minutes. When you get that information I want to know where they went. I also want to know if the Whitney Medical Center had any accident victims come in within the last hour. Get back to me as soon as you have any information."

He hung up the before McVittee could respond. Matt didn't want to hear another 'Well sir'. He was in a bad mood and knew he was getting no sleep for the rest of the night. He had a nagging hunch on his hospital idea and decided to head over there before McVittee did his digging.

⁓

Chase Adams sat in the cold office with its gray linoleum floors and big steel desk, thinking. What Fontaine had just told him was unbelievable and he was having trouble grasping it. Matt Hanson was dirty? Unbelievable! It just didn't jibe with the Matt Hanson he knew. Matt was a family man with a wonderful wife and a great career in law enforcement. There had to be an explanation for his betrayal. Could he be working the Russians from the inside and not telling the Bureau? Fontaine just looked at Chase and shook his head sadly. No, he'd replied. He wasn't sure how, but the Russians had something they were using to blackmail Matt. They also knew that one of the Russians, they weren't sure who, had threatened to harm Matt's family if he didn't cooperate. Fontaine explained that they'd had Matt under surveillance for some time now. He explained to Chase that about six months ago the Bureau suspected Matt had turned and put a tap on all his phones and a GPS tracker on his car.

"Why are you telling me all this?" he asked.

"Chase," he said, then paused a moment to organize his thoughts. Fontaine had a solemn look on his face and Chase could sense the weight of what he was about to hear. "Chase," he repeated, "Matt is going to use you. According to our intelligence there's been a shift in the Russian's organization and Matt plans to use you to remove one major player in the group. His name is

Vladi Cherkov. And we've been trying to build a case against him for the past two years. Unfortunately, we cannot put together enough evidence to get an indictment. We know, however, that Cherkov is one bad man. We also know that he holds a treasure trove of information on the Russian mob here in the United States.

"So what can I do?" asked Chase.

"Well, for now," Fontaine paused again and smiled. He was trying to break the tension so thick you could cut with a knife. "Just follow Matt's orders. Do whatever he says."

"Are you crazy?" cried Chase as he jumped out of his seat and walked to the window. He turned and pointed his finger at Fontaine. "I'm telling you now, I am not killing anyone. You got that? Not Vladi what his name or anyone else."

Fontaine stood up and walked over to the window and stood beside Chase. He told him he would not have to kill anyone and the Bureau would protect him. What was important was that Matt Hanson not learn the Bureau was on to him.

"I need you to act as if nothing is different. Follow his orders and just do as he says. Can you do that?"

Chase just kept looking out the window. The streets were quiet and he watched as two orderlies loaded someone into an awaiting ambulance. The men moved slowly to the front of the ambulance and drove away. Chase guessed there was no emergency because they drove off with no flashing lights or siren. For a moment he wondered who might be in the ambulance. Were they young or old, male or female? Perhaps they were dead and going to the morgue or a funeral home. Then he thought about Lisa, lying alone in the intensive care ward. She was so innocent and yet she'd been willing to put her life on the line. He also thought about Lisa's sister Julie and the other girl, Sonja. Their worlds' a living hell. He thought about the dead girl Julie had talked about and he thought about his own sister, dead because of bastards like this Vladi character. It was these Russians and others like them getting young kids hooked on drugs. Making them prostitute themselves to pay for their habits and causing them to die much too early in their young lives. Maybe he could make a difference. He turned and looked at Fontaine.

"Okay," he said, "what do I have to do?"

Fontaine repeated his instructions and reminded him that if he was with Hanson, Fontaine's team could hear him. He pulled a small microphone out of his pocket that was no larger than a dime and explained it was a transmitter. Fontaine took hold of Chase's belt buckle and placed the microphone behind it while Chase looked on, puzzled.

"Now we can record your movements and listen in on all your conversations. The buckle will effectively hide the transmitter if Matt somehow gets suspicious and runs a metal detector over you. Matt won't ask you to take off your belt and he'll assume it was the buckle that tripped the detector," he explained. "I will have a team within a mile of your location and if something goes wrong they'll be there in minutes."

Chase looked at him with a wry smile. He knew that minutes wouldn't cut it if they found out. He'd be dead in seconds.

Fontaine just shrugged knowing what that look meant.

"I'm sorry," he said, "it's the best I can do. If we get too close they'll spot the tail and we'll get nothing. We can't let Matt know. It will ruin everything."

Chase just looked at Fontaine as if to say 'I'm just a puppet to you, aren't I?'

He was angry and wanted to take it out on Fontaine but instead, all he said was, "how do I contact Matt?"

Fontaine smiled.

"You don't have to," he said. "He's on his way here right now." Fontaine glanced at his watch.

"He should be here in about twenty minutes," he said and looked up at Chase.

"What!" Chase screamed. He couldn't believe it. "You're kidding, right?"

"No Mr. Adams, I'm not," said Fontaine. "He's been one step behind you and knows about the shooting incident at your apartment. He's the lead investigator. He found your car and guessed with the blood loss at the scene, someone was in need of a doctor. At this point he's guessing, but he's on his way here to see if anyone came in with injuries consistent with a car wreck."

Fontaine turned and sat behind the large steel desk.

"So you see Chase, you need to get your head in the game right now. Can you do that?"

Chase turned and glared at Fontaine. The more time he spent in his presence the less he liked him.

"I'll be fine," he assured him. "I do have one problem though."

"What's that?" asked Fontaine.

"Well, it's my friend Nigel. He needs to get up to speed. I can't let him go into this blind or else he may screw it up," he explained.

"I've already dealt with that," said Fontaine.

Chase gave him a curious look.

"What do you mean?" he asked.

"What I mean is that your friend Nigel is in our care and is safe."

Fontaine held up his hand as he saw that Chase was about to protest.

"Chase you must understand this is for your own good. You're right about Nigel being a liability at this point," said Fontaine.

Chase was livid.

"I didn't say he was a liability at all," he argued, "in fact he could be an asset in the right circumstance. Besides, you can't just arrest him. He's a cop for Christ's sake."

"Well Chase, in fact we can. You see, since 9/11 the world has changed," he said then smiled. "And under our Homeland Security laws we can detain anyone as a suspected terrorist and there's nothing they can do. As we speak, your friend Nigel is on his way to a secure location for interrogation."

He paused, letting this information sink in and then continued.

"We've also taken care of his car," said Fontaine, and handed a set of keys to Chase. "Nigel won't be needing these anytime soon but when he does, he'll find his car at FBI headquarters. It's in our parking lot.

Fontaine smiled at Chase and continued to bring him up to speed on the whereabouts of his friends. He wanted to assure him the FBI was on his side.

"Chase, I want you to know that we have also secured your lady friend in the intensive care unit. I believe her name is Lisa. She's now under our protection," he explained. "We have a secure hospital nearby and we are taking good care of her."

Suddenly he rushed Fontaine and grabbed him by the front of his shirt.

"What the fuck do you think you're doing, you prick," he screamed, his face just inches away from the FBI man. "You lay a hand on Lisa and I swear I'll kill you, you bastard."

Suddenly out of nowhere and with the speed of a lightning bolt two men grabbed Chase. He resisted but the two men subdued him easily and placed him in a chair and held him securely.

"Mr. Adams, please relax," said Fontaine, straightening out his shirt. "I guarantee that no harm will come to her,' he said softly. "She's receiving the best care this country can provide. Our facility is world class so don't worry."

Chase just slumped in the chair knowing he could do nothing. He had only one choice. Cooperate with this bastard. At least for now.

"Chase, I want you to follow Matt Hanson's instructions and we'll figure out a way to get you out of this mess. Now, if you have no more objections, I suggest you get out of here and back to the waiting room. Matt should be arriving soon."

With that Fontaine got up and left the room with his two men, leaving Chase to organize his thoughts and prepare himself for the acting role of his life.

⁓

Goren decided it would be safer to make his way to the hospital by taking the final leg on foot. He'd asked the cabbie to drop him off a few blocks from the hospital. He was close to the emergency entrance when he stopped dead in his tracks. He was about a hundred yards from the entrance and hidden from view when he saw someone walking toward the doors. He was at an angle that put his face in profile. The sun was over the horizon but it was dark and there was a mist in the air. He couldn't see the man's face clearly. Goren was about to walk out into the open when he heard a voice call out. Suddenly the man, whose face he couldn't see, turned around and looked toward the main entrance as another man approached. As he turned, his face came into plain view and to Goren's disbelief he saw Matt Hanson standing there. What the hell was he doing here? He watched as the two men conversed for a brief time and then parted ways. Matt Hanson continued through the emergency entrance while the other man returned to the car waiting for him.

Goren waited about five minutes and then made his way toward the entrance. He peered through the glass doors, careful not to let anyone inside see him. From where he stood he could see no one in the hall or in any of the rooms alongside. He would have to take a calculated risk and enter the building if he was to have any chance of finding out what Hanson was up to. As he entered the wide hallway he could see a large opening to his left that led to a waiting room. In front of him, about fifty feet away, was a set of glass doors and to his right just past the waiting room was a nurse's station. He continued down the hall keeping his head down. Looking out of the corner of his eye he could see there were several people sitting in chairs in the large room. Out of the corner of his eye he saw Matt Hanson talking to another man. He was about to turn into the room and confront Hanson when he realized the man he was standing beside was Chase Adams! Without missing a step he turned on his heels and headed straight down the hallway toward the nurse's station. Neither man looked his way.

Dam, thought Goren. Adams must be with the FBI!

"Sir, can I help you?" shouted a nurse as he passed her station. Goren just ignored her and kept walking. He wanted to stay hidden so he kept moving toward the set of double doors just ahead of him. He kept his head down and picked up his pace.

"Sir," shouted the nurse as she walked after him. "Sir, you can't go in there." The nurse continued to run after him shouting. Goren hurried through the doors desperately looking for a way out. After only a few more steps he realized there was no way out. The hallway led to three glassed-in treatment rooms, which were empty. It was a dead end. The nurse was right behind him and was not about to back down. She was still shouting, trying to gain someone's attention, someone that might help.

"What the hell's going on?" asked Chase and looked down the hall. He saw the nurse bolt through the set of double doors and then noticed a tall man standing at the end of the hall, inside the double doors. He couldn't make out the face but there was something familiar about him. He watched as the nurse approached the man. From her actions Chase could see she was chastising him. The man stood there for a moment and it seemed as though he was about to follow the nurse back when he suddenly grabbed her around the neck and violently snapped her head sideways. The nurse just slumped in his arms and, as he let her go, she dropped to the floor.

"What the hell?" Chase shouted.

Matt had followed Chase to the hallway and when he saw what was happening he quickly went into action and ran to the cover of the nurse's station. Chase couldn't believe what he was seeing. He raced toward the man, ran right by Matt, and burst through the double doors.

"Chase, wait!" shouted Matt, but he ignored his order. Chase immediately recognized the man as he moved closer. It was the Russian! The one at the restaurant, the one who'd been looking for Sonja. What the hell was he doing here? How had he found them? His mind raced as he quickly closed the gap between him and the Russian. In seconds he was on him and when just a few feet away he leaped through the air and threw an old fashioned cross block. Chase hit the man with such force it propelled both back into the glass wall of one of the treatment rooms. This time Goren was not going to allow Adams to get the best of him. As they hit the ground he rolled over to his left and threw his leg up in a kicking motion, connecting with Adam's shoulder and knocking him back to the floor. With this maneuver Goren created just enough space between them to allow him to make his next move. Chase watched in horror as the Russian pulled out his gun and took dead aim. He closed his eyes and braced for what was coming! Then he heard the shot.

He wondered what happened. How could he still be alive? Instead of having everything go dark, he watched as the Russian dropped his pistol and slumped to the floor, a big red stain forming in the center of the man's chest. Chase turned around quickly and saw Matt Hanson holding his revolver in the firing position, the gun still smoking.

Chase scrambled to his feet and ran to the nurse. He placed a hand on her neck and detected no pulse. She was dead. Then he turned his attention to the Russian but he didn't have to touch him to know he was dead. A large pool of blood was forming beneath him and Chase's immediate reaction was anger.

"What did you do?" he screamed. "Why did you kill him, for Christ sakes?"

He was desperate to know what the man had been doing there. Why he'd been following him earlier? And how had he discovered them in the restaurant? He had many questions but now there would be no answers, thanks to Matt Hanson.

How convenient, he thought.

Matt couldn't believe the reaction.

"He was about to kill you Chase," said Matt defensively. "I had to take him out."

145

Chase didn't believe him and they argued. Matt couldn't understand why Chase would be angry at saving his life. Finally, he just threw his hands in the air and walked away.

"You'd think you'd be grateful to me for saving your life," he said over his shoulder.

Then Matt quickly turned around and faced him. Using an accusatory tone he asked harshly, "What is it Chase? Do you think I had some other motive to kill that bastard?" He ran toward Chase and confronted him. "Well, do you? You think I've got some other agenda, is that it?"

Chase immediately reversed his position, worried that he might somehow tip Matt off to what he knew.

"No Matt," he said. "Listen man, I'm sorry." He placed a hand on his shoulder. "I guess I was angry because I wanted to talk to the guy, okay? I wanted to find out what he knew," he explained.

Matt walked away unconvinced. Chase rushed past him and stood in front of him. He felt his explanation had to be credible.

"Matt," he said as he stood in his path, stopping him in his tracks. "Listen to me, please."

Chase shook his head and then he looked Matt straight in the eyes. "This is the guy who was following me earlier today. I also tussled with him in a restaurant tonight and now this. I can't prove it but I bet this was the guy who was at my apartment. I'm frustrated, that's all. I just want some answers."

Chase paused and looked down at his feet.

"You're right Matt. I know that you saved my life and I'm grateful. Thanks man."

Matt smiled and put a hand on Chase's shoulder.

"It's okay Chase. I understand," he said and moved past him. "Let's get the area secure and get you some answers."

Chapter 14

"We're sorry," was all he needed to hear. He'd heard the same recording for the umpteenth time. He hung up the phone and swore loudly. Vladi had been trying to reach Goren for the last two hours but he was not answering. After Dr. Tupolev had stitched him up, Vladi had taken refuge at a safe house he owned on the lake. Tupolev provided a nurse who would care for him for a few days while he convalesced. Dr. Tupolev knew he could count on her to be discreet. She'd arrived this morning.

The sun was up and there were a few wispy clouds in the sky. It was a beautiful morning and there was a light breeze coming off the water. It made the deck a comfortable place to sit. But Vladi wasn't paying any attention to the weather. He was too busy fretting. Where the hell could everyone be? Surely Goren would have found Sonja by now. And what about that damn detective Goren was talking about? Where the hell was he? He thought about contacting Stephan but dismissed the idea. He wanted to know a little more before he talked with him. It was better to have answers when you talked with Stephan because he was an inquisitive man.

His business was falling apart and all his luck was turning out bad. What else could possibly go wrong?

As he fretted the attractive nurse walked through the patio doors. She was wearing a crisp white uniform that clung tightly to her body. She had long blonde hair, a smooth bronze complexion and her bright blue eyes sparkled as she smiled at Vladi.

"Mr. Cherkov, it's time to change the dressing on that wound," she said as she turned to the portable medicine cabinet standing against the outside brick wall. Vladi was lying comfortably on a large wooden lounge chair in a reclined position with several pillows under his head for support. He smiled, feeling his blood flow as he became aroused by her gentle touch. In reaction he reached out and ran his hand along her tanned thigh. She turned to him and smiled.

"Mr. Cherkov, my name is Vivian and Dr. Tupolev has asked me to take care of you while you recuperate."

He could feel her hands as she held his head forward so she could inspect the dressing. They were soft and gentle and Vladi was becoming increasingly aroused. He relaxed and enjoyed the touch of this beautiful nurse.

Then she took hold of one corner of the bandage and abruptly jerked it from his flesh. Vladi screamed and his hands reached for his head in reaction to the intense pain. Vivian grabbed his arms at the wrist and held them down until the pain subsided.

"I'm sorry Mr. Cherkov, did that hurt?" she asked, frowning. Her tone of voice told Vladi she didn't care.

"Shit, you fucking bitch," he whispered harshly, out of breath from the shock. "What the fuck are you doing?"

Vivian gave him a look of disgust.

"Well Mr. Cherkov if you don't want that to happen again I suggest you remember what I am about to say," she said.

Then she tossed the old bandage into a plastic container, noticing the massive clump of her patient's hair sticking to it. Then looked at him in disgust and spat contemptuously.

"I'm your nurse. Not your whore!"

With that Vivian stood up and walked to the cabinet and pulled out a bottle. Vladi watched her suspiciously as she poured some of the liquid from the bottle onto a large cotton swab. She moved back toward him.

"This is going to sting Mr. Cherkov. I'm sorry but there is nothing I can do about it," she warned and began to tenderly dab the swab around the wound. Vladi winced but this time he held his tongue. He could feel the wound still oozing blood and it was still tender. He rolled over on his side and closed his eyes as the nurse finished redressing the wound. When she finished Vivian gave him a stern look and warned him again.

"Mr. Cherkov, I'll admit Dr. Tupolev is paying me handsomely, but my job is to provide you with medical care and nothing else. Do you understand?" she asked.

Vladi just nodded.

She smiled.

"Good. Then I think we'll get along nicely," she said and re-entered the apartment.

Well there you go, thought Vladi, gently laying his head back.

My luck is finally changing, he thought.

"It's just gotten worse," he said out loud.

His name was Goren ………and though Matt already knew this he allowed McVittee to give his report without interruption. It was noon and none of the men looking into the shooting had slept yet. McVittee and his partner, Jeb Stevens, sat opposite Matt in his small office and were going over the facts they'd gathered so far. There was a connection between Vasily, the dead guy in Adam's apartment and Goren, the man shot in the hospital. They just didn't know that connection. They did not understand why these guys had been in the apartment and Chase wasn't volunteering any information. He was in a safe house across town and was getting some much needed sleep. They would question him later. McVittee also explained that he'd been unable to find out anything about the woman he'd seen driving the Mustang in the park. She was gone, having vanished from the face of the earth.

"How is that possible?" demanded Hanson.

"Well sir," said McVittee, "I just don't know. There is no record of her admission to that hospital, or any hospital in the city."

"Well then, what the hell was Chase Adams doing there?" he asked. "Did he explain that at least?"

"Well sir," said McVittee, pausing. He knew he was on thin ice. "We didn't ask that question so I don't know," he admitted reluctantly and scribbled something on his notepad.

"Well sir," Matt sneered, his voice thick with sarcasm. "What the hell do you know?" he asked angrily. "Go find her, and don't come back until you do. She has to be somewhere," he bellowed and waved them away with his hand.

Both men quickly left the room without saying a word.

Matt sat there for a moment trying to regain his wits. How had these two ever made it through the Academy? He just shook his head and laughed. He came back to reality when the phone rang. Who the hell could that be?

"Hello?"

It was Fontaine.

"Well sir," he answered and grimaced, realizing he sounded exactly like McVittee. "I just finished a briefing with McVittee and Stevens," he continued, then stopped as Fontaine interrupted him and asked another question.

"No sir, they don't have any idea where she might be," he explained, becoming a little defensive. "I'll be right up sir," he said and hung up the phone.

Fontaine was standing by the window looking out over the water when Matt entered. He turned and motioned for Matt to take a seat.

Matt watched as his immediate superior moved nimbly to his comfy leather chair. He had never noticed how Fontaine could move so effortlessly. But now, watching him, he became aware of how muscular his physique was beneath his finely tailored white shirt. He'd always admired his boss's intellect but had never taken stock of his physical characteristics. For a man of his age he looked remarkably fit.

"Listen Matt," he said, picking up a file from his desk. "There are a few developments I need to update you on. First we received a strange police report this morning. It seems a man came into Whitney Medical early this morning with a head injury. He was treated and the doctors released him before the police arrived."

Matt looked at him, puzzled.

"Okay, so why are you telling me this?" he asked, clearly frustrated.

"Well, because the man was Russian," Fontaine replied, tossing the file across his desk.

Matt picked up the file and his heart pounded. He could feel the sweat trickle down his bicep and form a wet spot in the crook of his arm. On the front, secured by a blue paper clip was a picture of Vladi Cherkov.

"You recognize him Matt?" he asked.

"Of course," said Matt, trying to stay composed. "It's Vladi Cherkov," he said as he looked up from the file. "Was he the victim or the suspect?" Matt said and laughed nervously.

Fontaine stared at him for just a moment too long it seemed. Matt was wary. Was he being paranoid? Or did Fontaine suspect something? Matt felt his collar dampen.

"From the description we got it would appear he's our victim," said Fontaine and continued his briefing.

Fontaine explained that according to a duty nurse, Vladi, or someone who looked a lot like him, had come into the hospital with a severe head injury. He had asked to see Dr. Tupolev and when the nurse told him to sit he pulled out a gun and pushed her down the hall to the doctor's office. The nurse was eventually able to leave the room and immediately called the police. But when they got there he was gone.

Matt's jaw dropped as he listened.

"How the hell could that happen?" he asked.

Fontaine smiled.

"We don't know yet but as you can see by the doctor's name, he was also Russian. We're holding the doctor and we want you to question him. He's been uncooperative so far," Fontaine explained, and then suddenly paused. Matt watched as his boss tapped his fingers on the oak surface of his desk, thinking. He noticed Fontaine eyeing him carefully as if appraising him and saying nothing. To Matt, the silence was deafening. So quiet he could almost hear his heart pounding. The tension mounted as the seconds slowly ticked by. Matt could feel beads of sweat forming on his forehead. What was Fontaine doing?

Finally, after what seemed an eternity, Fontaine spoke.

"I want you to interrogate this doctor Matt. It's critical we find Cherkov and bring him in, alive. The Russians are going through a power struggle and Vladi could be a casualty. We also think he could be valuable to us in bringing these people down. If we can turn him."

Fontaine paused again and Matt felt certain that Fontaine was assessing his reaction. Was he onto him? Could the Bureau have discovered his betrayal? He'd been so careful. Besides, why would they give him this assignment if they knew? Wouldn't they just toss him in a cell and throw away the key? He decided he was just being paranoid. The stress of being up all night was getting to him.

"So where do I find this doctor," he asked, getting up from his chair.

"He's in the tombs Matt," said Fontaine and picked up his phone. "I'll arrange for clearance so you can start right away."

As he hung up, he stood and walked Matt to the door. Fontaine stopped at the opening and placed his hand on the doorframe trying to look relaxed.

"Matt, I want results on this. This is important and I want a report by the end of the day. Can you handle that?" he asked.

"Don't worry sir," he replied, feeling a sense of relief. "You'll have a full report by this afternoon."

"I knew I could count on you Matt," Fontaine said and he clapped his hand on Matt's shoulder. "I have another development as well."

He explained he had taken Chase's girlfriend Lisa out of Whitney Memorial and transported her to the medical facility in the FBI building nearby.

He also had any reports about her removed from the hospital's records.

"Matt, we also secured Chase's friend Nigel and two other unidentified women in the tombs," said Fontaine. "Once you've had a chance to interrogate the doctor and provide me with a report I want you to speak with the two women and find out who they are."

At the mention of the two women Matt stifled a smile. He knew who they were and keeping Fontaine in the dark might just work to Matt's advantage.

"I'll take care of Nigel," said Fontaine.

Then he ushered Matt out of his office.

"And Matt?

"Yes sir?"

"Mr. Adams knows we have detained his friend Nigel but please don't say anything about the two young women. Let's keep that our little secret."

Matt nodded his head and gave a conspiring wink as Fontaine dismissed him and stood in the doorway until Matt disappeared from view.

Fontaine smiled as he turned back into his office. He knew he'd given Matt something to think about. He hoped it would keep him off balance. While it had been some time since he'd been in the field he hadn't lost his touch. He was certain he had spooked Matt just enough. He desperately needed to keep him walking the tightrope he was on. It was the only way to control him. And control would be his greatest ally, at least for now.

Chapter 15

Nigel paced the floor. He had no idea how long he'd been here or where here was. He'd looked over every square inch of the windowless, nondescript square room and found no clues that would tell him where he was. It had gray carpet and walls the color of steel blue. If he'd had to guess he'd have said he was in a police interrogation room, but that just wasn't possible. He was a cop.

All he could remember was leaving the hospital cafeteria. He'd been on his way back to the waiting room to tell Chase about the two detectives he'd seen there. He'd overheard that some Russian had come into the hospital seeking treatment for a head wound. It seemed the victim was in a doctor's office and they were waiting to confirm his identity. Nigel was positive they'd mentioned the name Vladi Cherkov so he'd hurried out, eager to tell Chase. When he ran out of the cafeteria someone grabbed him. Two strong arms held him as a third placed a rag over his mouth and nose. He'd passed out in seconds.

From that point on, everything was a blank. That is until he awoke on the cot in the corner of the room where he was now. They'd taken his watch, his clothes, even his shoes and replaced them all with a pair of orange overalls and some soft soled slippers.

He punched a fist into the wall and thought about screaming again but decided against it. It was simply no use. Nigel knew the drill and when whoever had brought him here wanted to talk, they would. He also knew it would be on their time table, not his. So, resigned to his fate, he sat and waited.

Sonja continued to scream for help, pounding on the door, but it was useless. No one was coming to rescue her. Yet, for some strange reason she was sure she was in no real danger.

She and Julie had been making breakfast and wondering where the others were when suddenly the door burst open and four burly men in dark blue suits stormed the apartment. Sonja's first thought was Vladi but when she saw they were cops, she relaxed. But Julie was sure they were Vladi's men and became hysterical. They put handcuffs on their wrists and blindfolded them. Then they took them on a short ride. Sonja guessed they'd driven for about thirty minutes but she was unsure which direction they'd traveled. She also had no real sense how fast the van was traveling. Based on that information she had absolutely no idea where she was. Or where Julie was. When they got to their destination they separated the girls. They took Sonja to a small windowless room and left her there. What was confusing to her was why the police would kidnap her and Julie? If they were the police? Sonja didn't know why but, right now, she felt safer than she'd felt for some time. Sonja laid down on the cot in the corner of the room and closed her eyes, shivering inexplicably. She was almost asleep when out of nowhere came a vision of Vladi standing in the doorway with that evil grin of his. Was she dreaming? She wasn't sure, but in his hand Vladi held a bag of white powder and he dangled it like bait on a hook. Her body convulsed involuntarily, eagerly anticipating the euphoric effect of the cocaine he offered. Despite her fear of this monster she wished for the vision to be real. She could feel beads of sweat forming on her forehead, yet she felt cold and her body trembled uncontrollably. She realized then the immediate danger would not be coming from her captors. Instead it would be a battle from within as she began what would be a slow and painful withdrawal from her addiction to cocaine. The demons were coming, she could feel them. She shuddered once more, rolled herself into a fetal position and covered herself with a blanket. But she knew she would never keep these monsters at bay.

~

Julie was frightened. Who were these men? And what on earth did they want with her? She'd paced the room for the last half hour and had just sat down on a cot in the corner. Seconds later, the door opened and a man entered. Julie eyed him carefully as he walked to the center of the room and stood there.

"Hello Julie," he said in a quiet, almost soothing voice. "My name is Matt Hanson and I'm with the FBI. I hope my men have treated you well so far."

"The FBI?" she repeated, in disbelief. "Why am I here?" she asked, demanding an answer. "Am I under arrest?"

Her tone was growing shrill as she became more and more agitated.

"Please calm down Miss Eskin," Matt pleaded, becoming more businesslike. "Let me assure you that you are not under arrest. We've brought you here for your own protection and you will remain until it is safe for you to go. Do you understand?" he asked calmly. Julie nodded.

Matt then explained Sonja was nearby and was also there for her own well-being.

"Where's my sister?" asked Julie, feeling more relaxed. In some strange way Matt Hanson's voice had a calming effect on her.

Matt eyed her carefully, hesitated for just a moment, dropping his eyes to the floor. He was trying to think of how he should tell her about Lisa. But his hesitation had Julie visibly worried. She stood up and moved closer.

"What's happened?" she demanded, suspicious of Matt's pause. "Is she alright?"

"Julie, I have some bad news," he said struggling for the words to explain. And once again hesitated. Although his hesitation had only been for a split second, Julie screamed hysterically, moving forward and pounding her fists into Hanson's chest. She screamed out Lisa's name several times and cried. Matt grabbed her wrists and pulled her close. He realized Julie had misunderstood his awkwardness. She was thinking the worst. He cursed himself. He could ill afford to have this woman becoming even more hysterical. He needed information and he needed it now.

"Please Julie, calm down," he begged. "It's alright. Lisa's fine. She was in an accident earlier but she's going to be alright," he promised. He pulled her from his chest and looked directly into her eyes. "We're taking good care of her, I promise."

His voice, once again, reassured her.

He explained that Lisa was in a secure location and was receiving the best medical treatment money could buy. He decided not to give her the gritty details and omitted to include she was still in intensive care. He also decided not to tell her that her sister was in an induced coma and her life was still in grave danger. Why upset Julie any further?

"Can I see her?" she asked, taking a deep breath and feeling calmer.

"I'm sorry," he replied, thankful she was calming down. "She's in another location close to our medical team. But when it's possible we will arrange for you to see each other, I promise," he lied and smiled.

Julie turned and went to sit down but Matt stopped her, saying he needed to ask her some questions. He then moved to the door, opened it and motioned for her to follow.

He led her down a brightly lit hallway that went on forever. Every twelve feet she noticed a solid steel, windowless door and at the end of the hall there was a set of elevator doors. With every door closed Julie saw no sign of life, yet she had this eerie feeling that someone was occupying every room. It reminded her of an asylum, like the one in that movie.

What was it called? One Flew over the Cuckoo's Nest! The one where Jack Nicholson played the crazy guy, she thought. Or was it like the hotel in The Shining? No, she was sure it was One Flew over the Cuckoo's Nest.

The walls were bright white and the carpet was a nondescript beige. Even the doors and the frames surrounding them were the same bright white color. It was strange. Not once did she see any natural light entering the hallway and she noticed there were no windows to allow it. As they approached the elevator she took in something else that was strange. There were no numbers above the elevator doors and no up or down arrows either.

She watched as Matt inserted what looked like a hotel key card into a small slot next to the lift and then swiftly removed it. At once, the doors opened and Matt gestured for Julie to enter. The doors closed behind them and when she felt the elevator moving downward it surprised her. She thought she was in a basement but as the elevator moved she felt them descending into the bowels of this strange place. Since there were no floor numbers, only letters of the alphabet inside the elevator, she didn't know how far they'd traveled. Or whether they were above or below ground. She just felt the strange sensation of being deep below ground. The elevator stopped and the doors opened, revealing a hallway identical to the one they'd left just moments ago. If she had not felt the elevator move she would have sworn she'd arrived back at the same place. Matt escorted her to the first door on the right and asked her to sit in a chair on the far side of the room. The room itself was about the same size as the one she'd just left but felt much warmer. It looked more like a den or library and the entire wall opposite was an oak bookcase that held various vintage books and assorted paperbacks. There was a Persian rug on the floor and a small round table made of dark oak. Julie could see her own reflection in the polished table. Next to that was a chair similar to the one she was sitting in. He asked if she'd like a drink. She nodded, and a minute later a young woman brought her the drink and placed it on the table. She also brought a scotch and water for Mr. Hanson. At least that's what Julie thought it was. He took the empty seat opposite her and asked her questions about her involvement with the Russians. The atmosphere here was much different and she became more relaxed as she told him about her experiences with Vladi Cherkov and the others she'd met. He seemed genuinely interested in her story and as time passed she felt even more relaxed.

Matt listened as Julie told him about seeing the news coverage of the murdered young girl. He asked his questions in a manner that belied his intent. They sat together like in a coffee shop. Just friends talking. In reality he was subtly probing for information, determined to learn just how much she knew. After about an hour it became clear to him she knew little and wouldn't be a threat to his plans. He excused himself and told Julie someone would be by soon to take her back to her room. Before he left Julie asked once more about her sister. She had a worried look so Matt smiled and assured her he would arrange for them to be together when it was possible. Julie breathed a sigh of relief, smiled, and thanked him for his kindness.

He returned hers with his own warm, friendly smile and left her alone.

Like taking candy from a baby thought Matt. He felt he was making progress and he was happy with that. He chuckled to himself as he made his way to his next target, the lovely, yet pitiful Sonja.

As he entered the room he could see she was already feeling the effects of her withdrawal. Matt knew from experience that Sonja was no easy mark. She had lived a jaded life in her short time on this earth and Matt knew she would be difficult to break. However, because of the pain of withdrawal, he was sure Sonja would sell her grandmother for some cocaine. Christ, she'd sell her own children if she had any and wouldn't bat an eye. By now she'd be getting desperate and Matt knew it.

"Hello Sonja," he said as he approached the young woman lying on the bed. She was shivering uncontrollably and her hair stuck to her face from perspiration as she turned and looked up at him. She was so out of it she didn't even recognize him.

"How are you feeling?" he asked, knowing all too well that she was dealing with muscle cramps, stomach pain and the constant tension in her muscles caused from the tremors. He looked over at the far side of the bed and saw the floor caked with vomit. Thankfully, she hadn't eaten too much so there was just a small amount to clean up. Now she could only dry heave when her stomach cramped, making her belly ache.

Tears trickled down her cheek, smearing what little makeup she had on and making her appear even more emaciated than she was. Her eyes were dark and sunken. As he looked at her she reminded Matt of the young girl in the Exorcist. He was sure, that at any moment, her head would turn one hundred and eighty degrees and she'd spew green slime onto his expensive suit. She was not a pretty sight but Matt brought something that he thought would help the girl. At least for now.

"Please help me," she said in a hoarse whisper, her throat raw from all the dry heaves. She tried to sit up but had to deal with another bout of the shakes. Matt watched without pity as Sonja's stomach convulsed and she keeled over. Her mouth opened wide and her throat constricted. It seemed as though she was about to throw up the lining of her stomach. The force of this last convulsion caused her to fall to her knees in front of him as she held the bed for support and coughed several times. Finally, she looked up at him her eyes pleading for help.

He sat there without emotion as he looked at her on the floor. Instead he put his hand in his pocket and pulled out a clear plastic bag containing a white powdery substance. *Cocaine!*

"Is this what you're looking for Sonja?" he smiled as he pulled open the bag. She thought she was dreaming yet again as she watched the man pull a small mirror and a cocktail straw from his coat pocket.

"Oh God! Yessss," she hissed, as her tiny body trembled in anticipation. She watched carefully as he placed three lines on the mirror and handed her the straw. She felt a strange tingling sensation as she moved closer to the mirror, anticipating the delicious sensation of another cocaine high. Sonja placed the straw to her nose and took in a full line with one inhale. The euphoric feeling came immediately in a delicious wave and she quickly moved to do another line when Matt abruptly moved the mirror. She frowned and watched as he placed it on the floor a few feet away.

"Now, now Sonja," he said, "we can't have you getting too stoned yet, can we now?"

Sonja gazed up at him from the floor and smiled, slowly running her hand along his inner thigh. Matt returned her gaze. Even in this state, Sonja still had an allure he found hard to resist. Her sexual energy fascinated him and he remembered how it had trapped him in the Russians' web.

"I think we need to get you cleaned up a bit, Sonja," he said as he took her hand and lifted her onto the bed. She watched as he tipped the contents that lay on the mirror into the bag and placed it in his pocket.

"Maybe later we can play, okay?" he smiled.

She lay back on the bed and smiled up at him, a smoky, sexy look in her eyes.

"I'd like that," she whispered and closed her eyes.

"I'll come back soon, okay Sonja?" he promised and left her to enjoy the cocaine buzz.

Payback is a bitch, he thought as he sauntered toward the elevator, a satisfied smile crossing his lips.

~

"What the hell do you think you're doing?" screamed Nigel. He was angry and moved toward the door. "Do you have any idea who you're dealing with? I'm a police officer and I demand an explanation," he said and took another step closer to his captor trying to intimidate him.

Fontaine held his ground, feeling confident as the two men behind him silently braced themselves for any possible confrontation with their guest.

"Calm down Nigel," he said softly. "I know who you are and we are keeping you here for your own protection. I've spoken with your precinct commander and explained that you are on special assignment to the FBI. He knows you will not be reporting for duty for, at least, the next forty eight to ninety six hours," he explained.

"What are you talking about? What special assignment?"

Fontaine smiled and asked Nigel to have a seat.

"Please, let me explain," he said. "You see Nigel I have an important job for you."

"I'm listening," he replied, rather intrigued.

Chapter 16

He couldn't escape the confines of the car! The interior was quickly filling up and Chase struggled to pry open the door. It was dark and murky and the water surrounding him was freezing. It was rising rapidly and was now above his shoulders. In seconds the car would fill with water and Chase faced certain death. The car sank further into the abyss and he peered out the window. The body of a young woman passed by floating to the surface. As the woman passed, her face came in to plain view and Chase screamed in horror. It was Lisa!

"My God!" he screamed and sat up, suddenly realizing it was all a dream. No! It was a nightmare! His breath came in short gasps as he tried to calm himself, his heart racing.

"Jesus," he whispered, looking around the room trying to get his bearings.

Where the hell am I? His was unsure of where he was and confused by both his surrounding and the nightmare. Then he remembered Matt Hanson and his men bringing him to this place. He recalled someone talking about a safe house and it slowly came back to him. Though he had no memory of it he must have undressed himself at some point because his clothes were hanging over a chair in the corner of the room. The feeling reminded him of the first time he met Lisa and he longed to be with her again.

There were two large windows, framed by curtains, but no light came from them. He went to open one then saw that both had shutters locked from the outside. He saw a door leading to a large bathroom and went to explore. Next to the ensuite was a roomy exercise room filled with modern equipment.

"Impressive, huh?" said a voice from behind. Though the voice was familiar it startled Chase. He turned quickly to see Matt Hanson standing in the doorway smiling.

"Hey Matt," he said. "Where am I? What the hell is happening?"

Matt ignored the questions.

"How're you feeling, my friend?" he asked. "I thought I heard a scream and just wanted to make sure everything was okay. Are you alright?"

Chase looked at him, a little embarrassed. It was just a bad dream he told him and Matt laughed.

"Are you hungry?" he asked.

Chase nodded.

"Listen, why don't you take a shower and freshen up. I'll order us some dinner," said Matt.

Chase gave him a puzzled look.

"Dinner?" he asked.

"Yes Chase, dinner." Matt paused for just a moment. "Chase, it's almost seven. You've been asleep for nearly twelve hours. Maybe you'd prefer breakfast?" he asked with a smile.

Chase smiled back, sheepishly. "Maybe some steak and eggs, Matt," he replied.

"You got it buddy. It'll be ready in about half an hour," he said and started for the door. "I'll see you in the kitchen, okay?" Matt continued. "We've got a lot to talk about."

With that, Matt left the room and Chase was, once again, alone with his thoughts.

Almost twelve hours!

He wondered what had happened during that time. Where was everybody? Did Matt know where his friends were? How had Goren found them? He had questions and hoped Matt had the answers.

He smelled fresh brewed coffee as he entered the kitchen. Matt sat on a stool at the kitchen counter, reading the paper and sipping a cup of the dark brew.

"Here's your breakfast, my friend," he said and put a plate of food on the table. On it was the biggest steak Chase had ever seen. There were also three poached eggs, hash brown potatoes and two slices of toast. Matt placed it on the counter beside a fresh glass of orange juice and a tray of fruit spreads and butter. Chase just gazed at the feast in front of him.

"Wow," he said, as he poured himself a cup of hot coffee. "That looks incredible."

Matt just smiled.

"We provide nothing but the best here," he said. "Besides, you're going to need all that energy for this next assignment."

"What the hell are you talking about? What assignment?" he asked.

He didn't wait for an answer. Instead he bit into the juicy steak and dipped some toast into the soft poached eggs.

Matt remained silent and let his friend enjoy the meal.

No sense spoiling it, he thought.

"We'll talk in a little while," he said, "you just enjoy the food, buddy."

Chase, realizing just how hungry he was, ignored Matt and continued to eat everything on his plate.

Matt watched his friend eating. Chase ate as if he hadn't done so for a week or more. He was wolfing down his food like a ravenous beast. Matt smiled sadly. He felt a horrible sense of guilt, knowing this meal may well be Chase Adams' last! And he was responsible! After a moment he stood up, then slipped quietly out of the room. He needed to make a few phone calls and prepare for tonight's rendezvous.

Stephan was growing impatient. He was in his office looking out at that familiar view, the sailboats floating on the crystal surface of the lake as the sun slowly set in the west. People were out enjoying another glorious sun-drenched day in paradise. However, today held no enjoyment for Stephan. He was furious. There had been no word on the whereabouts of Vladi and he had yet to hear from Matt Hanson. He turned and was about to pick up the phone when it rang.

"Hello?" he asked with some anticipation, recognizing the voice at the other end immediately.

Things would get better. He could feel it.

Chapter 17

Vladi awoke and felt his beautiful blonde nurse, Vivian poking him. He was drowsy and disoriented, the room was dark. He sat up quickly, wondering where he was. Then felt the throbbing at the back of his head. He moaned loudly and lay back gently on the pillow.

"What are you doing, you bitch," he scowled.

Vivian ignored him and pushed at his shoulder to roll him on his side. She then went to work on changing the dressing on his head wound. He remembered what happened the last time and decided it was best to keep his mouth shut.

"The doctor asked that I make sure you don't sleep too long Mr. Cherkov. In case you've suffered a concussion."

She then gently removed the old dressing and applied a new one in its place. She turned away from him and walked to the television to turn it on for him.

"I brought you some movies to watch," she explained.

Vivian rhymed off the titles to several movies but Vladi recognized none of them so she just pushed the one in her hand into the DVD player and left the room.

As he watched the screen, Jack Nicholson appeared in a large, empty hotel ballroom and the scene cut to an outside shot that showed a large hotel covered in snow by a huge storm.

Although he had no interest in watching any movies he knew there was little he could do until he regained his strength. So he lay back on the soft pillows, got comfortable and let the movie play on.

The nurse silently entered the room to check on her patient. She checked the monitors and when she checked her vital signs, the patient stirred. The patient's arm was moving and the nurse ran out screaming!!

"Doctor!" she yelled as she ran down the hall. "She's awake, doctor!"

Lisa was coming out of the coma the doctors had induced to save her life.

They performed two separate surgeries over the past twelve hours and believed they had succeeded in stopping the bleeding in her brain. For twenty-four hours they had watched her closely and twice had to perform CPR. It had been touch and go but now it looked as though she was out of danger.

"Well young lady you put us to the test," said the doctor, explaining what they had done since she'd come in.

"But I believe the procedures were successful and you should make a full recovery"

Before the doctor entered the room Lisa had been hysterical and was screaming out her sister's name. She was also asking for her friend Chase Adams.

The doctor then called the two FBI agents standing outside the door of her room to explain what was happening. They told her about her friends and assured her that everyone was safe.

"The FBI is protecting you and your friends Lisa," said the tall blond agent in the dark blue suit.

"Are they alright?" Where's Chase?" the questions were coming a mile a minute.

"Everyone is fine ma'am," he reassured her.

"Please call me Lisa," she said. She gave the men a slight smile and thanked them for their help.

"Okay, Lisa it is. The doctors want to speak with you now so we'll be outside if you need us for anything, okay?" smiled the second agent.

She smiled back and laid her head down. She had a terrible headache and when she put her hand to her forehead she felt the thick bandage wrapped around her head.

"Hello Lisa", said the doctor, warmly. "I'm Dr. Stevenson. I'm the doctor who performed surgery on your brain Lisa."

"My brain? What the hell are you talking about? What happened to me?" Lisa tried to think back to what she last remembered and all she could remember was that night on the balcony with Chase.

"*What was it Chase was telling me?*" Lisa thought. She couldn't remember what he said but the memory of Chase warmed her heart. One feeling she could remember? The one she'd felt that night on the balcony.

Lisa tried to get up but as she did the doctor grabbed her and gently held her down. Suddenly she felt her head might blow apart and she got a stinging pain at her temple. The pain was so severe she stopped fighting.

"Lisa, you mustn't move too quickly. It's best to keep your head still. Your brain has suffered a severe beating and it's going to take time to recover. And you need to let that happen" explained Dr. Stevenson.

"Okay doctor," Lisa whispered. She squinted, hoping to relieve the pain.

Her head throbbed and her ears were ringing which made it difficult to hear what the doctor was saying. But when the ringing stopped the doctor had finished his explanation of the treatment so Lisa didn't know what was happening. Right now Lisa was too tired to care. She wanted to sleep so she closed her eyes to make the pain and the world go away for a while.

"Lisa! Lisa!" yelled Dr. Stevenson. "Lisa, you can't sleep right now! You need to stay awake for the next few hours. We need watch your brain at work in order evaluate your treatment," he explained.

The staff put a television directly in front of her and a nurse turned the set on. Then she adjusted the volume to low.

"You can watch some television for now," said the nurse. "We'll bring you some food a little later and if you want we can bring you some light reading."

"Sounds like fun," moaned Lisa.

―

"For Christ sakes you whore! This soup tastes like shit!"

Vladi was furious! For the past twenty four hours he hadn't moved and he was bored. On the positive side he was getting his strength back.

Vivian sat in the kitchen thinking. She worried that when this maniac got better she'd be in danger and did not want to be here when that happened. She had not heard from Dr. Tupolev either. It wasn't like him not to call and check on his patients. She knew this was different. She remembered him telling her repeatedly not to call him or the hospital. She made the call anyway.

"Dr. Tupolev's office" said the voice on the other end of the phone. It was a voice she didn't recognize.

"Who's this?" Vivian asked suspiciously.

"I'm a temp," she explained. "Alice called in sick this morning".

She asked who was calling and how she might direct the call.

"It's Vivian," she explained. "Is Dr. Tupolev in?"

"I'm sorry but he's on call at the hospital this morning," she replied. "Can I take a message?"

Vivian explained she had not heard from the doctor in twenty four hours and was worried.

"Are you sure he's okay?" she insisted, pacing the floor and feeling anxious.

"I can try to get him on the line, would you like me to do that?" the woman asked in a soft, warm voice.

"Could you please?" answered Vivian, suddenly feeling calmer. The woman's voice calmed Vivian and she felt more relaxed.

"Hold on," she said and explained this might take a few minutes. "Please be patient while I try to reach him. Okay?"

She waited a few minutes and wondered what could be taking so long. When the receptionist returned she explained the doctor was in surgery and couldn't take the call.

"Do you want me to leave a message that you called, Vivian?" she asked pleasantly.

"No, that's alright. I'll call back later."

Vivian thanked her for her time and hung up the phone. Then she dialed Dr. Tupolev's cell phone number, hoping he would pick up.

"Hi, this is Dr. Tupolev." It was the doctor's voice. *Thank God* she thought.

"Oh, Dr. Tupolev!" she cried. But before she could continue she heard,

"I can't come to the phone right now."

It was his voice mail kicking in!

This is crazy she thought, but there was little she could do. She'd have to wait for him to call. She left a short message and hung up.

Although she dreaded the idea, Vivian decided she should check on her patient again. This guy was a sick bastard and though she sounded tough, Vladi Cherkov frightened her, especially a healthy Vladimir Cherkov.

~

"I think we've got him sir!" cried McVittee on the other end of the line.

"Got who?" asked Matt.

"Cherkov, sir."

Matt had never heard McVittee this excited before but guessed it was because McVittee understood the stakes involved and knew what bringing in Vladi Cherkov could mean to his career path.

The thought excited Matt too, but he kept his emotions in check and gave McVittee and his team their orders. They'd found Vladi Cherkov and were planning to pick him up. The next step in his plan was both critical and difficult. He had to convince Cherkov that a meeting with Stephan was in everybody's best interest. If his plan worked he'd be rid of both of his problems and his family would be safe. As he hung up the phone he turned to see Chase Adams walk into the room and suddenly felt a twinge of regret at what might happen to him. Matt did not want to see him hurt but his family was more important than anything else in his life, including Chase Adams. Sacrificing a few lives was a small price to pay.

"What was that about?" Chase asked, taking a seat at the oak bar at the end of the room.

Matt turned to him and explained his men had been tracking Vladi Cherkov The leader of the fake bankcard scam involving his friend's sister.

"And?" interrupted Chase impatiently. "What's your next move?"

"We're picking him up soon," he said. "We have a location that we gained from a wiretap. Why?"

"Because I want a piece of this guy," said Chase, in a sinister whisper that caught Matt off guard. But, being the consummate pro, Matt quickly recovered.

"Relax Chase. You'll get your chance. But right now we've got some bigger fish to fry," said Matt.

"Chase, I'm sorry. I will explain later, but right now I've got to pick up Vladi Cherkov." As he left the room he said, "We'll talk when I get back, okay?"

Leaving Chase to wonder what would happen next. He knew Matt was up to something and he didn't like the fact he would be out there as bait. He didn't know the plan and it worried him. He hoped Fontaine would be keeping eyes on Hanson because he didn't like thinking he was on his own? And what was happening to his friends? The last time he'd seen Lisa she was still touch and go and he was not sure what had happened to Nigel, Julie or Sonja. Were they trying to find him? Or were they danger? Despite Fontaine's assurances.

He wanted answers but for now he knew he'd be going in blind until he could contact Fontaine. And that wouldn't happen until Fontaine contacted him. There was one part of the plan he knew. He was going to have the chance to confront this evil man known as Vladi Cherkov.

Chapter 18

The food the nurse gave him was garbage and sitting here watching movies was boring him. The combination frustrated him.

"Hey bitch," cried Vladi as he threw the bowl of slop at the wall. "Bring me something I can eat for Christ sakes."

"I'm coming," cried Vivian. She fretted for her safety because Cherkov was getting his strength back and it frightened Vivian.

"Who the fuck were you talking to just now," demanded Vladi.

Vivian stood tall and explained that she was trying to get a hold of Dr. Tupolev and had phoned his office.

Vladi couldn't believe what he was hearing. This dumb whore was going to ruin everything. He sat up in bed and demanded to know who she had spoken to. She told Vladi the regular receptionist had called in sick. The receptionist said that Dr. Tupolev was at the hospital.

"They put me on hold for a few minutes while they tried to find the doctor," explained Vivian.

Vladi felt something was not right and he needed to get out of this place.

"Vivian, I need you to get me out of here. Now!" he screamed. "Do you have a car?"

She nodded her head and he jumped out of bed and grabbed her by the arm. He grabbed her arm roughly and told her to pack whatever medical supplies she needed and they headed out the door.

Once in the car, Vladi relaxed.

"Don't worry Vivian I am not going to hurt you," he said with a calming voice that made Vivian feel slightly more relaxed. "Unless you screw up." Vladi looked at her with a smile and added, "So, for your sake, I suggest you don't screw up."

As they rounded the corner three dark blue sedans came barreling towards them and Vladi ducked below the dashboard. At six foot four he was a big man and it was difficult for him to get down that low.

"Keep driving," he cried and Vivian did just that without even looking at the three cars that rushed past them.

"Good girl," Vladi said with that syrupy calm voice of his. It gave Vivian a chill up her spine when he spoke like that. She knew all too well this crazy man could turn on a moment's notice. "I am going to reward you handsomely for this," he continued. Then he told her to get to another apartment he kept near the water.

Vladi tried to relax but his head throbbed from the wound and it made him think about how this had all happened. That little skank in the hotel room.

She would not see her next birthday thought Vladi.

He was going to personally see to that.

181

Vincent Fontaine waited impatiently in his office. He wanted to confirm they had captured Vladi Cherkov before he moved to the next phase of his plan. He'd thought briefly about what part the cop would play.

What was his name? thought Fontaine.

"That's right! Nigel Waters," he said aloud.

He was also arranging for Julie to visit her sister Lisa. Now that she was calm he had placed her in a more comfortable room in the basement of the building. For now, she and Lisa would remain in 'protective custody'. He would figure out what to do with the two sisters later.

~

Julie sat quietly in the room Fontaine had brought her to. Right now she wondered what was happening out in the world. The world she could not be a part of while she languished alone. Where was Chase? What had happened to Nigel? And Sonja! What was that conniving little liar up to? Her brain was going in a thousand directions thinking of all the possibilities. She had to get out of here somehow and find the others. But how? She did not know where she was. No escape plan. And the building was a fortress. But she had to find a way. Earlier, she'd noticed cameras in the first room she'd been in and in the hallways. But there was no camera in this room.

Was she locked in? she wondered. She tried the door and found it locked.

Dam, she thought.

"Worth a shot" she said aloud.

As she turned back to the chair, there was a knock at the door. Did she just imagine it? No, there it is again! Julie heard a voice from outside the door.

"Hello?" said a woman sheepishly.

"Julie, may I come in?"

Julie went to the door and asked, "who's there?"

Then she heard the swipe of a key card and the door opened slowly.

"Julie, would you please step away from the door for me?" said the woman, this time with a little more authority. Julie obeyed the command and moved back into the center of the room. She was wary and braced herself for whatever was coming. To her surprise a young woman, about the same size and build as her, walked into the room with a tray filled with food. She placed the tray on the table and told Julie to help herself to the array of fruits and vegetables and several types of breads and spreads. The young woman asked Julie if she was thirsty and offered her several drink choices. She told her, the choice was hers and she would be happy to get her whatever she wanted.

Julie paused a moment and stared at the woman.

"Who are you," she asked.

"I'm Heather Reardon. I am an agent working for the FBI," she said. Heather explained she was in training and was there to look after Julie's needs while she was a guest of the FBI.

Julie paused for a moment and smiled. Heather, looking puzzled, asked her what she was smiling about.

"You used the word guest just now. Does that mean I am free to go," asked Julie smiling even wider now.

"Well no," said Heather. "I'm trying to be polite but frankly you're in danger and it wouldn't be safe for you to leave. It's what we call 'protective custody' and used quotation marks with her hands as she said this.

"You're still in locked up, but it's for your own protection."

"So I'm a prisoner then, aren't I" stated Julie firmly.

"I'm afraid so," said Heather and shrugged. "But we're going to treat you very well and, as soon as we feel you're safe, we intend to let you go. So relax and enjoy the hospitality."

Then she smiled and asked.

"Julie, what can I get you to drink?"

Julie thought for a moment and asked for a soda with ice.

Heather turned on her high heels and left the room in search of Julie's drink.

Julie looked at the huge plate of food and wondered who could eat this. Then she thought about Heather and how uncanny it was that they were the same size and build. Even the same hair color!

It was a crazy idea but she thought about it for a moment and thought *this could work!* A plan of escape was starting to percolate in her brain but she realized she had to think of something in a hurry. Because Heather would be back any minute now! And to carry out her plan she would have to impersonate Heather!

~

He sat with his back to Nigel and looked out the window. He always loved the view. He felt it gave him inspiration. As he turned, he explained to Nigel how he could help.

"Nigel I need you to run some interference for Chase once Matt Hanson sets up his meeting with Stephan Corolev. I'm not sure what Hanson has in mind for Chase once the meet is on, so for now I need you to sit tight until I hear from him. Can you do that?"

Nigel was not happy but knew he had little choice, so he nodded, agreeing to follow the Deputy Director directions.

"Good," said Fontaine. "We will move you to another location. Somewhere you'll be more comfortable. Can we get you something to eat?" asked Fontaine.

Nigel hadn't eaten since dinner the night before so he readily agreed to his new digs and some food.

Fontaine called in the two men standing outside Fontaine's door. He told them to take Nigel to his new room and get him whatever he wanted.

Lisa was feeling better. The headache she had was easing and she felt hungry. Lisa pressed the call button at her bedside and asked the nurse if she could have some food.

She again wondered where the others were. The nurse said her sister Julie was nearby and would be visiting soon. But she did not know where the others were.

Although her memory was spotty she remembered the gunfire and trying to escape it in Chase's car. As hard as she tried she could remember nothing after that. Not until she awoke in this hospital bed.

Where was Chase? Was he alright? Did he know she was here and, if so, why hadn't he come to visit. Was she was the only one who felt that way. Maybe Chase was not feeling the same. Was she fooling herself to think he cared as much for her as she did for him?

A tear rolled slowly down her cheek and landed at the corner of her mouth. The salty liquid was like the feeling in her heart. It stung and she wiped it away just like the feelings stirring for Chase Adams.

The nurse returned with some food that looked like it belonged in a concentration camp. It was a bland looking porridge with some crackers in a cellophane packet. And a glass of apple juice. Lisa looked at the plate in disgust. Seeing the look on Lisa's face the nurse apologized and explained this was all she could to eat for now.

"Where's my sister Julie?" asked Lisa.

"Julie is at another location in the complex here and I believe Mr. Fontaine is arranging a visit. Right now I need you to try to eat what I brought you" urged the nurse.

Lisa looked at the food and took a spoonful of the slop, hesitantly. As soon as it touched her tongue she spit it back in the bowl and pushed the tray away.

"There is no way I am eating that," cried Lisa. "Please take it away!"

"Lisa, you need to eat," insisted the nurse.

"I want to see my sister," she cried. "I need to see Julie! Please let me see my sister," she screamed and she began sobbing hysterically.

"I'll see what I can do," said the nurse and left the room quickly in search of her supervisor.

⁓

Julie frantically searched the room for a makeshift weapon. Something to subdue Heather with but not something that would hurt her or might kill her.

There! On the book shelf, was what she needed. Two bookends made of what looked like brass and they looked heavy enough to do the job.

The bookend was like a globe and Julie was almost certain a blow from such an object would not do too much damage.

She grabbed one, just as she heard footsteps coming down the hallway.

Julie quickly ran behind the door and waited.

"Julie?" Heather opened the door but the girl wasn't there. Before she realized what was happening Julie came around from bchind the door and swung at her with something in her hand.

"What the hell!" cried Heather but it was too late. The blow caught her on the temple and she went down in heap on the carpeted floor.

Julie quickly grabbed her and dragged her away from the open door. Before she closed it, she looked into the hallway to make sure no one had noticed what had just happened.

Julie felt bad, as she looked down at the unconscious agent, hoping that she hadn't swung too hard and killed her. She bent down and checked for a pulse and felt relief at the throb she felt at her neck.

Good, she was alive. Just not kicking!

Julie checked the wound and saw there was some minor bleeding at the contact point. It did not look serious so she grabbed a towel and wrapped it around her head.

She hastily looked for something to tie her up but could find nothing suitable. Then she noticed the gun on her waist and the pair of handcuffs!

Julie dragged the agent into the bathroom and handcuffed her to the pipe under the sink. She grabbed a small wash cloth and stuffed it in her mouth hoping it would prevent her from crying out when she woke up.

Satisfied, Julie grabbed Heather's wallet and FBI identification. Then she saw the gun and holster and took those too.

"Shit," said Julie. She needed the woman's clothing and to get them she had to un-cuff her. Doing so, Julie then undressed the FBI agent and donned her slacks, blouse and jacket. But instead of leaving her there in just her underwear, Julie took the time to put some clothes on Heather. Then replaced the handcuffs on her wrists, shut the door to the bathroom and wedged a chair under the doorknob.

"That should do it," Julie said to herself.

Julie checked herself in the full length mirror and thought she looked good. She felt confident she would pass for Heather if nobody looked too closely.

Finally she took the leap, opened the door and peeked her head into the hallway. Seeing it empty she made her way to the elevator. Julie strode confidently down the hallway remembering a phrase she once heard that said "if you look and act like you're supposed to be there nobody will question your presence."

Or something like that she thought!

She reached the elevator and saw there was no up and down button beside the elevator door. She wasn't sure which floor she was on so didn't know where she should go. She decided to get the elevator and then figure the next move out. She took out the card she saw Matt Hanson use to call the elevator and open the doors. She swiped it once and waited for the elevator.

Thankfully she didn't have to wait long. The elevator doors parted and Julie just prayed it was empty. She hadn't realized it but she had closed her eyes as she willed the elevator to be empty and jumped when a voice asked her what was wrong.

She opened her eyes and smiled.

"Sorry, I was just thinking back to my last vacation and was in dreamland", she said as she entered the small enclosed space.

The woman smiled back and extended her hand.

"Jill Sykes," said the woman and Julie realized the woman did not know her alter ego Heather Reardon.

"Heather" she muttered haltingly, her eyes looking down. Then she straightened and looked the woman in the eyes and stated confidently "Heather Reardon."

"Well Heather Reardon, where to?"

"Pardon me?" replied Julie.

"You're on an elevator Heather, so which floor do you want to go to," asked a puzzled Jill.

Julie explained she was new to this place and wasn't sure what floor she needed. She was looking for the infirmary to question an injured suspect in a case she was working on.

Jill told her what floor she needed, quickly pushed the proper button and they were on their way. The short ride to the next stop was agonizing for Julie but she managed to smile and carry on a minimum of small talk until Jill reached her floor.

"It was a pleasure meeting you Heather Reardon," and smiled as she exited the elevator. "Hope to see you again soon," she said and disappeared down the corridor.

Julie breathed a visible sigh of relief and relaxed for the ride up to her floor. The relaxed feeling wasn't going to last long. She knew that if she met anyone who knew Heather she would not be so lucky.

She exited the elevator.

Chapter 19

"Hey Chase!" Someone had just called out his name and he turned to see who that might be. His chemistry class had ended and he was going to the gym for his daily workout.

He was a budding star in the hockey world and worked hard to stay in shape. Across the quad he saw Matt Hanson sprinting toward him and he smiled. Matt had always been the straight arrow. The moral compass for all of their buddies to follow. He remembered the night they had decided to have a little fun and pull a prank on a rival team in town to play a tournament. Although Matt wasn't the best hockey player on the team they appointed him captain of the squad because of his obvious leadership skills.

That night they had watched their rivals play their first game of the tournament and they'd won handily by a score of six to three! They were going out to celebrate! Now in this town, the only place for a group that large would be O'Halloran's, the Irish Pub, which was about a mile from the arena. There were other bars in town so, to ensure the team went to O'Halloran's, Chase and the others had printed some fake 2 for 1 beer tickets for the team and left them in their dressing room.

With their equipment stowed away and the players seated, the bus left for O'Halloran's. Excitement filled the air! It was routine for the visiting team to travel in suit and tie. They were grooming these players and the league felt this was one way to prepare them for the professional level. It was also normal in those days for the host team to play some elaborate pranks on visiting teams and Chase had come up with a good one.

His chemistry class discussed poisons recently. During the lesson they discussed cures you could use if you accidently took in a poison.

One common way was to immediately induce vomiting and they talked about the many ways one could do that.

One cure was a substance called Ipecac which was an oil extracted from the root of a plant too hard to pronounce. In the right dose, Ipecac induced vomiting in someone within 10 to 15 minutes of taking it. As a powder you could take it with water. The professor told them it was even more soluble in alcohol.

The idea had come to Chase when he watched a documentary on the date drug Rohypnol. The program showed you how to spike someone's drink without them knowing it.

Chase felt this was a solid plan because his team, as the hosts, would be serving the drinks. Chase knew there was no way the owner of the bar would allow them to do this so he recruited a few teammates to help with the prank.

That night Chase smuggled in a bottle of the powder.

The players from several teams packed the bar and some of the college girls also came out to party. Picking up a hockey player was a rite of passage for the girls in this town. The owner of the bar had even brought in a local band to play live music and the place was hopping.

During the festivities Chase and his teammates brought out several trays of beer in honor of the rival team's victory. To make the prank even better they challenged the players to chug the beer and most of the boys did. The party was on!

It didn't take long before all hell broke loose as many of the players started to vomit. And not just vomit. They were spewing just like that young woman in the exorcist. It was a mess!

Behind the bar Chase and his buddies were giggling like little girls as they watched their plan unfold.

But Chase and his friends stopped giggling when one player collapsed on the floor. He was shaking uncontrollably and it was obvious he was having a seizure.

Matt, who was not in on the prank, took control.

"Call 911!" he shouted, "Now!"

Within minutes several ambulances arrived and a paramedic gave the player a drug to stop the seizure.

"What the hell happened here?" asked the paramedics and everyone stared silently. Not looking at anyone or anything. Just staring into space.

One of his team members, who had stopped vomiting, came over and asked them if his friend would be all right.

"I don't know," said a woman EMT. "We need to know if they ate or drank anything unusual."

The paramedic caring for the young man said it could be an allergic reaction. It could also be something else. They needed more information to make the correct diagnosis.

"We'll find out more when we get him to a hospital," said the woman as they carted him off to the ambulance on a stretcher. They sped off with their lights flashing and the siren wailing.

Chase looked around the bar and realized he'd made a terrible mistake. The place was a mess, vomit covering most of the floor. It also covered the chairs and tables and almost everyone's clothes.

Matt saw the guilty look on Chase's face and immediately went to confront him.

"What the fuck did you do!" whispered Matt so no one else would hear.

Chase turned and walked behind the bar and confessed to Matt.

"This shouldn't have happened," said Chase, worried. "It was just a prank! We thought it would be funny," he explained. He told Matt what they had done and when he finished Matt went crazy.

"Are you nuts?" he cried. "We need to tell the doctors at the hospital what you did."

He grabbed Chase and told him to explain to the owner of the bar what they'd done and to promise he and the others would clean up the bar and pay for any damages. He took Chase to one of the other EMTs. He was giving fluids to those dehydrated from the vomiting.

The paramedic shook his head in disgust and radioed the ambulance to let them know.

At this point Chase was crestfallen.

"Is he going to be okay?" he asked, the shameful look noticeable to everyone.

Chase remembered the look of disgust on Matt's face like it was yesterday. Thank God everyone was okay and the young man who'd had the seizure made a full recovery.

They took a full day to clean up the mess and Matt stood over them and supervised them the entire time.

For the rest of the semester Matt was angry with every team member who'd participated in the prank. He told the coaches what happened and they disciplined the entire team, including Matt.

Chase jumped, as he came out of his daydream with the slamming of a door behind him. He turned around to see his friend Matt storm into the room out of breath and angry.

"What the hell, Matt?" Chase demanded, surprised to see his friend in such a state.

"We lost him," screamed Matt and threw his keys across the room.

"Who?"

"Cherkov. He wasn't there when we conducted the raid. Someone must have tipped him off." Matt explained and moved across the room. He picked up his keys and flopped down on the sofa.

"I can't fucking believe this!"

Chase sat down in the chair across from him.

"What happened?"

Matt put his face in his hands and then ran them through his hair in frustration. He explained how they had put a trace on the doctor's phone and got, what they were sure was, Vladi Cherkov's location. But when they got there the place was empty. After a thorough search of the house they determined that someone had been there. And that someone received some serious medical treatment, judging from the supplies they found.

"We knew someone had injured him," Matt explained. "And we knew Dr. Tupolev, a doctor on Vladi's payroll had treated him at the hospital. That's when we put a trace on the doctor's phone hoping Cherkov would reach out.

"Don't beat yourself up," he said. "I'm sure you'll get another chance."

According to Fontaine the capture of Cherkov was an integral part of Matt's plan and Chase knew this. He didn't know if this set back would mean that Matt would need a new strategy but he didn't care. He knew he had to confront Matt about his betrayal of the FBI. And he had to do it now.

Matt was his friend. He was someone with the moral compass of a saint. Why on earth was he betraying the FBI? And working with scumbags like Stephan Corolev and Vladi Cherkov.

There had to be a reason! he thought.

"And I'm going to find out what that reason is," he mumbled under his breath.

"What did you say?" Matt had moved from the sofa and was standing across the room, a puzzled look creased his face.

"Matt, we need to talk."

Chase got up and moved to the kitchen. Then sat down at the table and asked Matt to join him.

Chase talked about the old days and even recounted some pranks they'd pulled back in University. He explained how the other night, before they'd met up at the hospital, he'd met with Fontaine.

"I see?" said Matt eyeing him with some suspicion. "And what did you two talk about?"

"He told me something I'm having trouble believing and, even worse that if it's true, I just can't understand it,"

"So what did he tell you?"

Chase stood up and paced the room. He turned to Matt and recounted what Fontaine had told him.

Matt sat there with a look of shock on his face. He tried to deny it but realized it was useless so with a resigned look on his face he confessed that what Fontaine had told him was true.

Chase looked at him sadly.

"Why Matt?" he asked.

He needed to know because this was not the Matt he knew. He looked at him in total disbelief and asked again.

"Matt you were our rock back in the day," he said sadly. "What the hell happened?"

Matt stood up and walked to the window and the room was still. For several minutes Matt thought about what he should say and Chase sat there patiently, waiting for what was to come.

Matt turned, looked at Chase and told him how he'd become embroiled in this mess.

"They've got me Chase," he told him. He explained how he had messed up. How Corolev had set him up and made a tape. A tape exposing the sexual liaison he had with Sonja. He recalled the moment the tape had come to him and the call from Corolev, threatening to expose his indiscretions.

"It was a moment of weakness Chase!" said Matt, "and I'm paying for it. And it's not just me, it's my family."

Tears were forming in his eyes as he told Chase about the brake mishap with his wife's car and the threat it posed. His family was everything to him and he would do anything to protect them.

"I'm sorry, but I just don't have any other choice," he protested.

Chase looked at him sternly and said,

"That's just not true Matt. You always have a choice."

He then moved across the room and put his hands on his good friend's shoulders.

"Look at me, Matt."

Matt slowly raised his head and looked Chase in the eyes. Ashamed of what he had done Matt shed a tear. He hated the man standing in front of his friend Chase.

"I can help you," said Chase and, once again, paced around the room. He stopped and said, "We can figure this out together Matt. But first I need to see Lisa."

Chapter 20

"Her name is Lisa. Lisa Eskin," Julie told them.

Feeling more confident Julie flashed the badge she'd taken from Heather and insisted she needed to see the woman now.

The nurse was reluctant. She explained that even though Lisa was conscious she was not ready to answer questions.

"I understand," said Julie. "I need just a few moments with her. I have a few important questions," she insisted.

"Okay then," replied the nurse but then cautioned her to be quick and to not create any stress for the poor girl.

Julie promised to do so and headed for Lisa's room full of anticipation.

As she entered the room her heart fell out of her chest as she saw her sister lying in the hospital bed. She looked so frail. It seemed like she could break with just a touch. She felt this so strongly that she barely caressed her shoulder, trying to awaken her.

Lisa stirred and slowly opened her eyes. Although she could barely move, the look of shock on her face was obvious.

"Julie!" Her raspy voice barely above a whisper.

"Ssh," said Julie quietly, "Lisa, please let me do the talking right now."

Julie then told her what had transpired over the past twenty-four hours. She told her about the FBI agents who swarmed the apartment and took her and Sonja away.

"I don't know where Sonja is," she explained. "And I don't have a clue where Nigel and Chase are," she continued.

"Oh my God!" cried Lisa. "How did you get here?" she asked.

Julie showed Lisa the FBI badge and Lisa freaked out. She was still feeling the effects of the concussion and the drugs she'd taken and seeing those two men earlier had confused her.

"You're an FBI agent?" she asked. She couldn't believe what she was hearing! Her sister was with the FBI!

"No," said Julie. "That's not me. It's a woman whose name is Heather Reardon."

She explained what had happened. How she had overpowered the FBI agent, then tied her up in the room where they had been holding her.

"I felt bad about hurting her but I'm sure she'll be alright. What I need to do is get out of here so I can find Chase and the others."

Lisa looked at her sadly knowing Julie would have to leave her there. She knew she was in no shape to leave the hospital. She would have gone in a minute if she could but she was safe here and that was comforting.

She also explained to her sister that Chase was with his friend Matt Hanson, the FBI agent. She told Julie she did not know the whereabouts of the others so she could not be of much help there.

Lisa was about to elaborate when a nurse entered the room. The nurse gave Julie a stern look signaling it was time for her to go.

"Thank you Miss Eskin," Julie smiled at the nurse and turned back to Lisa. "You've been a real help."

Julie could see she was tiring but Lisa smiled weakly and replied, "you're welcome Miss Reardon and I hope you can help my friends."

"Listen, I should let you get some rest but let me assure you the FBI will do everything in its power to find your friends and bring them back safe."

With that Julie turned, smiled once again at the angry nurse and scurried down the hall to the elevator.

"Excuse me," yelled Julie, trying to gain the attention of a nurse.

The nurse turned to her and put her finger to her lips warning Julie. Then she moved closer so she didn't have to speak too loudly.

"I'm new here. Can you tell me what floor I need to get out of the building?" she said quietly.

The nurse looked at her suspiciously again but said "Just go to level G. You should be able to find your way out from there"

"Thanks," said Julie but then realized she needed something more as she went to slide the card reader into the slot beside the elevator.

"Sorry," she said sheepishly, "but is that up or down from here?

'We're on Level H right now so it is down one floor," as she eyed her again.

Julie thanked her again and quickly hit the down call button beside the elevator door.

While she waited she could feel the eyes of the nurse staring at her.

"C'mon, C'mon" said Julie whispering to herself quietly.

"Miss Reardon is it?" the voice coming from directly behind her.

'Excuse me?" Julie was suddenly wary. Who was this behind her?

She turned around slowly and saw it was the other nurse she'd met earlier.

The nurse stepped closer and was about to ask a question when the elevator doors parted.

"Heather Reardon. That's correct."

Julie quickly stepped inside, explaining to the nurse she was on a tight schedule and needed to hurry. She flashed her badge to the nurse as the elevator doors closed ensuring that no real scrutiny was possible.

Julie smiled again and breathed a sigh of relief once the doors had closed.

Julie exhaled loudly as the elevator moved down the shaft to the next level.

That was close she thought.

⁓

Lisa lay in her hospital bed, frightened. Frightened of what was happening to her. Would she be okay? Or would this injury be a life sentence.

But more than that she was afraid of what might happen to Chase. She knew what she was feeling for him and she hoped he felt the same way. But neither had expressed their feelings to the other yet. She knew there was a spark. But was it enough to light the fire of love in them both?

Lisa closed her eyes suddenly feeling very tired. But just as she did the doctor came in.

"Ah Lisa, I see you're awake," said the doctor as he moved into the room. "How are you feeling?"

"Not so good," replied Lisa and closed her eyes.

"I understand you had a visitor," replied the doctor and eyed her, gauging her reaction.

"Yes, she was an FBI agent," she explained. "She was here to ask me some questions."

"Are you sure of that Lisa?" he said. "Because I spoke with the lead investigator about that and he told me he didn't send anyone here to ask you any questions. And there's something else that's puzzling."

"What's that?" asked Lisa.

"The nurse tells me the woman who came to see you looked a lot like you."

Lisa couldn't hide the look of fright on her face and the doctor knew something was amiss.

"Lisa you need to tell me what is going on here," the doctor insisted.

"Nothing is going on," said Lisa with some conviction but she wasn't convincing the doctor.

He had a hunch that something was amiss. He told Lisa he'd be right back and walked quickly to the nurse's station to use the phone.

Lisa called after him but it was no use. She knew he was onto them and prayed that Julie got away.

Someone answered the phone and the doctor explained why he was calling, telling the agent on the other end of the line to check on one of their detainees.

"Her name is Julie Eskin," he told him. "Her sister Lisa came in with the head injury. Yes, Mr. Fontaine said she was down in holding on Level C. Can you check to see if she's still there?"

Ten minutes later two large, beefy men walked briskly into Lisa's room. One was taller than the other but other than height they looked almost identical. The taller one introduced himself as Agent McVittee and demanded to know where her sister Julie had gone.

"I don't know what you're talking about. I haven't seen my sister since I got here. The last time I saw her was at a friend's apartment."

Lisa moaned as if in pain and pressed the small call button at her bedside.

A nurse came in and Lisa told her she was feeling nauseous and that her head was throbbing.

The nurse turned to the two men and asked them to leave this woman alone.

"She is still in serious condition and getting her agitated like this isn't going to help her recover," rebuked the nurse and she ushered them out of the room.

As the nurse escorted them out, one of them yelled over his shoulder.

"We know she was here Lisa, and we're going to find her with or without your help. It would be better for everyone if you cooperated and told us what you know."

Lisa thought about this for a moment and asked the men to come back. The nurse, who was angry with them shrugged her shoulders and let the men return.

Lisa looked at them with tears in her eyes.

"You won't hurt her will you?" she asked. "She's a victim in this, just like me," she insisted.

Agent McVittee gazed at her with a sympathetic look on his face and said, "we're the good guys here Lisa. We're not going hurt her. It's our job to protect her but we can't do that without knowing where she is and what she has planned."

Lisa then confessed that it was Julie who'd been there. She wasn't sure but she thought that Julie was trying to find their friend Chase Adams.

The men listened to her explain what Julie had done and told them she didn't know where she was or where she was going. Only that she was trying to find Chase.

"Lisa," said the shorter man. "Chase is with our boss Matt Hanson."

McVittee gave her a suspicious look.

"But you knew that already, right?" he asked.

Lisa feigned ignorance claiming she only remembered Chase mentioning that name and saying he was a friend. Someone who could help. But she wasn't certain where they were.

McVittee eyed her again but decided that perhaps her concussion had affected her memory after all and he didn't press her any further.

"Chase knows you're here Lisa, and he knows we're taking good care of you," explained the shorter man.

"I'm sorry," said Lisa, "but my sister worries about me. She's just trying to, ah." Lisa abruptly stopped in the middle of the sentence. She realized that Julie was also a fugitive from the law, having worked for the Russians, helping them with their bank card scam.

"She's trying to what?" asked the McVittee.

"I don't know," cried Lisa. "Please stop asking me questions. I'm tired and my head hurts. Can I please get some sleep now?" she asked harshly.

Just then the nurse who attended to her earlier came into the room and saw how upset Lisa was and ushered the two agents out once again.

The agents obliged quietly. The shorter man turned to the nurse and handed her his card.

"Let us know when she's up to answering some more questions. There are lives at stake here and we need answers to prevent any more people getting seriously hurt or even dying."

The nurse looked at them suspiciously. She told them Lisa was still in serious condition and it would be some time before they could interrogate her again.

"Fellas, you're going to have to find another way to get your information," she explained, "she needs some time to recuperate and adding the stress you've already caused will not help. So please leave her alone."

"Yes ma'am," replied McVittee.

McVittee left the room frustrated. Earlier that day they'd raided a house they thought Vladi Cherkov was convalescing in but he was gone when they arrived. His boss Matt Hanson was not happy and when his boss was not happy McVittee and his partner Jeb Stevens suffered.

He turned to his partner.

"We have to find her," he said, thinking maybe that would make his boss happy.

~

She pored over the newspaper looking for some news on the death of the Russian mobster. When she had come to rescue of the young girl in the hotel room and saw all the blood, she was sure Cherkov was dead. She feared what might happen to Melanie but she had to admit, that if she killed the pig, Anya would be happy.

"Tell me exactly what happened," she asked Melanie.

Anya Senkin was a beautiful woman and had been in charge of the girls here for the past eight years. She knew Stephan Corolev and had once been his favorite. Then she was carefree. But now was different. While a dead Vladi Cherkov was good news, she knew someone would pay. Most likely with their life.

Melanie had just awakened from a deep sleep and was still groggy. But Anya needed information and pushed her to explain the events of the evening.

Melanie explained that earlier that evening Vladi had called, asking for her. It seemed she had become his favourite. He asked her to meet him at the hotel so they could spend the evening together. She told Anya she wanted to kill him since she'd learned he was the animal who had killed her sister. So she gladly obliged. She said that he drank several glasses of champagne and snorted some cocaine. She admitted she had some cocaine but told Anya that every time he offered her more she refused. She explained to him she wanted to be her best in bed. He liked that idea so he stopped offering. What she really wanted was to have a clear head when the chance came to kill him.

After having sex with her he left the room and when he returned he was talking on the phone.

When she saw him she laughed and made fun of him. This made him angry. When she tried to calm him he hit her hard and she hit her head on the headboard. As she recovered from the shock of the blow, he came to look at her and realized he had hurt her.

"He said he was sorry," Melanie said.

When he went to the bathroom to put on his clothes Melanie knew he was angry and she was afraid. He returned and picked up his phone to make a call.

"He killed my sister," she screamed, and sobbed. "She was just an innocent girl and he threw her in a dumpster like she was trash."

Melanie looked up, her eyes filled with tears, and told Anya the rest of the story. She told Anya that while he talked on the phone she grabbed the bedside lamp and waited. As soon as he hung up she hit him.

"There was blood everywhere," explained Melanie. "But I wanted to kill him so I hit him again and again."

She said she must have passed out because she remembered nothing else until she awakened a few minutes ago.

As she listened Anya realized the call Vladi made was to her. She remembered their conversation and how she argued with him. Reading about the young girl found in the dumpster several weeks ago she did not realize the young girl was Melanie's sister then. Thinking about it now, it made sense that Melanie started working for the organization just over a month ago but Anya knew little else about her.

"Hi," said the young woman standing outside the doorway. "A friend suggested I come and see you about a job."

Anya looked at the girl and smiled.

"What work are you looking for and who told you to come here?" she asked.

She told Anya her name was Melanie Wentz. Then said she'd been working at a local strip club, which was a lie.

"One of the men there said I could make a lot of money working as an escort," she explained. "And he told me to come and see you." This was also a lie.

Anya stepped back and looked this beautiful young woman over from head to toe.

Whoever told her that, was right she thought. The girl was beautiful and Anya was confident, that with some polishing, this girl would be an asset to her business.

She invited her in and they went into her office. They talked together for about an hour before Anya offered Melanie a job.

In just a few short weeks Melanie developed a reputation with the Russian customers. She was a girl who could show a man a good time and the rumor was that she didn't mind the sex being rough.

While Anya was skeptical, she was happy to have such a beautiful girl willing to spend time with the Russian clientele. Even Stephan Corolev knew of this young woman, though he had not used the services of an escort since Anya had retired.

Stephan and Anya would often go to dinner and if asked she would still satisfy any of Stephan's demands when it came to his sexual appetite.

~

Anya thought about what she should do next. She should have checked his pulse there in the hotel room.

That was stupid, she thought.

Should she call Stephan? He would know whether Vladi was alive or dead.

Or would he? She knew that Stephan was having some problems with Vladi. He'd lamented his hiring during an intimate dinner at his favorite restaurant just a week ago. The recent killing of the young girl, who Anya now knew was Melanie's sister, had made Stephan angry. He also complained about the number of times Vladi's terrible temper had created problems that became more and more public. Stephan was a man who liked to fly under the radar and Vladi made that harder and harder to do. She decided to wait and watch the news later that day. Maybe then there would be news of the Russian's death.

~

Vladi was angry but knew he needed the nurse's services so he didn't do what came natural to him. He would not hurt her. At least not just yet.

"That was close," he said to Vivian. "But you did well to get us out of there so quickly."

He smiled and Vivian visibly relaxed her tense shoulders and returned the smile.

Vladi could feel something warm dripping down his neck and slid his hand across it to see what it was. Blood!

Vivian saw his hand and quickly took Vladi by the arm and sat him down in the kitchen.

He was bleeding heavily through the dressing she'd applied not more than an hour ago.

She grabbed a dish towel by the kitchen sink and used it to stem the flow while she carefully removed the bandage.

"Mr. Cherkov, you've torn the stitches in your wound and it is bleeding badly. You'll need to have someone re-stitch it and soon," she explained as she put some pressure on the wound.

"Fuck, that hurts!" he cried, and pushed her arm away forcefully. "Can't you stitch it up," he asked and grabbed the towel from her, applying some delicate pressure to the back of his head.

Vivian explained that she had no training in stitching wounds but said she would give it a try.

"Mr. Cherkov, I don't have anything to freeze the area before I stitch the wound."

"I don't care," he said. "Just do what you have to do."

Vivian shrugged and went to the bedroom. When she returned she told him to lay his head on the kitchen table with his face in the pillow. Then she started to stitch the wound.

The pain was unbearable but Vladi held his tongue as the young nurse delicately stitched the wound.

When she finished her work she inspected it and declared it a solid effort. After cleaning the excess blood Vivian put a new dressing on the wound.

"Thank you for being still Vladi," Vivian stated and gently touched his shoulder. "I know it must have been painful."

Vladi just nodded and asked her to take him to the bedroom where he could lie down. He was genuinely grateful and thanked her as he lay on the bed face down.

Vivian left and returned with a shot of morphine which she thought might help with the pain for a while. However, she knew he would be hurting for some time.

Soon Vladi was asleep and Vivian sighed with relief. She was safe for now. But she knew she had to leave this apartment sooner rather than later. An animal like Vladi Cherkov did not change his stripes and once he had his strength back he would be that dangerous animal once again.

She decided she would stay just long enough to give her patient one more shot of morphine and another dressing change. Then she'd be gone!

Chapter 21

Stephan Corolev was a patient man when it came to almost anything but his patience was wearing thin when it came to Vladimir Cherkov. He had been calling him constantly for the past twenty-four hours and it was not like Vladi to leave his phone unanswered.

What the hell is he up to? he thought. He'd just seen the news about Goren Skolotnev dying at the hospital and he needed some answers. It seemed this entire scheme of Vladi's was falling apart. He reviewed the events that had unfolded over the past few weeks. First, one of Vladi's girls dies mysteriously. And of all places, he puts her in a dumpster. When they found her she had over twenty bogus bank cards so they tied her to Vladi's bankcard scheme. What was Vladi thinking? Stephan knew Vladi had killed her, even though he denied it. Then one of Vladi's other girls is missing with no explanation from him. And he'd been avoiding him since then.

"Where in the hell could he be?" he muttered, pacing the office floor. He knew Vladi well and knew that with the events of the past few days his stress levels would be off the charts. And he knew that his go to stress relievers were sex and drugs. Those being number two and three. After his number one stress reliever, killing!

With that in mind he walked across the room to his large desk and dialed a number he was familiar with.

The phone was answered on the first ring.

"Hello my dear," said Stephan, moving around his desk so he could sit in his comfortable leather chair. He placed his feet up on the desk and continued.

"You sound surprised to hear from me," he continued, after hearing the woman on the other end hesitate in her greeting.

"Hello Stephan," said the woman on the other end of the line. "To what do I owe the pleasure?"

"Well Anya, I have a problem and I am hoping you might be able to help me."

"Oh?" questioned Anya. "What is the problem my love?"

"Well," he paused. "In the past twenty-four hours one of my employees has disappeared and another found dead."

Anya's mind immediately turned to the image of Vladi Cherkov lying on the floor in a pool of blood with one of her girls lying beside him. The girl semi-conscious and holding a brass bed lamp in her hand.

She hesitated again but continued the conversation by asking why Stephan would think she would know anything about the death of Vladi Cherkov.

"Why would you think the dead employee would be Vladi," he asked, suspicion now seeping into the tone of his voice. "Anya, is there something I need to know?"

Anya began to cry quietly into the phone, but remained silent, desperately thinking of what to say. She did not want this innocent girl to become the target of a man like Stephan Corolev. She was only avenging her sister's death.

Stephan was a man who was worldly and did not dirty his own hands in such matters but he, too, had a temper. Anya witnessed this temper on several occasions and saw what happened when Stephan Corolev was angry.

"Anya," he said softly and waited patiently. She remained silent on the other end and Stephan counted to twenty, waiting for Anya to respond.

"Anya, please tell me what is going on," he asked again.

With no response, Stephan spoke, telling Anya that Goren Skolotnov was the dead employee he was referring to, not Vladi.

"I have been looking for Vladi for almost two days. That was when I last heard from him," he explained. "Do you have any idea where I can find him?"

"Stephan," she replied and hesitated once again.

"What is it, Anya," he spat loudly making her flinch. She was thankful she was having this conversation over the phone and not in person.

"Please tell me what you know! Now!" he said forcefully, demanding an answer.

Anya sobbed and told Stephan what had happened at the hotel the night before. Vladi had called and asked for the new girl Melanie. Anya had not taken the call so she was unaware that Melanie had gone to meet Vladi and that she was with him at the hotel for the evening.

She told Stephan she had no idea that Melanie had plans to kill Vladi. She only found out where Melanie was when Vladi called just past midnight. He told Anya that one of the girls was with him at the hotel and she needed to come and get her. He explained the girl was hurt and Anya was furious. She protested but Vladi just laughed and hung up the phone. That's when Anya drove over to the hotel.

"When I arrived she was lying there with the lamp in her hand," she explained. "And there was blood everywhere!"

She sobbed again.

"I was so afraid Stephan that I quickly cleaned up as much as I could and took the girl home. I didn't check to confirm but I was certain Vladi was dead! He had to be with all that blood."

Stephan stayed silent as she explained that when they got home she cleaned up Melanie and put her to bed. She then made an anonymous call to the police.

"But I've been watching the news and there has been nothing about any incident or any report of a mysterious death at the hotel."

"Anya, you should have called me and not the police," he said sternly. "I would have taken care of it. I am disappointed in you Anya."

Anya begged for forgiveness and explained her concern for the girl. She reminded Stephan of the death of the young girl less than a month ago at the hands of that beast Vladi.

"The young girl he killed was Melanie's sister," she cried. "I only found this out this morning when she awakened and told me what had happened."

"Please calm down Anya," said Stephan. He hoped his tone would soothe her fears. "If Vladi is dead I will not be unhappy. But if he is alive, which I fear is the case, he will seek revenge on this girl."

Anya shuddered at the thought. But the way her old lover was speaking she felt she had an ally in Stephan. Perhaps he would spare this young woman. As long as Vladi didn't find her.

Stephan gave her the address to a house where both she and Melanie could hide and told them to get there as soon as they could. For now, she should have one of the other girls take care of business.

"Anya, I will meet with you and Melanie later," he said and hung up the phone.

Anya looked at the phone she held in her hand. A moment ago she felt safe but now she had her doubts. Did Stephan have revenge in his heart as well? Or did the feelings between them mean something more? Something that would save Melanie from death at the hands of a vengeful monster.

She placed the cradle down and called out to Melanie.

"We have to go, Melanie," she said. "I will explain on the way."

She told her to pack some clothes and she did the same. Within minutes they were out the door and on their way. Anya prayed that everything would be okay.

~

Chase gazed at Lisa's smiling face. She was asleep and while he wanted desperately to talk to her he just stood there and watched her smile. A smile so out of place given the large bandage wrapped around her tiny head. A bandage so wide it kept her flowing red hair from cascading on her pillow. Instead it fell straight down the sides of her face and rested on her shoulders. To Chase she looked like a refugee from some war torn country.

As she slept Lisa mumbled. Mumbled words that Chase could not make out but the smile told him she was dreaming happy thoughts which warmed his heart.

In the past he'd been with other women. Some he cared for deeply and others were just flings along the path of a well-known sports figure's life. But no one had pulled at his heartstrings the way this beautiful woman had. He loved everything about her and as he'd promised when he was waiting to hear of her fate, he now vowed to devote his life to her.

As he held her hand patiently, she stirred. She whispered his name and then looked up at his face and smiled the brightest smile he had ever seen.

"Hi," she smiled and looked into his sea blue eyes with her emerald greens.

"Hi," he smiled back and bent low to give her a delicate hug afraid he might break her.

She put her arms around him and hugged with all the strength she had.

"I'm so glad to see you," she cried and lay back down to stare at him lovingly. "I've been so worried."

Chase pulled up a chair so he could sit close enough to allow eye contact without Lisa having to strain.

His mind was racing with a million thoughts and he had to take a moment to sort them out. He wanted to tell her everything that had happened but instead looked her in the eye and said, "I love you Lisa."

Before she could answer he said, "I don't know if you feel the same way but I don't want to wait any longer to tell how much you mean to me."

He started to say something more but she sat up and put her finger to his lips. Then she gave him her answer with a kiss. Delicate at first but then probing, her tongue darting along the outside of his open mouth then it deepened. Their mouths pressed warmly together and their tongues began a sensuous duel. Her arms enveloped his neck in a warm embrace and he place his hands around her and held her tight.

As their lips softly separated she looked deeply into his eyes, smiled and said the words he hoped to hear.

"I love you too," as she gave him a quick kiss on the lips to seal the sentiment.

Lisa smiled but Chase could tell she was tiring quickly and he gently laid her back down on the bed and sat down beside her.

Chase held her hand as he explained the events of the last twenty-four hours. He told her about the gunfight at his apartment. How he and Nigel had escaped death but that one guy was not so lucky. He asked if she remembered crashing the car. She shook her head and told him she could remember nothing after she heard the gunshots in the park. He talked about how frightened he was when they found her in his car. How they raced to the hospital with her cradled in his arms. He told about the gunfight in the hospital where Matt shot and killed the guy named Goren. He told her about his meeting with FBI Director Fontaine and finally he told her about Matt. And Sonja!

"He's in way over his head," said Chase, shaking his head and thinking about how Sonja had compromised Matt.

"I know he's your friend Chase but it sounds like he made his own bed." She smiled and said, "If you get my drift."

Chase smiled in return but said he had to help the guy. He was his friend and he'd helped him out of a jam a time or two in the past. He owed him one.

Plus I'm up to my eyeballs in this he thought, but said nothing to Lisa.

Chase told her the FBI was holding the others for their own safety. He explained to Lisa they were here in this building and would be staying until everyone was safe.

"Oh shit," cried Lisa. "I forgot to tell you! Julie was here earlier! And she was posing as an FBI agent. Her name was Heather Reardon!"

"What the hell!" Chase stood up, shocked at this revelation. "Do you have any idea where she was going?"

"She was going to try and find you," Lisa moaned and turned away, a frightened look clouding her face.

Chase paced the room, thinking. He turned to her and asked if she had any idea where she might go. After all Julie was her sister. She had to have some clue about how her sister's brain worked.

"No, she said. "But the FBI knows that she's escaped and that she's posing as Heather Reardon. Maybe they can help."

With that, Chase stepped up to the bed and told Lisa he had to go. Then he gave his new found love another kiss and turned to leave.

"I'll be back," he said in his best Schwarzenegger impression, smiling.

She called out to him and told him to be careful. He waved over his shoulder as he left the room and walked quickly down the hall.

Chase now had a new mission. He had to find Julie and bring her back to Lisa. Lisa's happiness was of the utmost importance to him now, so he had to make sure Julie was okay. He strode down the hall looking directly at his friend Matt Hanson.

He was sure Matt could help him find Julie.

~

Julie breathed in the fresh air as she exited the building. What in the hell was she thinking!! And where in the hell was she going to go??

She felt conflicted and the conflict gave her pause. She hesitated. Should she go back in and give herself up? Or was it possible she could help herself and the others by being on the outside taking action?

She decided to take action and with that she pressed the panic button on the key fob she had taken from FBI agent Heather Reardon. Suddenly a cacophony of sound came from her right and she saw the flashing lights of a blue sedan about four rows away.

She noted where the car was and immediately hit the panic button again to silence the alarm.

Walking quickly, but not fast enough to draw attention, she made her way to the blue sedan. As she got closer she hit the unlock button and the parking lights flashed twice to let her know she was at the right place. At this point she did not know what she was doing or where she was going. All she knew now was that she had to go and get as far from here as she could.

As she left the parking lot and headed west, looking for anything that would tell her where she was, she glanced over her shoulder and saw two men exiting the building she'd just left.

But the two men were too far away. She couldn't see them clearly so she had no way of knowing one of them was Chase Adams, the man she was looking for. When Julie hit the gas, she realized she was escaping one captor and hoped she was not running into the arms of another.

When she was still with Vladi, one of the girls told her about an escort service the Russians owned. While she drove she tried to remember what the girls had said about it. Did they mention a location? She just couldn't think right now. Her adrenaline levels had been off the charts ten minutes ago and though she didn't realize it her body was coming down off that adrenaline high.

She felt dizzy and light headed. Her stomach growled and she felt herself sweating. In her present state there was no way she could continue to drive around aimlessly. She knew it would bring attention to herself if she continued. She had to get off the street. She noticed a coffee shop down the block and decided she should stop there for a drink. And a short rest. It would give her time to remember something more about the escort service.

Julie pulled the car around the back of the plaza. She wanted to keep the car hidden from the street. Looking around to make sure no one had followed, she quickly entered the café, intending to buy herself a drink and some food.

As she approached the counter she put her hand in her pocket to pull out some money and realized she had none.

Shit she thought. Without missing a beat she changed direction and went straight to the ladies room instead. Julie needed to sit and think. Everything was moving so fast! She opened a stall door and sat down on the toilet. She put her head in her hands and began to quietly sob, tears falling down her cheeks soaking her hands.

She wasn't sure how long she sat there crying. Through her tears she didn't hear the woman enter. Julie thought she was alone, so when she heard a light tap on the stall door it startled her.

A tiny voice asked if she was okay in there and Julie froze! Now what should she do? She tried to ignore the woman but she knocked and once again asked if she was okay.

"I'm fine," Julie said sheepishly.

"You don't sound fine my dear," said the woman from outside the stall. "Is there anything I could do to help?"

"No thank you," Julie said quickly and then thought m*aybe this woman can help me.*

Julie stood and opened the stall door to see a little old lady standing there. She couldn't have been more than five feet tall and had to be in her eighties. The woman smiled at Julie as she wiped the tears from her eyes and cheek. She sniffled and ran her sleeve across her nose to wipe it.

"Oh, you poor girl," whispered the woman as she took Julie's arm and led her to the sink.

Julie began to invent a story in her head as she splashed some cool water on her face.

She explained to the old woman that she'd had a fight with her boyfriend. She was angry when she left the house and she'd forgotten her purse.

"Come along dear," said the woman taking her hand and leading her to the door. "Let me buy you something to eat and drink."

Julie knew she needed to eat something and thought she might pass out. She followed the woman and picked out a sandwich and a soda.

The old woman wanted go outside to enjoy the sun but Julie insisted they stay indoors and moved to a table in the corner.

As Julie ate her sandwich the woman watched warily. But she was wise enough and kind enough to stop with the questions while Julie ate.

When Julie had finished her meal the old woman talked about herself. She told Julie she lived only a few blocks from here and came to the coffee shop often.

"I don't know why I'm telling you everything about me," she said. "But I guess it's because you have an honest face."

As the woman talked, Julie secretly gazed through the window hoping not to spook the woman.

The woman eyed her.

"Is there something you're not telling me," she asked and followed Julie's eyes.

"No," replied Julie. "I'm just afraid that my boyfriend might find me here. He has a temper and has hit me before," she lied.

Hearing that, the old woman stood up, took Julie's hand and led her to the door. She insisted that Julie come and stay with her until they could figure something out. She wanted to make sure her boyfriend had calmed down and, if not, they would call the police.

Julie protested, saying she couldn't impose, but gave in quickly and followed the old woman through the front door of the café.

She knew this was not a solution but right now she didn't know where to go or who to turn to. She hoped that hiding out at the woman's house would allow her time to put a plan together. But a plan for what?

Chapter 22

"Let's go!" cried Chase as he ran past his friend.

"Where to?" asked Matt and followed Chase to the elevator.

"We need to find Julie."

Matt grabbed his arm.

"Whoa buddy," he cried. "I know where Julie is. She's safe, here in the building."

"No! She's not!" Chase yelled as he stood there willing Matt to use his card to open the elevator.

"Open the door, Matt," screaming so loud that one of the nurses gave him a nasty look.

As a confused Matt opened the door, Chase told him that Julie had escaped by masquerading as FBI agent Heather Reardon.

"Lisa told me she was just here! Maybe we can catch her before she leaves the building."

As he the elevator moved to the ground floor Chase was shaking his head.

He just couldn't understand what Julie was thinking. What could she possibly do out there on her own? The fact was she was the one who had started all this. The reason he had gotten involved. How could she think she could do anything without his help and that of the FBI? But he knew how much Lisa loved her sister. So for that reason alone he was going to find Julie.

Chase was the first one out of the building. He looked to his left and scanned the parking lot looking for any sign of Julie but saw none. As he looked to his right he could see a blue sedan in the distance. It was leaving the western edge of the parking lot and heading west on the main road.

"There," he shouted. "Could that be her?"

He couldn't see the driver of the car so he had no way to know if it was Julie.

Matt gazed into the distance too, but said he couldn't tell if it was Julie either. For all he knew it was just another agent leaving the parking lot.

"People come and go from here all the time," he explained. "But right now it's our only lead so let's see if we can catch that car."

He smiled as he said this and quickened his pace.

As they drove, Chase and Matt talked about what had happened so far and where they stood in the overall picture. Now that Matt knew Fontaine was on to him he felt there might be a way out of this. And without having to follow through with his original plan.

Maybe now they could take down Corolev and Cherkov, as well as some of the lower level grunts of the organization. With what Chase told him, he now had enough information to take down these scumbags and free him from the grip of Stephan Corolev.

~

Vincent Fontaine could not believe what he'd just heard. He'd put far too much faith in this amateur sleuth. Why on earth would he tell Matt Hanson what he knew? Had he forgotten there was a bug in his belt? Or was he underestimating the sleuth? Did he think I would forgive Matt after hearing his confession? Or was there another reason. Could it be that he was on to him?

"There's not a chance this amateur could have figured out what is really going on," he said to himself as he looked out his office window. *Is there?*

It was time to make a call. Fontaine pulled the burner phone from his desk drawer and dialed the only number on it.

～

He awoke from a deep sleep, disoriented and unsure of where he was. The room was dark and as he looked to the window he could see the sun sinking into the west. He sat up in bed but a wave of nausea dizzied him so much he had to lie back. When his head touched the pillow he screamed and sat up quickly putting his hand to the back of his head.

"Jesus Christ," he whispered loudly putting it all together. He remembered the nurse and smiled. Then he thought back to the events that had brought him to this place. That horrible wench at the hotel.

"When I find her I will kill her slowly and painfully!" he vowed, then turned his body slowly and put his legs over the side.

"Vivian," he yelled loudly. No answer.

That's strange he thought and tried to stand. Feeling shaky he sat back down to get his bearings and try again.

He touched the back of his head lightly and felt the bandage wrapped around his head. It was protecting the wound from bleeding. When he pulled his hand back and looked it had no blood on it. That was a good sign.

"Vivian!" he screamed at the top of his lungs. Still no answer.

"Where is that bitch?" he said to no one but himself.

He was in pain, angry and confused which was never a good combination for Vladi. He sat still for another minute and then cautiously stepped onto the floor and stood. His head still hurt but over the last minute he felt the pain subsiding. To the point that he could tolerate it.

Vladi slowly walked down the hall to the kitchen calling out for his nurse Vivian but nobody answered.

Just then his cell phone rang from somewhere in the living room.

"Goren!" he said, again talking to himself. "That idiot better have some good news for me," he said aloud, then slowly made his way to the living room. That's when he saw his phone on the end table. Without taking the time to look at the call display he snatched up the phone and answered it.

"Goren!" he screamed into the phone, demanding to know what was happening with the search for Julie and Sonya. And that pussy private detective who'd been nosing around!

"Well hello my friend, Vladi," said the silky smooth voice on the other end of the line. "I see you are still alive. Unlike your poor friend Goren"

"Stephan, I am so sorry. I thought you were someone else"

"Clearly."

Vladi hesitated unsure of what Stephan had said just a moment ago.

"What did you say about Goren just now?" he asked.

There was a moment of hesitation on the other end of the line and Vladi waited impatiently. He was anticipating that syrupy sarcastic voice but instead a deafening scream came through the phone causing Vladi to flinch. Now his headache was back!

"Goren is dead you idiot!"

Vladi couldn't believe it! He stepped back and slumped into the sofa. He sat there trying to make sense of what was happening while Stephan went over the events of the last thirty six hours.

Though stunned by the news, Vladi quickly recovered and listened in earnest to what his boss was telling him.

At one point, part way into the explanation Stephan was providing, Vladi interrupted him.

He began to explain but Stephan took control and interrupted Vladi.

"I am well aware of what you've been doing for the past thirty-six hours," he said sarcastically. "Do you think there is anything that happens in my organization that I am not aware of?" he asked, again with a slight hint of superiority in his voice.

Vladi always marveled at how much information Stephan knew about his businesses but on this occasion he was more than surprised. How could this man possibly know what had happened to him?

Stephan could tell by his reaction that Vladi did not understand how he could possibly know about what had happened at the hotel. He decided to keep Vladi in the dark.

Then Vladi started to explain but Stephan stopped him again.

'Mr. Cherkov, I don't need any more explanations from you. What I need now is some action. I presume you are fit enough to carry out some orders," stated Stephan and waited for an answer.

"Of course Stephan," he replied, knowing he wasn't fit enough to do much of anything. But he would not let this prick know that. Vladi would do what needed doing, no matter. "What is it you need me to do?" he asked.

Stephan explained what he needed from Vladi and the more he listened the more frustrated he became. He interrupted him twice, both times asking Stephan, simply why. Why did he want Vladi to do this? At the first interruption Stephan told him that was none of his concern. When he interrupted for the second time Stephan let his temper get the best of him and in uncharacteristic fashion screamed into the phone.

"Just do what you're told," Stephan stated forcefully. "No more! No less! Do you understand your instructions Vladi?" he stated.

Vladi answered yes to his question and disconnected the phone, puzzled. He sat down trying to wrap his head around what had just happened. None of it made sense. The whole idea seemed absurd to Vladi and frankly Stephan Corolev was getting on his nerves.

The man was nothing like his father. After working for him these past few years he had lost all respect for him. But Stephan was still the boss and while he did not respect him he did fear him. If Stephan Corolev wanted something he just took it. If that was Vladi's life then so be it. But before he would do anything for Stephan he had to exact his revenge on two individuals. The nurse Vivian and the whore named Melanie. He had a reputation to uphold and he would not let these two bitches tarnish it. They would both pay a precious price for their actions.

Chapter 23

An hour before he called Vladi, Stephan Corolev had received a phone call of his own.

"Hello," said Stephan Corolev. It surprised him when he heard the voice on the other end of the line but as he listened his surprise turned to concern.

He sat down at his desk and gazed out the window. But at that moment he couldn't enjoy the view.

"I see," he whispered, growing angrier by the second.

He continued to listen for another five minutes as the voice on the other end caused a major headache. One forming at his temples. Then without saying goodbye the voice on the other end abruptly hung up the phone.

Stephan hung up the phone and swore to himself. Vladi Cherkov was becoming a problem and now was the time to get rid of his problem. He needed to think. Based on the information he'd just received he had more than just one problem. Perhaps he could kill two birds with just one stone.

He called down to the restaurant on the main floor of his building and ordered lunch.

"Yes Henri," he said softly. "I'd like the usual please. And can you send it up right away?"

He needed to think and he thought best on a full stomach. Besides, he was never one to act hastily. He had learned over the years it was better to think before you speak. And more importantly to think before you act.

As a plan percolated in his head the waiter from downstairs came into his office with his order.

He thanked the young man and gave him his usual, generous tip and dismissed him.

As he ate the finely prepared meal he smiled. A plan was slowly coming together in his mind.

~

"Anatoly here."

With Goren dead Vladi called on his second in command, Anatoly Levkin.

"Hello Anatoly, Vladi here."

It surprised Anatoly to hear Vladi's voice. He usually only spoke to Goren. He liked it that way because he knew how easy it was to get on the bad side of Vladi Cherkov.

"Hello Mr. Cherkov," said Anatoly, his voice quivering just slightly.

"Please Anatoly there is no need to be formal with me. Call me Vladi"

"Yes sir," he replied and immediately corrected himself and said "I mean Vladi."

"That's better."

Vladi then explained why he called, telling him that Goren was dead and he was his new right hand man.

Anatoly cringed at the thought of being that close to Cherkov. The idea frightened him so much that, at first, he didn't react to the news of Goren's death.

"What happened to Goren?" he asked after gathering his thoughts. Goren had been a good boss and Anatoly considered him a friend.

"What difference does it make?" he screamed into the phone. "All you need to know is that he's dead don't you?"

Anatoly apologized and asked how he could help.

Vladi calmed down and explained that he needed him to get some information for him right away. He told Anatoly the he also had another important job for him.

Anatoly wrote down every word spoken. He wanted to make sure there were no mistakes. He had seen what happened to people who made mistakes when working for Cherkov. He remembered dumping the girl's body in the dumpster about a month ago. She had made a mistake and now she was dead.

"And when you ask, tell them I want to send the nurse a thank you gift so I will need her home address," Vladi told him. "And Anatoly, I want this to be a surprise so make sure the office doesn't let Vivian know," he smiled.

Then he hung up the phone and lay down on the bed, eager to hear back from Anatoly. He needed to rest and recuperate. He would need all his strength before taking on the strenuous work of killing.

~

Sonja was slowly coming down from the cocaine high Matt Hanson had given her. Her head ached and her nose was running.

She was glad there was no mirror in the room because she was afraid to see what she looked like. The earlier withdrawal had taken a real toll on her and her body was having a tough time coping.

Sonja was hungry too. But she knew there was no chance she could keep any food down at the moment. What she needed was more cocaine. It would make her feel better. She was sure of it.

As she lay there hoping beyond hope that her wish would come true the door to the room opened and a well-dressed man stepped inside.

"Hello Sonja," said the good-looking man in the doorway. "I hope you're feeling better than you look, my dear," he commented as he sat down on the bed at her feet.

She slowly moved her feet back and sat up, leaning against the headboard.

"I don't feel well," she whispered hoarsely and leaned her head back and moaned.

Vincent Fontaine couldn't believe that even in this state Sonja could still radiate a sexuality that made him feel the beginnings of an erection. She had filthy clothes on, her hair was a mess and she wore no makeup, yet something about her made men want her in the worst way.

"Do you have anything for me?" she begged as she sat up on her shins and moved toward him.

Fontaine pulled a clear bag out of his suit pocket. "You mean some of this Sonja?"

Her eyes lit up and she smiled.

"Yesss," she hissed almost silently and crawled toward him.

"I don't think it would be wise for you to have any more of this, do you?"

The look in her eyes made him shift in his seat and adjust his pants so he'd feel more comfortable.

Shit he thought as she put her hand on his leg and moved it sensuously along his thigh.

"Please may I have some," her sensuous voice cracking as her hand moved closer to its target. Fontaine stood up quickly but uncomfortably and stepped back.

"Soon Sonja," he replied feeling a tinge of guilt. "But I need you to help me first."

He reached out and gently nudged Sonja back to the head of the bed and sat down. When Fontaine explained what he needed her to do, it frightened her.

"Sonja, you don't have to worry. I will protect you and when this is over you will never have to fear Vladi Cherkov again. But first we need to get you cleaned up. Then I will take you to a safe house nearby and I can assure you everything you need will be at that safe house."

Vincent stood up and told her that someone would be in soon to clean her up and give her some medicine and food.

"I need you to be strong Sonja," he explained. "I need you to be that sexy little minx I know you can be," he added and left her sitting on the bed, sniffling.

She wiped her hand across her nose and waited impatiently for someone to come.

A few minutes later a young woman came into the room. She looked at Sonja sympathetically and smiled. She told her she was there to help clean her up.

For the next hour they worked together to reinvigorate her spirit and get her feeling better. They gave her something to calm her stomach so she could eat. They brought her new clothes and put some make up on her face. When they finished Sonja looked like a different person.

Excellent thought Fontaine as he watched the transformation from his office. He had turned off the camera during his visit, but now he was watching this stunning change take place before his eyes.

Soon she would be working her magic on the subject of his choosing.

~

Vivian heard the knock on the door and jumped out of her skin. Since she'd left that bastard she was constantly looking over her shoulder, sure that he was right there behind her.

Who could it be? She moved to the front door but before she could get there the door burst open and she realized her worst nightmare.

"Hello Vivian." The smile on his face was pure evil and she screamed and ran toward the back of the house. If he caught her he would kill her! She knew that! But what she feared most was what he would do to her before he killed her. She ran, hoping beyond hope she could escape. But Vladi was just too quick for her.

As she opened the patio door, she felt a hand grab her hair and pull her back. The force was so strong that she fell backward and hit the tile floor hard. He pulled her back down the hall by her hair as she screamed. She was screaming so loud Vladi thought the neighbors would hear. So before another scream left her throat he punched her in the face and knocked her out.

When Vivian came to she felt cold and confused. She couldn't understand why until she looked down and saw she was on the bed naked. She tried to get up but she couldn't move. Vladi had tied her by her wrists and ankles to the four-poster bed. She screamed! There at the end of the bed sat her worst nightmare! Naked! Her body convulsed involuntarily at the sight of him. She sobbed knowing her life was over.

"Vivian," he said quietly, smiling that evil smile. "I am so glad you are awake. I've been waiting patiently. I didn't want to start while you were unconscious because it would not be nearly as much fun if you weren't awake to enjoy it."

"Why are you doing this to me?" she asked even though she knew the answer. "Please Mr. Cherkov I'll do anything you ask."

He slapped her hard across the face.

"You're damn right you will, you filthy bitch," he screamed.

He held her chin in his hand and softly caressed her reddening cheek. He smiled that evil smile once again.

"And Vivian. You can call me Vladi. Trust me, over the next few hours we are going to get to know each other well. In the most intimate ways."

Then he reached across to the night table and picked up a spoon filled with a white powdery substance. He added a few drops of water and used a lighter to heat it up. Once liquefied he reached for the syringe and filled it with the warm liquid.

"I have something for you Vivian," he smiled as he flicked his finger on the syringe to make sure there were no bubbles. He didn't want her to die before he had some fun playing with his new toy.

"You know Vivian, I found this syringe on the floor of the flop house where I bought this heroin," he whispered as he wrapped the rubber ban around her upper arm. "I think it has been used a few times already Vivian. But you don't need to worry, you are not going to live long enough to get HIV." He gently tapped her arm to raise the vein.

"I promise you," he added as the syringe hit its mark.

Vivian felt the pinprick as the warm liquid entered her body and an incredible feeling of euphoria swept over her when Vladi pulled the elastic band from her arm.

She moaned as the feeling hit her even though she knew, that before this night was over, she would die a horrific death at the hands of this monster.

She felt his hand along her upper thigh as it moved slowly toward the area between her legs. She was powerless to protect herself, tied to the bed with legs opened wide. She felt his wet tongue brush her nipple as his hand reached its target. This time she moaned loudly as her body reacted to his touch, knowing she was helpless to save herself.

Matt drove, while Chase was on the lookout for Julie and the car they were sure she drove out of the parking lot. Since getting on the road they had checked in with McVittee and his partner Stevens. The two confirmed Julie had taken agent Reardon's keys and her badge. She also took her gun so they suggested Matt and Chase be careful approaching her.

They took the same route they felt the sedan had traveled and followed that main road. As they approached a plaza on the left side of the road Chase noticed a dark blue sedan parked haphazardly across the rear parking lot.

"There," he cried as he pointed at the car in the lot. "That looks like the car we saw leaving."

Matt got on the phone to confirm the license plate on the car was the same as Reardon's assigned car.

They both got out of the car and slowly walked around to the front of the building. They were looking for somewhere that Julie might have gone. They spotted the coffee shop and decided it would be the most obvious place.

Matt entered the shop first thinking, that since Julie had only met him once, she might not recognize him. That way she would not be alerted to their presence if she was there. He looked around and saw no Julie. Then he motioned for Chase to come in.

"She not here," said Matt as he moved toward the cashier's counter. He pulled out a picture and showed it to the young barista, asking her if she'd seen this woman in the last little while.

The young girl looked at the photo for a moment and called a fellow worker over.

"Hey Josh," she said. "This is the girl that was in here just a few minutes ago? Right?"

"Yeah," said the young man. "I saw her leave with an older lady who always comes in here. I think her name is Marion."

Chase looked at the young man.

"Do you have any idea which way they went?" he asked, desperately hoping he knew.

"I'm sorry but I don't." He explained that he just saw them leave but then went back to making up his orders. "We've been busy."

Chase stood there, thinking of what they should do next.

"You mentioned a minute ago that she comes in here all the time," he said and looked at the young man. "Do you know if she drives or walks?"

"I'm almost certain she walks," he replied, thinking. Then said, "you know what? I know she walks. I remember her saying how pleasant it was to walk over here for her afternoon tea."

Matt and Chase looked at each other.

"If she lives nearby, the tech guys can perform a search for women named Marion who live close by," explained Matt. He pulled out his cell phone and punched in the speed dial number for the office.

He suggested they both have a coffee and wait to see if the tech guys could find a Marion who lived nearby.

Maybe they'd get lucky and find Julie hiding out with this old lady. Matt knew they had more pressing matters but felt this was important to Chase. He could tell Chase cared for Lisa and he knew if it was important to Lisa it was important to Chase.

Anatoly was driving and thinking. He had called Dr. Tupolev's office and passed on the address of the nurse named Vivian. Dr. Tupolev had come to the phone to ask Anatoly how Vladi was feeling. Since he didn't know, he just lied and said he was feeling much better. He didn't know what was wrong with Vladi and wasn't about to ask. He knew Vladi well enough to know the fewer questions Anatoly asked the better.

Just do what you're told Anatoly, he thought. But he did wonder why Vladi was giving this woman a gift. From his experience that was not his style. Normally a job well done meant you would live. To Vladi that was thanks enough because if you screwed up you died.

As Anatoly drove up the quiet suburban street he saw the house he was looking for. He drove by slowly to check it out and see how he should approach it. His new boss had asked him to undertake a delicate job so he needed to carry it out carefully. No bull in a china shop approach this time.

As he drove by he could see the young boy and his mother talking in the kitchen. Anatoly turned around at the end of the street and went back the way he came.

He'd come up with a plan to gain access to the house and slowly pulled his car into the driveway.

He approached the door and knocked, waiting for either the boy or his mother to answer. It took only a moment and the young woman came to the door.

Anatoly noted she was attractive and before he could introduce himself the young boy, who looked to be around six, came and stood beside the woman.

"Who is it mommy?" the boy asked.

His mother rubbed the blond hair on his head and smiled.

"I don't know Jeremy. Let's ask him."

The woman looked up at the man and asked him how she could help.

Anatoly gazed at her, a solemn look on his face.

"Hello Mrs. Hanson."

Chapter 24

Vladi exited the shower watching all the blood red water flow into the drain. Although he'd killed many people he still marveled at all the blood a body could hold. It would have been impossible to get that much blood out of his clothing so he was happy he'd removed his clothes at the beginning. Even after a long, hot shower there were still remnants of Vivian's blood on his skin.

He walked back into the bedroom and laughed as he eyed his handiwork.

The body was unrecognizable. He'd slashed her throat and there were deep cuts along her thighs and on the insides of her upper arms. Spots of dried blood were caked on her breasts where her nipples once were. Vivian had tried hard to fight the fated responses but her body betrayed her as Vladi used her as his personal sex toy. During one of her orgasms he used his knife to cut off both nipples. At that moment he wasn't sure whether she screamed in agony or ecstasy. It didn't matter either way to him.

Vladi wasn't sure what had killed her but based on the volume of blood that spurted from her neck when he cut her throat he guessed that was the killing blow. A needle stuck out of her arm which he hadn't bothered to remove after giving her the final dose of heroin. He cut her face savagely along her cheek lines and the cuts made her once beautiful face a grotesque mask. The blood in her blond hair made the color pink.

Vivian's death had been a slow and painful one. Vladi used her sexually for hours. When he was finally spent he viciously tortured her before brutally killing her. In her final moments Vivian only wanted it to end and begged to die. But before Vladi granted her that wish he shot her up with another dose of heroin. Even in her state of incredible pain Vladi saw a look of ecstasy on her face just before he viciously slit her throat, ending her misery. He laughed knowing he denied her a chance to enjoy that final feeling of euphoria.

His phone rang and brought him out of the trance like state he'd fallen into recalling his time with the nurse.

"Hello?"

It was Anatoly who simply said "It's done," and hung up the phone.

Vladi smiled. Anatoly was quickly earning the faith Vladi had reluctantly put in his new right hand man. Vladi finished dressing and left the bedroom, not bothering to clean up. He knew he had left some of his DNA in and on the body but he was just as sure that no one in the United States had his DNA in any database. He was certain the Russians had his DNA but he did not think they or the Americans were sharing the DNA of their citizens with any foreign jurisdiction.

As he left the bedroom he turned back and, once more, admired his handiwork. He felt strong and that surprised him. The pain in his head was gone and when he touched the dressing, put on by Vivian earlier, it was still dry.

He smiled an evil smile thinking Vivian did have her good points.

"Too bad she had to be such a bitch," he said aloud and walked out the front door, determined to win back the trust of his boss Stephan Corolev.

And with the work already completed by Anatoly he was more than half way there.

He made the call to update Stephan.

He felt the phone buzz in his pocket. He wondered who might be calling and then saw who it was and smiled.

"Hi sweetheart," he said. "What's up?"

A male voice responded.

"Isn't that a lovely way to answer the phone," said the male voice softly.

The sound of that voice surprised Matt and he panicked!

"What are you doing? Are you insane?" he cried, recognizing the voice instantly. He stopped in his tracks causing Chase to do the same. He frowned as he listened to Matt's end of the conversation.

"Where's Amanda," he demanded, visibly shaking.

"Mathew, Mathew," the voice of Stephan Corolev said, this time with a little more force. "There is no need to worry yourself," he assured him.

"Your wife and son are fine."

Matt couldn't believe this was happening!

"Why do you have my wife's phone you fucking bastard!" he screamed. "I swear if you harm my family I will kill you!"

Chase stood there watching his friend lose it. He'd never seen him like this and felt helpless to do anything for him.

"Relax Mathew," said Stephan once more, in a firm voice, taking charge of the conversation. Surprising Matt had served its purpose. "As I said your wife and child are fine. And will remain that way as long as you do what I tell you to do." Stephan gathered his thoughts. "My sources tell me that you have gone," he paused again. "How does the American phrase go? Oh yes, gone off the reservation."

"What are you talking about?" Matt demanded.

"I understand, my friend, that you are not living up to our agreement," Stephan paused once again, this time for dramatic affect. "And I have decided that a reminder of what can happen when you don't do as you're told is in order. Mathew, your decisions are consequential so I suggest you make the right ones."

With that Stephan hung up the phone.

Matt looked at the phone, disbelief showing in his wide eyes.

"What the hell was that about?" asked Chase.

Matt's look didn't change as he continued to gaze at his phone. He said in a fog of disbelief "the Russians have Amanda and Jeremy."

"What!" Chase couldn't believe what he was hearing. "Why would they take Amanda and Jeremy?"

Matt continued to stare at the phone but his mind was reeling. Chase was asking questions a mile a minute but Matt wasn't listening to a word.

What was Stephan talking about? What's changed since the last time they talked? He was confused by the conversation that just occurred.

"Chase, would you shut up for a minute!" he cried. "I need to think!"

"Something must have spooked him," Matt said.

He was talking to himself but Chase responded saying, "what would have spooked who?"

Finally he looked up at Chase, fear in his eyes.

"Stephen Corolev, the head of the Russian mafia in this city. That's who has my wife and son."

"What do you think we should do?" asked Chase, still confused.

"I don't have a fucking clue but I need to figure this out," and turned to go back to the car. Chase grabbed his shoulder.

"Where are you going?" he asked. "We've got to find Julie."

Matt pulled away, giving him a death stare. He told Chase he could continue to look for Julie if he wanted but there was no way he would abandon his wife and kid.

"Chase I need to go," he insisted and turned away. Without looking back he said, "You can come if you want."

Chase stood there a moment. What should he do? As far as he knew Julie was safe. She was spending time with some old lady in the neighborhood. What difference would it make? As long as Julie was out of sight of the Russian Vladimir Cherkov she was out of mind. And based on what Matt had told him it sounded like Cherkov might have other problems to deal with.

Matt was already halfway back to the car when Chase decided to join him.

"Hey Matt! Wait up!" he yelled and started running after him.

Although Chase couldn't see it, Matt smiled. He was happy his friend was coming to help.

Since Chase had told him about his conversation with Fontaine he felt a renewed and deeper kinship with his friend. They had grown apart over the past several years, their lives going in different direction. Chase, chasing his dream of a career in professional hockey and him following his lifelong goal of law enforcement. It was good to have Chase in his life and he hoped the partnership would grow.

Matt got to the car and turned to see Chase only a few feet away. They got into the car and headed for the FBI building.

"Thanks Chase."

"For what?" Chase looked at him and smiled. "I figure Julie is as safe where she is now as she would be at FBI headquarters."

Chase clapped him the shoulder.

"And besides, it's obvious we make a great team," he laughed, hoping to lighten Matt's load.

"I don't know about that my friend but I do appreciate you sticking by me like this. I know you care about Lisa and, for her, finding Julie is priority numero uno."

Chase smiled.

"As I said, she's safe for now so let's figure how we can get Amanda and Jeremy home."

Since Chase had not heard the other side of the phone call, he grilled Matt on the details. After hearing the entire conversation he asked Matt what Corolev meant by going off the reservation.

"I don't have a clue," he replied.

"Well," said Chase. "What's changed since the last time you spoke to him?"

"Nothing," Matt replied.

Matt thought about the last time they'd talked and what had transpired between that time and now.

"Wait!" cried Matt. "The only variable I can think of is the talk you and I had."

He looked at Chase and asked him if he thought Fontaine had been playing him knowing that he'd confront him about his betrayal of the FBI.

"I don't think so Matt. He told me clearly not to breathe a word of it to you and I'm sure he meant it."

Chase then went over the events of the day as well and suddenly it dawned on him.

"Shit!" He'd forgotten all about the belt.

"What's the matter?" asked Matt, as he watched Chase slowly take off his belt and place a finger to his lips signaling Matt to stop talking.

Once he removed the belt he tried to show Matt the bug in the buckle.

When Matt gave him a puzzled look Chase took another path.

"Can we pull over here," said Chase. "I need to pee."

Matt pulled over and Chase got out the car and slowly put his belt on the back seat, motioning for Matt to follow him. About twenty yards from the car Chase abruptly turned to Matt, stopping him in his tracks.

"What the hell, Chase," he said, looking even more puzzled.

"It's my belt!" whispered Chase urgently.

"What about your belt?" said Matt in a loud voice, confused by what Chase was saying.

"Ssh!" whispered Chase and again put his finger to his lips. "Fontaine put a bug in the buckle," he explained.

"You're kidding me!" Matt was furious. "Why didn't you tell me this earlier?"

"I'm sorry Matt but I forgot. There's been so much going on! He wanted to watch what we were doing without you knowing so obviously I couldn't tell you earlier." He knew his explanation would do no good so he shut up. He waited for Matt to speak and when he didn't he finished his thought.

"So Fontaine obviously knows what you told me earlier and that you've been working with Corolev." continued Chase, thinking back to earlier. "Could he be dirty too?"

"Nothing else makes sense Chase. He has to be." Matt was busy thinking back, looking for clues. Was there anything in Fontaine's behavior over the past few days that pointed to him being dirty?

Chase asked Matt if he thought kidnapping Amanda and Jeremy would be something that Fontaine would be part of. Matt said he didn't think so but couldn't rule it out.

"We have to play this out as if he's part of this Chase."

He swore in a whisper aware the belt wasn't far away. "Fontaine knows that they've kidnapped Amanda and Jeremy if for no other reason than he overheard us talking just now."

"Based on what we've just figured out Fontaine must be the one who told Corolev about our conversation!" said Chase. "It has to be him. Could Fontaine be in this guy's pocket too?"

Chase couldn't believe how stupid he'd been. And his stupidity might give somebody a chance to kill them.

Matt couldn't believe Fontaine had fooled him too. He recalled their chat earlier in the day. When Matt thought that Fontaine suspected something. But to be working with Corolev? That just didn't make sense.

Matt turned to Chase.

"Change of plan my friend." Matt explained that they needed to head back to the safe house and put together a plan of attack there. With Fontaine in the picture the landscape had changed and they needed to rethink their strategy.

As they drove to the safe house Matt made a call.

"Listen McVittee, something's come up and I need you and Stevens to handle the search for Julie Eskin."

He explained that they'd recently traced her to a coffee shop and gave him all the details.

"Follow up on that lead and see if you can't bring her back safe."

Chase looked over at him and said thank you.

"Listen," Matt smiled. "They work for me so I might as well have them doing something useful."

⁓

He listened to the conversation and couldn't believe what he was hearing! What the hell was Corolev thinking? Kidnapping an FBI agent's family? This would cause a major problem. He was about to call the Russian when he heard the conversation between the two men turn. As he listened his heart raced and he could feel a bead of perspiration trickle down his neck dampening his shirt collar.

They cannot connect the dots he thought.

That fucking idiot! This Russian idiot would ruin everything. He realized now, he should never have called Corolev. He should have kept the information about Hanson to himself. He picked up the phone and was ready to call Stephan Corolev. He wanted to rip this asshole a new one, but then he hesitated. He stopped for a moment, thinking about the pawns he had yet to play in this deadly chess game. Maybe Sonja was the pawn to move now. Her moves could make the entire game turn on its head. This pawn could take out one important piece for him. The Knight! And with the Knight out of service the King would become vulnerable.

Fontaine turned off the audio on the buckle bug and made his way out of the office.

He could listened to the rest of the recording later.

⁓

Sonja gazed at her image in the mirror and couldn't believe it. The young woman sitting beside her had performed a miracle. She was at the safe house now and was putting the final touches to her look. Her black hair shone with a healthy glow and the makeup the young girl had applied made Sonja's eyes brighten to accentuate her already radiant beauty.

When she got to the safe house a doctor had given Sonja some pills to take. She hesitated but the doctor explained the drug, called Propranolol, would help her with the cocaine cravings she was experiencing. Sonja wanted the cocaine not the drug but the handsome man named Vincent told her it would be too dangerous for her to take the cocaine now, given what he needed her to do.

Vincent Fontaine entered the room and commented on Sonja's new look.

He felt a certain stirring as he gazed on this vision of beauty and sexuality.

"Please come with me Sonja," said Vincent Fontaine and he led her down the hall to a large kitchen. The island countertop held an array of food and Fontaine urged her to eat. Her stomach was still queasy but she sat down on a stool and nibbled on some fruit and took a drink of juice.

Fontaine couldn't help but stare. Sonja looked incredible and he could understand how she could have seduced Matt Hanson. No matter how strong his devotion to his wife and family. And while Vincent knew the pitfalls of playing with Sonja and enjoying her company he would not dismiss the idea just yet.

"I don't know if I can do this Mr. Fontaine," said Sonja. She explained the circumstances of her escape from Vladi Cherkov but Fontaine just smiled.

"He will be more than angry with me," she added. She looked terrified but Fontaine insisted she would be all right.

"Sonja, as I said earlier we will be close by to protect you. You are the only way we have to find out where he's hiding. We know he's injured and we assume he's convalescing somewhere so I don't think he poses a threat to you or anyone else at the moment."

Vincent handed her a burner cell and told her to make the call.

She took the phone reluctantly and dialed the number from memory.

"Hello," said the voice on the other end of the line.

"Who the hell is this?"

"Vladi?" she whispered. "This is Sonja."

Chapter 25

Dr. Tupolev had been trying to find Vivian for the past few hours without success and it frustrated him. He'd finally been able to track down Vladi but when he asked if she was with him he told her he had dismissed her because he was feeling much better.

"Maybe she's at home," Vladi suggested, smiling to himself. "I can tell you doctor that she is a miracle worker. She was the one who gave me the incentive to get out of bed."

Tupolev said he was glad Vivian had been helpful and explained he'd been calling her home phone and her cell but was getting no answer.

"Doctor she was more than helpful. She was an inspiration. But she was looking beat up the last time I saw her," he said and had to stifle a hearty laugh.

"She could be sleeping. I know that when I am as tired as she looked I can sleep like the dead." This time unable to hold back, he chuckled into the phone.

"You're right," said the doctor, a little confused by the tone in Vladi's voice. "I think I'll go by the house and see if I can rouse her out of bed."

"You do that doctor," replied Vladi this time laughing. "You do that."

Vladi was just picturing the scene. Seeing Tupolev's face when he found Vivian would be priceless. He was thinking maybe he should be there when his phone rang. His mind was still picturing the moment and he didn't look down at phone.

"Hello," he stated forcefully, upset the phone had interrupted his pleasant thoughts.

The voice on the other end said his name meekly, then hesitated a moment, before saying, "It's me."

A frustrated Vladi yelled into the phone.

"Who the fuck is this?"

"It's Sonja," said the voice, unsure of the reception her voice would elicit.

"Sonja!" cried Vladi, now recognizing her voice. He kept his tone light so he would not scare the poor girl away again. He was genuinely happy to hear her voice but not because he was happy to hear from her. He had other reasons.

"Where have you been?" he asked, suddenly feeling the anger rise to the surface.

"I'm sorry I ran away Vladi. But you frightened me. I was so afraid you would kill me like you did that other girl. You were so angry."

Vladi was livid but he kept his voice calm and steady.

"I am so sorry Sonja," he said softly. "I did not mean to frighten you. I treated you badly and you were right to leave."

Keeping his voice steady he told her how frustrating business was recently and he knew he should not take it out on her. She had been a wonderful companion he said and he wanted her to come home.

"Okay," she said meekly. "I still have the money I took so is it okay if I take a cab home?" She steadied herself and then said in her sexiest voice, "Maybe we can have a little fun tonight?"

When he heard that Vladi remembered another reason he should punish this bitch. Stealing his money! But instead of lashing out he merely said that it was 'only money' and told her he'd be home later tonight.

"Wait Sonja," having another thought, "don't go to the apartment," he said and gave her the address to a property he had access to on the west side.

"There's a key under the planter at the front door, okay?"

Once again he said he was glad she had called and then disconnected the line.

Sonja listened to the dial tone for several seconds trying to read Vladi's mood from the conversation she'd just had. He seemed okay on the phone which relaxed Sonja but only slightly.

Vladi felt some mixed emotions which was not like him. As he drove to meet with Anatoly at the property he was holding Hanson's family he thought about what had happened these past few days and wondered if he could ever change. Lately, he'd felt oddly remorseful for some of the pain he'd caused in the past few months. Was it somehow his fault that Goren was dead? Did his action cause the ATM scam to fall apart? This was not an emotion he felt normally and it caused him pause for a moment.

"Maybe I need to change," he said aloud, feeling his regret grow a little stronger.

The feeling didn't last long for Vladi though. Instead, as he sped down the interstate in his black Porsche, he grabbed a cocktail straw, set the mirror on dashboard and took a healthy snort of coke and laughed.

He took notice it was the last of his stash and made a mental note to stop by his supplier to pick up more. Maybe he'd stop by that flop house he'd visited earlier and grab some smack too! He smiled as he hit the gas pedal. He was going to have some fun with Sonja tonight!

~

It was Stephan calling. Vladi stared at the number deciding whether to answer or let it go to voicemail. He did not like having to serve this man but knew it was his only way to the top. He did not understand the need for kidnapping the FBI agent's wife and kid. As far as he knew Hanson was keeping up his end of the bargain. The FBI agent had consistently looked the other way when it came to looking into any of Stephan's businesses. And when necessary steered those investigations in another direction, causing them to hit a dead end. He'd been a good soldier. So why this?

When his phone buzzed with Stephan's call Vladi had just arrived at the house. At that precise moment he was speaking with Anatoly. He explained that picking up the mother and her child had gone smoothly, and told Vladi he'd locked them in the second floor bedroom.

"Aren't you going to answer that?" Anatoly asked.

"No Anatoly, I do not want to speak to anyone right now," Vladi explained. He felt tired.

Maybe he'd done too much he thought and smiled. Killing could sure make you tired.

He let the phone go to voicemail deciding he would speak to Stephan later. He wanted to visit with Amanda Hanson for a few minutes and then take a nap before meeting with Sonja.

He had plans for Sonja and wanted to be fresh so he could enjoy the fun.

He knocked on the door and asked if he could come in. There was no answer so Vladi opened the door and entered. Amanda Hanson and her son were cowering on the king size bed wrapped in each other's arms. The boy was whimpering.

"Hello Mrs. Hanson," he said, "or may I call you Amanda?"

Vladi smiled and moved into the room causing the boy to move in closer to his mother and sob loudly.

"What do you want from us?" Amanda demanded, sheltering her young son. "Where is my husband? Does he know you've taken us?"

"Please calm down Amanda. I do not want to hurt you or your little boy," Vladi said, ignoring her demands. "But if you don't do as I say I will do what is necessary," he warned. "Do you understand?"

Amanda, although frightened of the kidnapper, would not back down. She demanded to speak to her husband. She told Vladi her husband was with the FBI and that he would make them pay if they did not let her and her son go. All the while cowering on the far side of the bed with her arms around her little boy.

Vladi smiled.

"I know who your husband is Amanda and what he does for a living," he explained. "And I do not think that you can make demands. So I would suggest you," Vladi paused a moment then leaned in close to his captives, "shut the fuck up!" Vladi spoke the last four words so loud and with such anger that spittle flew across the room and landed on Amanda's arm.

At that moment Amanda wished she was invisible and if she could crawl any deeper into the corner she would. She pulled her son in close to her and then cried quietly.

Vladi then calmly asked if they would like something to eat. Amanda couldn't believe what she was witnessing. One minute this man was calm and collected and the next he was a raving maniac. But what disturbed her the most was how the raving maniac disappeared as quickly as it appeared. Watching this man's was like watching a duck on a pond. Calm one minute, like a duck floating serenely on the water. But just beneath the surface there was a frenzied madness.

"Why don't I order us some pizza?" he asked, looking at the boy. Jeremy nodded silently in answer to his question. His mother said nothing.

Vladi clapped his hands together, which made both mother and son flinch.

"Pizza it is!" he cried and walked out the door.

Amanda breathed a sigh of relief when the angry Russian left the room. She wondered if Matt knew their fate. And if he did, what was he doing about it? How did a man like this maniac know her husband? He must be lying.

She held her little boy and prayed a silent prayer, willing her husband to come to the rescue.

~

Matt looked at the telephone debating his next move. Both he and Chase had arrived at the safe house and were sitting in the living room. He was trying to decide which of his enemies he should confront first. At this point he knew that Stephan Corolev was holding his wife, trying to bring him back into line. But he had no idea where. He and Chase had talked in the car and both agreed there were only two ways the Russian could know. Either Stephan Corolev had a bug in this safe house which seemed unlikely or Fontaine had overheard their conversation. The second scenario made more sense, since they knew he had placed a bug on Chase's belt buckle. If this was the case then the only way Stephan could know about their conversation would be from Fontaine. What didn't make sense was why? What possible ties could these two men have? Vincent Fontaine was the Deputy Director of the FBI for God's sake! Could they be wrong?

"I just don't get it," said Matt. He got up off the couch and paced the room. "What possible motive could Fontaine have for getting into bed with the Russians?"

Chase watched as he continued to pace the room not knowing what to say.

Matt turned to him in frustration and said, "It just doesn't make sense!"

"Listen Matt we can't just sit here and do nothing," said Chase, stating the obvious. Then he suggested it would be wise to keep Fontaine on the sideline and see if he shows his hand somehow.

"Maybe we need to figure out what this Corolev guy wants. Then we can work out a way to get your family back," suggested Chase. "Shit, maybe we can even get this guy to tell us what he has on Fontaine."

Matt was thinking. He turned to Chase and told him he agreed with his idea.

"But we can't just go straight at a guy like Corolev," he explained. "He's too smart for that."

Matt knew there was no way the Russian mob boss would trust him now. It was obvious the arrangement he had with him was over. There was no going back. But he also knew that what Stephan wanted badly, was to have Vladimir Cherkov out of the way, permanently! Maybe he could win back his trust by making sure that Stephan got what he wished for. Maybe.

"I think we need to figure out where Cherkov is," said Matt.

"Why Cherkov?" asked Chase.

"Because he's the key cog in this machine, Chase," explained Matt. He told him about Stephan's wish to remove Vladi and that doing so might get them back on the right path.

Chase smiled, thinking that arresting Vladi Cherkov was a great idea.

"How do we find him?" he asked.

Matt looked at him with a sly smile, "I think I've got an idea."

Chapter 26

He knocked on the door. There was no answer so he knocked again, this time harder, causing the door to open.

That's strange he thought and slowly made his way into the foyer.

He called out her name but got no answer. Stepping further into the house he detected a strange smell in the air. It smelled like burned rust and he could almost taste it. It didn't make sense to him. How could you taste what you smelled?

In the kitchen he noticed her coat laying on the back of a chair and her purse sitting on the kitchen counter. Her keys lay beside the purse suggesting the woman who occupied the house must be home. He called out again, thinking that perhaps she was sleeping as Vladi had suggested. But as he moved slowly down the hallway the rust taste turned to something else. It was a smell he was familiar with. Death!

Dr. Tupolev's senses became heightened! Concerned something was wrong, he moved cautiously down the hall. At the door he hesitated, then slowly moved into the bedroom. At first, confused, he saw blood everywhere! As he moved closer to examine the scene, his foot stepped in a pool of blood, causing him to slip and fall on his back. Frantically, he turned and put his hands on the floor and tried to get up but slipped once again, this time with his face hitting the floor. As he got up off the floor awkwardly he saw the blood all over him. Seeing what had become of Vivian, he threw up and collapsed beside the bed.

"What have you done?" he cried. Shouting at the top of his lungs, he cried for help but there was no one there. He was alone. He immediately realized it was that pig Cherkov who'd done this.

"Why?" he cried out. "Why would you do this? You bastard!" Suddenly a wave of guilt swept over him. He was responsible for this! He should never have asked her to take care of that monster. An innocent, beautiful young woman he had thrown to the wolves.

He looked down at her, his emotions in turmoil. He couldn't call the police. With all this blood on him they would undoubtedly suspect and detain him. It would take hours, even days, to prove he had not been the person who mutilated and murdered this poor young girl. He needed to avenge her death. But how? What could a man like him do to a monster such as Vladi Cherkov?

~

As Matt led them through the front door of the vast FBI building, Chase Adams expressed confusion. Matt tried to explain but realized showing was better than telling.

"Chase, just trust me okay?" Matt pleaded. "Come with me. I want you to meet someone. Once you see her it may become clearer.

They entered a small office where a young woman was sitting behind her desk. Her back was to them and she was reading something on a computer set on a credenza. The name plate on the desk identified the occupant as FBI Special Agent Heather Reardon. As she turned to face them Chase couldn't believe his eyes! Sitting before him was Julie Eskin, Lisa's little sister. Then he did a double take and realized it wasn't Julie but someone who looked a lot like her.

"Chase, I want you to meet Agent Heather Reardon," said Matt Hanson, smiling.

Heather looked at both men with a confused look on her face.

"You look like you've seen a ghost," said the female agent.

Heather was looking directly at Chase when she made the statement and then waited for an introduction.

Matt immediately realized his blunder and his lack of manners.

"Heather, this is a friend of mine. Chase Adams."

"I'm sorry," said Chase. "But you look a lot like someone I know."

Heather smiled with understanding.

"Ah yes! You must mean Julie Eskin," she replied. "Yes, I am well aware of the similar look we share," she added and laughed.

She began to tell her story but Matt interrupted her, telling her they knew the circumstances surrounding Julie Eskin's escape.

Heather looked at them sheepishly and asked what they were doing in her office and how she could help.

Matt turned, closed the door to her office and explained. He laid out a plan that involved Heather posing as Julie. He explained that, while this would put her in danger, they would be working as a team with the two men close by if needed.

Heather listened carefully and cut him off several times, asking questions. After a full explanation and Matt responding to her questions, she felt comfortable with her role in Matt's plan. Even though she had only been with the bureau a short time she felt confident she could pull off the charade.

Matt smiled. He, too, was confident in the plan and Heather's ability to pull it off.

"Okay!" he said. "Let's go find the final piece to this puzzle and solve it."

Matt led the way as the three went to find an important part their scheme. Someone Matt knew well.

Anya heard the key enter the lock and listened as the door to the house opened. She turned to Melanie, her finger to her lips and motioned for her to head upstairs. Anya followed close behind.

"Hello?" cried the voice at the door. The girl noticed signs of life in the house when she entered. There were coats hanging on hooks by the front hall and two pairs of shoes.

She called out again but there was no response. Timidly, she moved down the hallway and turned into the kitchen. From there she could see that someone had eaten a meal. There were dirty dishes in the sink and the unfinished portion of a meal that sat forlornly at the kitchen table. From what she could see there were two occupants and they were both women. She decided it was time to explore.

The house was a two storey affair with four large rooms on the main floor and a bathroom. She guessed the bedrooms were upstairs but before heading that way she made a sweep of the main level. There was also a basement, which she peeked her head into but saw no one in the unfinished space.

Anya recognized the voice from somewhere but couldn't place it. She told Melanie to hide in the bathroom off the master bedroom and lock the door behind her. Then she slowly crept to the top of the stairs and saw the eyes of a woman familiar to her staring back. A surprised look on her face!

"Sonja!" she cried. "What on earth are you doing here?"

"Anya? Is that you?" Sonja couldn't believe what she was seeing. Since the day the Russians lured her into this life, Anya had been the only one who cared. She took care of all the girls but Sonja had always been her special one. At least that's how Sonja felt. Looking back on it, it was likely how Anya made all the girls feel. Special.

"Anya, what are doing here?" she cried racing up the stairs to give Anya a great big hug.

The two women hugged and held each other close before separating and looking deep into the other's eyes.

Just like old times thought Sonja. She was happy to see her old friend.

"Melanie! You can come out now," Anya cried out, smiling at the new arrival and breathing a big sigh of relief. "It's okay. It is a friend," she explained.

Melanie came out of the bedroom and stood in the doorway, afraid to come any closer. The young woman who had just arrived was a stranger to her and that made her wary.

Anya smiled at her and motioned for her to come closer.

"Melanie, I want you to meet an old friend of mine," signalling her to join them. "This is Sonja," she continued. She looked at Sonja as she said this and smiled. "How can I call you an old friend when you are so young," she exclaimed and laughed aloud.

Anya put her arms around both girl's shoulders and ushered them down the wide staircase and into the kitchen. She offered Sonja some food which she refused. Sonja sat down heavily on one of the kitchen chairs and declared her need for a drink.

"Melanie, can you get Sonja something to drink?" asked Anya. The she suggested an ice tea, to which Sonja heartily agreed.

Melanie moved to the fridge and took out the ice tea. Then she took out a glass and was about to pour when Anya asked Sonja what she was doing here.

"I am meeting Vladi here," she said and smiled. "Why are you here?" she asked, happy knowing there would be others here. It made her feel safe.

Without warning Melanie screamed and dropped the glass and the bottle of ice tea, both crashing to the floor.

Anya and her old friend jumped from the table to escape the flying glass and ice tea but had little luck. The glass and the sticky liquid covered the floor around them. Melanie standing dead still, screamed hysterically.

"He's coming here?" cried Anya incredulously. "Why is he coming here?"

She took hold of Sonja by the shoulders and with a face as white as a ghost asked again. What possible reason could Vladi Cherkov have for coming to this house? Her mind reeled. Had Stephan set her up? Was this all a plot to kill Melanie? Why would Stephan do this to her? He cared about her? Didn't he? None of this made sense.

Anya's reaction confused Sonja and the sheer look of terror in Melanie's eyes frightened her.

"He told me to come to this address and said he would meet me here later," she explained.

Sonja told the two women about the events of the past two days and explained that she was just trying to make amends. She knew she had been wrong to leave Vladi like that and to have angered him. At first the idea of seeing Vladi frightened her but she felt much safer with two more people in the house. She didn't tell them it was the Assistant Director of the FBI that ordered her to come and that he was close by, recording her movements. She didn't know if she could trust them with that.

"This can't be happening," Melanie said, coming out of her fugue state. She turned to Anya and screamed once again.

"Anya, this can't be happening," clutching her shoulders and shaking her. "What are we going to do?" cried Melanie. She was out of control. She paced the room frantically and was mumbling to herself. Sonja watched this, trying to understand her reaction.

Anya turned to her and told her she needed to calm Melanie down and once she had she would explain everything.

"Melanie, let's go upstairs and lie down," Anya pleaded. "I'll give you something to relax you and perhaps you will get some much needed sleep."

"Sleep?" screamed Melanie, now apoplectic. "If Vladi finds me here he will kill me Anya. There's no way I can sleep!"

Anya pulled Melanie in and hugged her tight telling her everything would be okay. She promised she would call Stephan Corolev and assured her he would take care of them. But before Anya could do that, Melanie needed to calm down.

Anya turned to Sonja and asked her if she knew when Vladi was arriving. Sonja shrugged her shoulders, signaling she didn't know.

"Okay then," she said and moved Melanie into the hallway, "let's find a place upstairs where you and I can hide."

Then she gently put her arm around the girl and led her to the stairway and up to the master bedroom. She tucked Melanie into the large bed and gave her a glass of water and a sedative.

"Here, take this," she insisted and left the room, promising to call Stephan right away.

Anya was more relaxed when she returned to the kitchen. She wanted to explain what had happened to Melanie and in doing so hoped to gain Sonja's trust. For them to survive, she needed to have Sonja's help and she needed to have her trust.

Sonja sat at the kitchen table listening to her old mentor, all the while recounting the horror she endured in Vladi's bathroom just days earlier. That frightening experience helped her understand the fear these two women were feeling.

As she listened she also thought about the handsome FBI agent and wondered if there was a way he could help them. Did she trust him enough to put the lives of these women in his hands? Then decided it would better to let his plan play out and if conditions changed she could always ask for his help. Her 'mission' as he called it was to keep Vladi happy and to stay close. That way Fontaine could follow his movements.

"I need to meet with Vladi," Sonja said. "Since he is expecting only me perhaps the two of you should hide. I will make sure he doesn't find you."

She gave Anya a smile and a wink and said, "I know how to keep him busy. Trust me he will not be interested in anything but me."

Anya returned the smile and decided she had to trust her old friend and join Melanie in the upstairs bedroom. All she could do now was hope that Sonja was true to her word and could keep the monster busy.

She climbed the stairs and opened the bedroom door to find Melanie sitting up in bed shaking.

"Melanie, I told you to take that sedative! You need to stay calm and you need some sleep."

"Are you kidding me?" she exclaimed. "There is no way I am going to sleep knowing that monster is going to be in the same house as you and me!"

Knowing that Vladi Cherkov was on his way here agitated Melanie and her voice rose with every word. Anya put her finger to her lips, begging Melanie to be quiet, when suddenly she heard the front door open and the voice of Vladi Cherkov invade their sanctuary.

Anya grabbed her companion and quickly put her hand over her mouth and pleaded with Melanie to be quiet.

~

"Sonja?" Vladi cried out. "Where are you my lovely?"

Sonja stepped out into the front hall looking much more confident than she felt.

"I'm here," she replied, her sensuous voice falsely suggesting she was happy to see him.

"Sonja, look what I have brought for you," holding out a bag of cocaine, a bottle of vodka and a small bag, filled with what she guessed was heroin.

"We're going to have a party!!" he shouted loud enough for the two others to hear. The two others in the house that Vladi was, blissfully unaware of.

Sonja smiled. She then turned and called him to join her in the living room.

Upstairs Anya hugged Melanie close, the two shaking and hoping beyond hope that Vladi would remain ignorant to their presence.

But Anya needed more than hope so she took out her phone and hit the speed dial number for the only person who could save her.

Hearing the voice on the line calmed Anya and she whispered into the phone,

"Stephan, you must help us! Vladi is here," she said and hung up the phone.

⁓

Heather Reardon held up the rear as all three walked down the hall. The hallway was familiar to her because it wasn't long ago that she'd walked it in shame. When they found her handcuffed to the plumbing in the bathroom, a washcloth in her mouth. At the time she was thankful that Julie had at least dressed her. Her mistake was embarrassing enough. Having your colleagues find you in your bra and panties was too much to endure.

Reading her mind, Matt called out over his shoulder.

"Don't feel too bad Agent Reardon. We've all had incidents we're not proud of. When your career is over I'm sure there will be plenty more to add." and with that he turned to her and smiled.

What they needed now was a way to contact Cherkov and Matt was hoping Sonja could provide that information.

They moved down the hallway toward the room that housed Sonja. Matt opened the door in anticipation. Sonja was the reason he betrayed the organization he loved and the family he cherished. But despite that, the girl could stir feelings in him that were hard to control.

He moved into the room steeling himself against any feelings that might surface. It shocked him to see the room was empty.

He turned to agent Reardon.

"Where the hell is she?" he demanded.

Reardon shrugged her shoulders, saying she didn't know and suggested they check to see if someone moved her to another location. She explained that after her interview with Julie they'd moved her to more comfortable quarters on another floor.

"At least until she escaped," Reardon said sheepishly. "Maybe they moved Sonja too."

Chase and Matt followed as Reardon led the way to the elevator and up to the floor where they had held Julie.

Once on the floor they went to the office to ask the whereabouts of Sonja. The young girl at the desk explained Sonja had been here earlier but had left after getting cleaned up. When Matt asked where she had gone the girl told him she didn't know but said that she'd left with Assistant Director Fontaine.

"Fontaine?" Matt asked. "Why would she be with Director Fontaine?" Matt was clearly upset while the conversation confused Chase and Reardon.

The young girl said she did not know why Sonja was with the Director and could only tell them she overheard the two conversing and had mentioned the name Cherkov.

"I think Sonja was going to meet him for some reason," explained the young girl. "But I don't know any more than that," she said and turned away, continuing her work on her computer.

Matt looked at Chase knowingly. Fontaine was up to something. Something that involved Vladimir Cherkov and that meant something no good.

What was Fontaine up to? And how did Sonja fit in? Cherkov was the key and a determined Matt Hanson wanted to get ahead of whatever was going on. Finding Cherkov was now his priority and to do so he had to call Stephan Corolev. He would know where to find him.

Before he could come up with a plan Chase interrupted his thoughts.

"Listen Matt, I'd like to talk to Nigel and let him know that everyone is okay. Can I do that?" he asked.

"Sure," said Matt. "Just ask the girl we just spoke to. I'm sure she can get you into see him. And while you're doing that Reardon and I can figure out our next move. So come back here when you're done.

Chase smiled and moved off to speak with the girl so he could check up on his good friend.

~

"Chase!" cried Nigel as he saw his good buddy standing in the doorway. He ran up and embraced his friend in a great big bear hug.

"Where the hell have you been?" he cried, holding Chase by both shoulders and smiling. He was happy to see his friend and peppered him with a million questions.

Chase looked at him and held up his hand as if to say now was not the time. Nigel didn't understand the signal at first but then saw someone else behind Chase. From his look Nigel guessed he was another FBI agent.

"Hold up Nigel," Chase said and pulled away, looking around the room. He turned and looked at his escort and politely asked him for some privacy. The agent wasn't sure he should allow that but Chase reminded him he was on their side. That he was working with his boss, Matt Hanson. The reminder was all he needed to have the agent give him and his friend the space he sought.

Once alone with Nigel, he sat down on the sofa and motioned for Nigel to join him. For the next half hour he explained everything that had happened since they last saw each other. Nigel continued to interrupt by asking questions but Chase ignored him.

"Thank God Lisa's alright," he said once Chase had finished going over the events. "Can you get me outta here?" he asked.

Chase looked around making sure they were out of earshot of the agent in the hall. He wasn't sure he could get Nigel out but said he would try.

"Has anybody talked to you," he asked Nigel.

"Yea, that big shot. What's his name?" he thought for a moment then, remembering, cried out, "Fontaine!"

Chase looked at him with concern.

"What did he want?" asked Chase.

Nigel explained that Fontaine had asked him to sit tight. That he had a plan in the works that Nigel was part of.

"What do you mean?" he asked. "What plan?"

"I'm afraid he didn't say Chase," he replied. "But he did mention you and agent Hanson"

Knowing what he now knew, the idea of Fontaine having a plan concerned him. He didn't trust the man and was sure that he was up to no good. And he didn't want Nigel caught in the middle.

"Nigel," Chase looked at his friend, his expression serious. "Wait here a second and follow my lead. I'm going to get you out of here."

Chase went to the doorway and asked the agent to come in. He told him he wanted to ask him a few questions. The agent smiled and entered the room ready to answer any question this friend of his superior asked of him.

Chase stepped back and allowed the man to enter closing the door behind him.

As soon as the door had closed Chase grabbed the agent from behind and placed him in a choke hold. He couldn't remember the name of it but he knew it was dangerous. He remembered the police had outlawed the maneuver years ago after it had killed a suspect. The agent struggled mightily but Chase was stronger and held on until he felt the man go limp. Then he placed him gently on the ground and felt for a pulse. Feeling one he felt relief and quickly motioned for Nigel to help lift him onto the bed in the corner.

Chase ran to the door and quickly opened it. Seeing it empty, Chase moved into it and motioned for Nigel to follow. Before he did, Chase grabbed the agent's gun and stuffed it in his jeans. They quickly and quietly made their way to the elevator where Chase used the key card Matt had given him and took it to the ground floor.

Once outside Chase turned to Nigel.

"Here you go," he laughed and handed him a set of keys.

Nigel looked at them, a surprised look on his face.

"Where did you get these?" he said. They were the keys to his car! His pride and joy! He loved this car almost as much as Chase loved his. It was a black, matte finished, Chevy Camaro. A sweet ride!

Chase laughed.

"I thought you'd be happy!" he stated, knowing how much Nigel loved his car. "Fontaine gave them to me!" he exclaimed and clapped him on the shoulder. "It's should be over there somewhere," said Chase, then looking out at the sea of blue sedans he laughed. "I don't think you'll have any problem finding it."

Chase explained that he wanted Nigel to move the car close to the exit of the parking lot and wait until he saw them coming out. He wanted him to follow. He needed him to be his back up if something went wrong.

"Nigel, I trust Matt," he said. "But right now he's under serious stress and having you close by feels like a good idea."

"No problem Chase."

He watched as Nigel walked into the parking lot and saw the lights of his black Camaro flash, signaling the car unlocking.

Suddenly Chase felt a surge of confidence, knowing his friend was out there backing him up. He walked back into the building and headed back to find Matt and Reardon. For now he would keep his back up to himself. A secret ally might come in handy.

~

"Mathew, of course I know where my employees are."

It was Stephan Corolev. Matt didn't like Stephan calling him Mathew but he hated the way he used that syrupy voice when he said it. It just frustrated him.

He wanted to jump through the phone and strangle the bastard. But he couldn't. So instead he seethed quietly.

"Well," said Matt in a superior tone. "There's something that I didn't tell you the last time we spoke."

"I see," was the syrupy reply. "And what is that young Mathew," he asked.

"We have one of Vladi's girls here," he smiled. "Her name is Julie. You know her. She's one of the girls Vladi used in his ATM scheme."

"And why would that interest me Matthew?" Stephan's voice changed slightly. Not as syrupy and confident as it was a moment ago.

"Well, my colleagues are about to interrogate her and my concern for you is that she'll talk. She looked frightened when they brought her in. Now in my experience, when someone is in that state of mind they can be much more cooperative. Sometimes they tell their captors everything they want to hear. I'd hate to have her share any secrets that could hurt you Stephan."

He waited for Stephan to answer, hoping he would take the bait. He did.

Stephan told Matt there was a safe house where he could take the girl. At the moment there were two women at the house waiting for instructions. The girl would be safe there.

At first Matt objected to the idea, wanting instead to deliver her to Vladi. He was about to refuse when Stephan reminded him that his wife and son were safe right now.

"But that could change," warned Stephan, his confidence at a high point once again.

Matt cursed himself knowing he was not in control just yet. But he knew the only way to gain that control was to keep the play moving.

He grabbed the pen and paper sitting by the phone and jotted down the address of the house. He was eager to get moving but he couldn't find Chase. He paced the room as Reardon looked on. Matt gazed at the clock wishing time would stand still, only to hear the door slowly open.

"Where have you been?" he demanded as Chase entered the office. He was worried and it was getting to him.

"Whoa," Chase replied, raising his hands, palms out as if in defense.

"I just finished talking with Nigel. All is good. Do we have a plan?"

He looked over at Reardon, his look seeking some answer to Matt's mood.

Reardon just shrugged her shoulders. Matt looked at them both and explained that for now they would take "Julie" to a house across town the Russians owned.

"Stephan tells me there are two women there now who are awaiting his instructions so we're going to head over there and see what happens," he explained.

Chase didn't understand how this was going to help them since their primary target was Vladi Cherkov, not two random women working for Corolev. But seeing the look on Matt's face told him now was not the time to object.

Just go with the flow he thought. He looked over at Reardon. He couldn't believe how much she resembled Lisa's sister. He just hoped the likeness would be enough to fool the Russians.

Matt moved toward the door and signaled the other two to follow. They left the building and went out to Matt's car. Down near the exit to the parking lot but hidden from view was Nigel's Camaro, its driver patiently waiting.

~

Stephan hung up the phone. He couldn't believe his luck. Not two minutes before the call from agent Hanson he'd spoken to a frightened Anya. Vladi Cherkov was at the house! Mathew and Vladimir colliding! Death and destruction would result from such an event. Too bad the women would be collateral damage.

There were other women in this world, weren't there? thought Stephan.

He smiled.

Chapter 27

Vladi was in the mood to party! Life was good. His new right hand man Anatoly was working out just fine and it looked like his boss was finally off his back. He had work to do to get his little ATM scheme back on track but was confident his new right hand man was up to the task. He was so happy at the moment that he'd forgotten about the girl who got away. The girl named Julie! What he hadn't forgotten was the bitch who clocked him at the hotel. She was going to pay!

But for now Vladi would have some fun. He had his favorite party girl with him and all the drugs they needed to have a good time. Revenge would come later.

"Did you say you brought something for me?" smiled Sonja, having taken a spot at the end of the sofa. Sonja, dressed to kill with a sheer white blouse covering her white skin and pair of black leather pants that looked painted on. A perfect look to show off that fine ass and those lovely long legs. Her jet black hair cascaded across the beige leather as she lay back at the far end of the sofa.

Vladi smiled.

"Sonja, Sonja," he whispered as he moved toward her and set a large bag of white powder on the table. "Of course I have something for you."

Sonja looked at the bag and her body shivered, anticipating the coming high. She wanted the drug so fiercely she abandoned herself to it. Forgetting the justifiable fear she had for her life. She didn't care. All that mattered right now was that high! And nothing, not even the fear of death, would deter her from that.

As Vladi removed some powder from the bag and cut the drug into lines of white powder, Sonja slid across the sofa and took a rolled up hundred dollar bill from Vladi.

She bent over and drew in the first line of the four spread out on the glass surface. The effect was immediate. Her body convulsed subtly and a wave of euphoria swept over her.

"Isn't it fine Sonja," laughed Vladi, watching her drift into ecstasy. Vladi couldn't believe the effect it had. Sonja was a beautiful girl and had such a sensuous way about her. One that would bring any man to his knees. But when under the influence of cocaine? That sensuality rose tenfold.

"Yessss," she hissed quietly and bent over for a second line. She inhaled it deeply and lay back on the couch. She looked over at Vladi with a smile and a sexy look that said 'come over here, I want you'.

Vladi smiled back and took the rolled up bill from her and took in a line for himself.

"Now Sonja, don't be greedy!" he said and immediately felt the rush of euphoria himself.

He stared at Sonja, the sexy waif, and felt an erection coming on. When Vladi was on cocaine, the sex he had was incredible no matter who it was with. But with Sonja! There was just no comparison.

He moved over beside her and grabbed her viciously by the hair and pulled her to him. With her head slung back she exposed the milky white skin of her long neck. He gazed at her then he slowly ran his tongue along the smooth skin and up the side of her face. When he reached her cheek he turned her roughly toward him and kissed her hard. Sonja didn't resist but instead moaned into his mouth, opening hers to allow the dueling of their tongues to begin. She grabbed at his belt wanting to remove his pants but he took her hands away. She looked up at him, her eyes smoking, and ran her fingers up his chest unbuttoning his shirt as she went.

"Sonja," he whispered. "Why don't we take this party upstairs and get comfortable?"

Vladi did not wait for an answer. Instead he grabbed her by the hair once again and pulled her to her feet. Before leaving the room he grabbed the bag of white powder and the other drug paraphernalia he'd brought.

"Let's go!" he demanded and grabbed her roughly by the arm. And quickly moved toward the staircase.

As they reached the top of the stairs Vladi dragged her toward the master bedroom. Something in Sonja's head screamed out a warning and she gently pulled him toward one of the smaller rooms.

"Let's go to this room Vladi," she said pressing her body into his and rubbing her breasts into him. She suddenly remembered. The two women were hiding in the master bedroom!

"I want to be close to you," she whispered, "not in such a big bed."

Vladi laughed and told her he wanted to party and with that he pulled her into the master bedroom and threw her onto the king-size bed.

"And we need room to party!" he laughed and jumped on the bed beside her. He tore at her clothes and began to take off his own. He knew what pleasure Sonja would bring him, her naked body under his. He would use her in every way possible. Use her until she was useless and then enjoy one of his other pleasures! Killing!

He didn't know that deep inside the walk-in closet next to the bathroom were Anya and Melanie. They heard them coming up the stairs and swiftly ran for the bathroom and jumped into the first place they could find. They had barely made it before Vladi and Sonja walked into the room. Both knew that Vladi was unpredictable and if he caught them in here there would be no escape. They were certain he would kill them. Anya hoped beyond hope that Stephan would get to the house before Vladi discovered they were there. But Melanie had other ideas. Down on the floor next to her, and out of Anya's sight, was the long silver plated letter opener she had taken from the night table. Her fingers brushed across the cold steel and she was trying her best to call on the courage to use it.

~

Nigel watched as the large blue sedan, carrying his friend Chase, swept past him. He waited a few moments then started the car, put it in drive and move in behind it. He had done this before so he knew he had to keep some traffic between him and his target. Most of the time tailing another car needed several follow cars so they wouldn't alert the target. But in this case that wasn't going to happen. From four cars back he watched the sedan move down the street and take a right hand turn two blocks ahead. He wasn't sure how this would play out but he was certain he would do everything he could to have his friend's back. He took the right hand turn and slowed to allow another car to get between them. If he got too close he worried they might see him and he didn't want that to happen.

Reardon sat quietly in the back, concerned. Matt Hanson was losing it. He was on edge and wasn't taking any precautions with this hastily put together plan. She listened as the two men talked and tried to figure out what they would do once they arrived at their destination. While Matt's friend Chase Adams was in control of his wits, he was not the one in charge. The unhinged one was. She decided it was best to stay vigilant for now. She'd keep her head down and act when it was necessary to act and not before. Hopefully these two were not propelling the three of them into a disaster. As she listened to them she turned to look out the rear window, again.

There it was she thought. Could be a coincidence? She didn't think so. Four cars behind them she could see the familiar car. The black Camaro she'd seen as they left the parking lot of the FBI complex!

Matt was oblivious to his surroundings. In the state he was in he had complete tunnel vision. His mind was racing! He had to figure out a way to get his wife and kid back. How had he gotten them into this? A good husband and father wouldn't let this happen. But he knew had to accept responsibility! The blame! Could he fix this? He was going to kill that bastard Cherkov. But only after he told Matt where his wife and son were. He didn't care what he had to do. He would do whatever it took to get them back. And he'd do it with or without his friend's help.

Chase took a stealthy look in the passenger's side view mirror. He was happy and relieved to see that Nigel was still behind them. Matt was so focused on getting to where they were going he was unaware that Nigel was following them. He worried about his friend. He wasn't the same. Matt was acting irrational and Chase worried that Matt's actions might put them in danger. He wanted to calm Matt down but he didn't know how right now.

They were just a few blocks away from their destination when they passed another blue sedan parked on the side of the street. No one in the car noticed as they passed and the occupant couldn't believe what he was seeing. What the hell were they doing here? He panicked but then he suddenly realized that if Matt and his friend were going to the house where Cherkov was, this could work out fine. Fontaine didn't notice the black Camaro following a few cars behind.

~

Vladi got up from the bed, spent. Covered in sweat, his legs felt like rubber. Standing there he looked down at Sonja lying there on the sweat soaked sheets. Her body was a mass of bruises and strings of his DNA spread across her breasts. A dirty hypodermic needle dangled from her arm. Vladi had filled it with the large dose of heroin now coursing through her worn out body. She had put up a good fight but in the end he was just too strong for her. This time he'd been careful not to shed any blood. The needle in her arm had sent an overdose of heroin into her body and it was killing her slowly. She let out a low moan. It wouldn't be long.

He marveled at how much sex appeal, even in the throes of death, exuded from this young girl. So much so he almost felt sad knowing he could no longer enjoy this wonderful creature's talents. He moved away from the bed and started toward the bathroom on his tired legs. He stood by the sink and splashed cold water on his face, trying to rejuvenate his tired body. Then he heard someone open the front door of the house and suddenly the synapses in his brain brought his body to full alert. He moved quietly to the bedroom and quickly donned his clothes. His gun and knife were on the night stand and he grabbed them both and with stealth, moved toward the top of the stairs!

~

Anya heard the front door open and waited. She and Melanie huddled in the corner of the closet when Vladi had entered the bathroom. A tear was slowly crawling down Anya's cheek as she realized that her friend Sonja was dead. They had been ear witnesses to the devastating treatment she had suffered at the hands of this monster. They heard the moans of ecstasy and the screams of despair as the monster used her for his filthy pleasure and then discarded her like trash. Throughout the ordeal Melanie had to battle the urge to save Sonja. She desperately wanted to jump out of the closet and stab the bastard with the letter opener she kept hidden from Anya. But she knew it was not the right time. Patience was her friend and she knew she must wait for just the right moment. One that insured success and the death of this pig. She thought of her sister and vowed this time this monster would die!

The girls listened as Vladi moved from the bedroom and when they were sure he'd left, they slowly made their way out of their hiding place. Anya's hand covered her mouth and stifled a cry of despair when she eyed the naked and bruised body of Sonja lying on the bed. She quietly moved to the bed. She covered her body with a sheet and gently pulled the syringe from her arm. How could anyone do this to another human? Hate boiled inside her for this man and she vowed to avenge Sonja's death. Perhaps Stephan would share her disgust once he witnessed the aftermath of this innocent girl's grisly execution. And just maybe he would mete out a just punishment.

Melanie stifled a scream of sheer anger as she looked down at the body that Anya had covered so gently. Adrenaline coursed through her as she gripped the weapon she held by her side. Then gunshots rang out!

~

Matt opened the front door carefully. But the door creaked and he knew their presence was no longer a secret. He swore silently, knowing the noise was loud enough to alert anyone who was in the house. As he moved into the large front foyer he looked for any signs of life but saw none. Chase and Reardon were close behind and together they moved toward the kitchen at the back of the house. To the right was an open stairway leading to the second floor. It went straight up to a landing then turned left and continued to the second floor.

At the top of the staircase was a half wall that blocked their view to the floor above. They could see two open doors they assumed led to a bedroom or perhaps, a bathroom. From where they stood it was hard to tell. Standard procedure dictated they clear the main floor before moving upstairs. They continued along the far wall, staying out of sight. They saw the kitchen and a large family room that stretched across the back of the house. As they reached the end of the foyer they could see there was no one in the kitchen. Matt held up his hand causing the other two to stop. Chase was no expert in tactical maneuvers but he was not happy being out in the open. He saw movement at the top of the stairway. He cried out a warning but not before the figure at the top of the stairs fired an automatic in their direction.

As bullets peppered the wall above them, Matt and the others scampered to the relative safety of the hallway leading to the laundry room. Heather followed the two men but she couldn't make it to cover. A bullet struck her thigh, tore through the muscle and exited out the other side. Luckily, it missed the major artery there but she was still bleeding badly. Chase quickly reached out to her and hauled her to the safety of a small hallway. He quickly looked around the laundry room next to him, hoping to find some first aid. He knew he needed to stem the bleeding quickly so Chase took off his belt and made a tourniquet with it. Reardon was grateful but when he tightened the belt around her leg she screamed in pain and cursed him. While Chase was helping Reardon, Matt moved toward the edge of the wall to look but the shooter showered him in a hail of bullets. His quick reflexes took over and he ducked back to safety just in time.

"Fuck," he cried out and looked back at the blood soaked pant leg of his colleague. He knew the shooter had the advantage. They couldn't stay where they were. He had them pinned down and without cover they couldn't move either. If they did they'd be like targets in a shooting gallery. Matt motioned for Chase to join him.

"How's Reardon," he asked, keeping his voiced hushed to avoid her overhearing.

"It's bad," whispered Chase, "I've stopped the bleeding for now but she needs a hospital."

Behind them Reardon let out a low moan.

"What's going on?" she asked. As she looked at the two men she grimaced in pain and slumped against the wall.

"I need to get to a doctor," she whispered, "and fast!"

"Just hang on Reardon," said Matt. "We'll get you out of here."

His confident bearing belied the concern he had for his colleague and he hoped what he was saying was true.

He told Chase to grab Reardon's gun and explained that he needed him to set down some cover fire. That way he could move to a better, more strategic location. Instead Chase pulled the gun he had in his waist and was ready for action.

"Where did you get that?" demanded Matt.

Chase shrugged and said he would explain later. If he told his friend how he got the gun he would be blowing Nigel's cover so he stayed silent. Instead of confronting Chase, Matt shrugged his shoulders and turned to deal with the man taking shots at them.

"We can't stay here," he explained. "I need to find a better position so we can gain some advantage. We need to get on the offensive."

Chase nodded, signaling he could handle that. Matt got to his feet and moved to the end of the hall closest to the foyer and motioned for Chase to follow.

"When I signal I want you to lay down some fire directly at the opening at the top of the stairs," he said. "You got that?"

"I got it," Chase assured his friend.

Matt yelled go, and ran toward the far side of the foyer. Simultaneously Chase rounded the wall and opened fire, sending a torrent of firepower toward the top of the stairs.

When Chase had emptied the clip he reloaded, ready to continue. But before he could, the shooter got up and fired furiously in all directions, essentially pinning them both down. Being in separate positions now, Matt knew that this guy couldn't cover them both effectively.

Behind him Reardon moaned loudly. Chase knew she couldn't hang on forever. They had to get her out of there. And soon!

Suddenly the firing from above abruptly stopped and Chase wondered what was happening. Based on the weapon the shooter had he couldn't be out of ammunition. Something else was happening.

~

Nigel watched as the car pulled into a driveway so he slowly moved past the house and parked on the opposite side of the street, about fifty yards beyond. From his position he could see the driveway clearly. He saw the three occupants of the car exit and make their way to the front door. He could see that Matt and the female agent had their guns drawn and were moving stealthily toward the front door. Chase was just behind them. Nigel's gut reaction was to help his friends but at this point he felt he had to wait. He'd seen Fontaine nearby and felt he needed to have his friend's back. Right now Fontaine was an unknown. And Nigel didn't like unknowns.

~

For the past hour Fontaine had listened to the muffled sounds of Vladi and Sonja. Without realizing it Sonja had lost the necklace that held the listening device and it was now laying under a pile of Sonja's clothing. Several times Fontaine thought he heard Sonja scream but it was hard to tell whether she was screaming in agony or ecstasy. He'd heard Vladi tell Sonja he wanted to party so he assumed the screams were of the pleasurable kind. But now he heard something that made him take action! Gunshots! He'd seen Matt and his posse pass by a few minutes ago so given the timing, this meant something was happening at the house! Something he needed to control. He didn't need a spotlight shining on him and a shootout involving the FBI was sure to make that happen.

Vincent Fontaine's survival instincts kicked in and he started the car. He needed to protect his secret and that meant he needed to take control. Whoever got in his way would pay with their life. Gunning the engine he squealed the tires and catapulted into the street. Within seconds he was in front of the house where the shooting was coming from. He quickly exited the car and made his way toward the front door. Neighbors who had heard the shots were peering out their windows so Vincent pulled out his FBI credentials and flashed them. Then he motioned for them to stay out of sight. As he approached the door he could hear the gunfire so he slowed his pace. He needed to be careful. He did not want to rush into a gunfight without knowing what was happening. You could die doing that! He opened the front door and a barrage of gunfire came down on him from the top of the open stairway. There was no way he would be able to enter the fray from the front door. He made his way around to the side of the house and found a side door to the garage. There was a window in the door so he broke it with a rock, slipped his arm in and opened the door. He was sure that, with the noise coming from that much gunfire, no one would hear the glass breaking. He slowly made his way to the door on the other side of the garage. The one that would lead into the house. Based on his knowledge of this style of house he was almost certain it led into a short hallway that housed a small laundry room or mud room. He was also confident that no one would lock this door from this inside because the garage door had an automatic opener. His hunch proved correct when he turned handle and the door opened.

He slowly made his way into the short hall and immediately saw agent Heather Reardon sprawled against the wall, her pant leg soaked in blood. In her state she didn't notice the FBI Director. The gunfire was so loud that Fontaine didn't notice the figure coming up behind him either.

He slowly moved in behind Chase Adams his gun drawn ready to fire when someone grabbed him from behind and threw him to the floor. It took him by surprise but he quickly recovered. He wrestled with the figure who jumped him and tried to overpower him but the assailant was too strong.

With all the noise created by the furious gunfight. Chase didn't hear the commotion behind him but he felt it and turned to see his friend Nigel grappling with Director Fontaine. As the two men struggled they moved closer to Chase causing him to step back. From here he saw the two men struggling for control of the gun Fontaine was holding. In all the confusion Chase was not aware that he was now an open target for the shooter at the top of the stairs.

At that same moment, the shooter peered over the half wall and saw Adams out in the open. He smiled and raised his weapon, aiming at the man's head.

Matt couldn't believe what he was seeing and cried out, "Chase get down!"

Chase turned just in time to see the shooter level his gun at him. He knew he had no chance. Then came a woman's bloodcurdling scream from the top of the stairs and the shooter froze! Just for a split second, his attention lost! Then a young woman came into view wielding some kind of knife which she raised above her head and plunged it into the shooter's back. Luckily for him the weapon plunged into the soft tissue near his shoulder blade.

He screamed in pain and fired his weapon but the bullet meant for Chase slammed into the wall not more than a foot above his head. He felt the searing pain in his right shoulder blade and in his rage turned and shot the woman, hitting her in the midsection. The impact of the gunshot sent her backwards and she fell against the far wall blood spreading from her wound and pooling on the floor around her.

Vladi looked at the woman in total disbelief! Then realized it was Melanie! The girl who tried to kill him at the hotel. He saw Anya rush to the aid of the wounded young woman and became confused by the scene.

Where had they come from? he thought.

Then he heard the shot from below! Right then he forgot all about the women and concentrated on saving himself.

―

Chase couldn't believe what he was seeing and was about to move on the shooter when the shot rang out behind him. He ducked for cover but turned in time to see Fontaine and Nigel in a hostile embrace. Then suddenly, there was a look of shock on Nigel's face. The two men staggered together toward the door to the garage but before they reached it, Fontaine fell to the floor, blood flowering on his white shirt. He was dead before he hit the ground.

In the confusion Vladi, bleeding badly from the wound in his shoulder, made his getaway. He hustled down the hall and made his way to the back bedroom. Opening the window he saw a ledge. He climbed out on the ledge and then scaled the downspout down the side of the house, making it safely to the ground.

Lights in the house next door shone a path for him to follow. He moved away from the house and down a narrow lane that ran behind the row of houses. He could hear sirens in the distance and knew they were coming for him. He needed to move! And move fast! His shoulder ached and he could feel the blood pulsing out of the wound. He had to get help if he was going to survive. But who could he trust? Not his boss Stephan Corolev. Stephan would not be happy to know that he had fucked up, yet again! He pulled out his phone and looked at the list of speed dial numbers there. He smiled to himself as he hit the newest number on his list. He called his new right hand man, Anatoly, and hoped he'd made the right choice.

Chapter 28

"Help!" she cried. "Please help," Anya pleaded, pressing a wet towel on the wound in Melanie's gut.

Downstairs Matt and Chase couldn't believe the devastation surrounding them. There were bullet holes everywhere and the smell of cordite was thick and sickening. Nigel was in shock, gazing down at the dead FBI Director.

"My God," cried Matt when he saw the dead body of Vincent Fontaine.

"What the hell happened?" he asked, a look of disbelief on his face. "And where did you come from?"

Matt raised his gun and stepped toward Nigel who immediately put his hands in the air.

"He was going to kill Chase," he explained. "And I didn't mean to kill him, I swear!"

Chase moved between them and grabbed Matt by the shoulders.

"Matt! It's okay! I had Nigel follow us. He was my back up in case something went wrong!" he explained. "And guess what?" Chase then paused for effect. "Something did go wrong and he saved our lives!"

Chase turned and gave his friend a hug of thanks. Hearing the sirens in the distance he moved over to Reardon and told her help was on the way.

"Hang in there Heather," he said. "You're going to be fine. Heather Reardon just looked up at him and grimaced in pain.

"Please help us!" came the cry from the top of the stairs.

"Nigel, stay here with Reardon while we check on the people upstairs," commanded Matt.

Matt and Chase ran to the stairs and bounded up them two at a time. At the top they discovered two women in the hallway. It looked like the shooter had tried to kill one and the other was trying to stop the bleeding caused by a bullet to her friend's abdomen. Unfortunately, her efforts to do so were not effective. It was clear the woman had lost a lot of blood.

"Please we must save her," cried Anya. She could hear the sirens coming closer and silently prayed for them to make in time.

Melanie looked up at Anya and smiled.

"Did I kill him Anya?" she asked weakly. Then she lay back and closed her eyes.

Matt looked at the woman, puzzled and asked, "kill who?"

Anya stared at him in disbelief. "That was Vladi Cherkov," she cried.

"You're kidding," cried Matt and started for the stairs.

Chase grabbed by the arm and said, "Matt! We'll get him later. Right now we've got to help these women."

Matt looked at him, knowing he was right. But what about his family?

The woman named Anya cried out.

"Melanie, stay with me! Stay with me please," she pleaded.

Then held her and said another prayer.

~

"Anatoly!" It's me," Vladi shrieked into the phone.

"Vladi what is wrong?" he asked.

"I need you to come and get me."

Anatoly listened to his boss's instructions and was ready to hang up when he thought of something.

"What about the woman and the kid?" he asked.

"Shit," howled Vladi. He'd forgotten about them.

He thought for a moment then said, "don't worry about them. They'll be fine. Just lock them in the bedroom and we will deal with them later. Now, get in the damn car and pick me up."

The pain in his shoulder was getting worse and he knew that he was losing blood. He felt faint and sat down in the alleyway and waited for Anatoly to arrive. Anatoly wasn't that far away so he was sure that he'd be here soon. He heard the sirens stop their wailing and he closed his eyes to rest.

~

Amanda heard the man talking on the phone and wondered what was happening. She feared, not for herself, but for her young son Jeremy. Something like this could scar the young boy for life and she hoped her actions had helped calm him. Keep him calm and hopefully save his life.

As she sat there comforting her son she heard the front door open and moments later heard a car start up. She quickly got to her feet and looked out the window. She watched in shock as the man, who had taken her and Jeremy, was leaving. What was happening? Slowly she moved to the door of their room and listened for any sign of life. Hearing nothing, she tried the door but found it locked!

"Dam it," she said.

She swore to herself and looked around the room for something she could use to pry the door open. After searching for a few minutes she realized there was nothing here. She looked at the window thinking maybe they could escape that way. But they were on the second floor. There was no way Jeremy could make that jump without serious injury. She was feeling an overwhelming sense of despair when she had an idea.

"Maybe Jeremy can't make the jump but I can," she said quietly.

"What did you say mommy?" asked her son.

"Nothing Jeremy," she replied. Then she moved onto the bed and looked Jeremy in the eyes.

"Listen Jeremy. Mommy needs you to be brave for just a minute."

"Why mommy?" he cried, fear registering in his voice.

"Mommy's going to climb down from this window."

"No!" said Jeremy and he cried. His mother held him close and calmly explained that she would come right back and open the bedroom door so they could go home.

After adding some assurances Jeremy calmed down and Amanda made her way to the window and pried it open.

She crawled out and stood on the small portion of roof that over hung the porch at the back of the house. It was only nine feet to freedom but it looked a lot longer. She hesitated a moment, unsure of her ability to make the jump. When she looked back and saw Jeremy looking on, frightened, she decided it was time to act. She had to save her baby!

She felt her ankle crack as she landed hard on the ground below and she cried out. Gingerly, she moved to stand and tentatively put her injured foot on the ground. She didn't think she broke it from the fall but it was painful to walk. Now she had only to get back inside and get Jeremy!

She ran to the front door to get her son. Locked! Panic set in and Amanda was frantic. What could she do? There were no other houses nearby and though she could see some lights in the distance she was afraid to leave Jeremy alone. She ran around to the back of the house, looking for another way in when she saw the big picture window. She needed to break it! She looked around, becoming more hysterical by the second.

She heard Jeremy cry out and she ran over beneath the bedroom window.

"I'm coming Jeremy!" she whispered loudly, trying to calm him, then ran toward the side of the property where a stand of trees stood. She noticed that her ankle didn't hurt anymore but then realized the adrenaline in her body was working overtime. The fight or flight response. Right now she was preparing for flight but if she had to she would fight to the death to save her baby.

There!

Just at the edge of the treeline she saw a large rock she knew would do the trick. Running back to the house she stood in front of the window and heaved the rock as hard as she could. She closed her eyes and braced as the large glass window crumbled into a million pieces. She was grateful the window was shatterproof glass as she jumped through the opening and raced up the stairs to get Jeremy.

When they returned to the main floor Amanda looked for a phone. Finding none she grabbed Jeremy and started slowly heading toward the lights off in the distance. She wasn't sure where she was or when her captors might return so she made her way to the house in the distance. The one she could see through the forest that surrounded them. She kept her eyes on the lights ahead and slowly made her way to what she hoped was freedom. As they made their way, a car came racing by on the road in the distance. Amanda grabbed her son and crouched down behind a tree. She stood still and watched as the speeding car pulled into the driveway of the house they had just left. With a sense of urgency she quickly picked up her young son and ran toward the lights.

"Vladi! Vladi, wake up man!"

In his dream he heard the voice begging him to wake up but he was too tired. He batted a hand away. The man was shaking him but he told whoever it was to leave him alone.

"Vladi!" cried the voice in a harsh whisper. "You need to get up. We have to get out of here! There are cops everywhere!"

That brought Vladi to life and he looked up to see his new right hand man standing over him.

Anatoly breathed a sigh of relief and gently pulled his boss to his feet and led him to the backseat of the car. Vladi looked at him and smiled as he slowly laid down in the backseat and, once again, lost consciousness.

Anatoly swore, realizing his predicament was not good. First he had to get out of the immediate neighborhood. And once that happened he could figure out what to do with Vladi. But he needed to act fast! He could see the knife wound in Vladi's back and knew he needed medical aid. But there was no way he could take him to a hospital. There'd be questions. Questions he was afraid to answer!

He was thinking of his next move as he made his way out of the alley. Then he saw two police cars drive slowly by, heading east. He immediately turned in the opposite direction and slowly made his way to the corner, making a right hand turn. The ramp to the highway was only a few blocks away and when he got there he would call Stephan Corolev. He would know what to do. He pulled out his phone and was about to dial when he realized he didn't have a number for Corolev. He thought for a moment then reached behind him and pulled Vladi's phone out of his pocket. A quick search brought him to the speed dial number for a Stephan with no last name. Anatoly guessed it was the number he needed and hit the button.

When Stephan picked up the phone he immediately chastised his underling.

"Vladi, where the hell are you," he demanded but before he could continue another voice broke in.

"Mr. Corolev, this Anatoly Levkin," he explained meekly.

"Ah, Anatoly," replied Stephan. "Yes, Vladi has told me much about you."

The fact was Stephan didn't know this man. But he had learned a long time ago it was better to feign knowledge of someone and praise them rather than act like an ignorant oaf. Knowledge someone like Vladi Cherkov would obviously benefit from. Unfortunately Vladi could only act like an ignorant oaf.

Anatoly puffed out his chest. Hearing those words made him happy and pleasantly surprised. Stephan Corolev knew who he was.

"Sir, I have a problem and I am hoping you can help me," he stated, more confidence in his voice now.

"I'm listening," smiled Stephan.

Anatoly explained the events of the past hour. But when he told Mr. Corolev that he'd found Vladi with a knife wound in his back, Stephan interrupted him.

"How badly is he hurt?" he asked.

"He's unconscious in the backseat of the car," explained Anatoly. "And he's bleeding a lot."

Stephan smiled at his good fortune.

"Anatoly," he began, "I know just the right doctor."

When Stephan mentioned the doctor's name, Anatoly cursed himself.

Why hadn't he thought of that?

"I know him, sir. I will take him to the doctor right now," he stated confidently and hung up the phone.

Stephan looked at the phone and smiled.

"Yes Anatoly," he said to himself. "The doctor will take good care of Mr. Cherkov."

~

The two paramedics rushed through the door and when they saw agent Reardon lying there, immediately started providing her medical assistance.

"No," cried Reardon. "I'm okay but there's someone up there," pointing to the top of the stairs. "They need your help now!" she insisted.

They told Reardon another ambulance was on the way, then they hustled up to the second floor.

Melanie lay there in a pool of her own blood but Anya had not given up and was applying pressure to the wound and urging her to stay awake. Melanie had already lost consciousness twice but was awake now, though barely.

The paramedics moved in! They gently pushed Anya aside and worked on the young girl. They put in an I.V. to stabilize her then laid her on a back board.

"We need to get her to a hospital," said the paramedic as they lifted her and carried her gently down the stairs. It was tricky but it was obvious these people had done this before. In minutes they had her in the ambulance and were on their way to the hospital. As Matt and Chase looked on they hoped the young girl would make it. She reminded Chase of his younger sister, Joanne. The young girl, known on the streets, as Luna.

The two men stood there at the top of the stairs looking down at the second pair of EMTs working on Reardon. Although it would be a while before she was up and walking she would recover. Nigel looked on as they prepared to take her away and told Matt and Chase he would stay with Heather.

Chase smiled.

"Looks like my buddy has his eye on Reardon," he laughed.

"He could do a lot worse," chimed in his buddy Matt and they both had a laugh.

They stood there a moment longer alone. Anya had gone with Melanie so the place seemed eerily quiet.

"Maybe we should look around," said Matt and he made his way to the other rooms upstairs.

They both entered the master bedroom to see a body under the sheets. They quickly ran over and removed the sheet hoping to find someone sleeping or unconscious in the bed.

"Oh my God." Chase said, stunned. He couldn't believe that someone could do what he was looking at to another person.

Matt stood there mute. Even though Sonja had been the one to compromise him he felt sadness. He looked down at her lifeless body. It was obvious she had suffered a brutal death and he felt sorry for this poor girl. She been a vibrant young woman who did not deserve this. To him it was such a waste.

"This is the work of that monster Cherkov," said Matt as he turned away and moved out of the room.

"I just hope the bastard gets what he deserves," muttered Chase as he followed his friend out.

With all that had gone on Matt forgot about the plight of his family but now suddenly remembered. He ran down the stairs, calling after Chase to get moving.

"I need to find Amanda and Jeremy!" he cried.

Stephan was feeling smug! Finally his problems might have some solutions. He went to the bar and was about to pour himself another drink when he realized something was wrong! The young woman and her child!

He suddenly realized that his captives were no longer supervised! They were alone! He needed to get out there, and quickly. He still needed leverage on his young FBI agent Matt Hanson. And his wife and son were that leverage.

He called down to his driver and ordered him to bring the car around.

"Quickly Sergei, quickly!"

When the car arrived he jumped into the back and Sergei hit the gas.

"Bring him in here," commanded the doctor.

Anatoly was dragging Vladi into the room. He had Vladi's arm around his shoulder and was propping him up by holding tightly to his waist. He grabbed him and threw him, rather roughly, onto the hospital bed.

"I see you have your own operating room right here in your offices," noted Anatoly.

"That's right," smiled Dr. Tupolev and paused. It's Anatoly? Am I right?" he asked pleasantly.

Anatoly nodded.

"Now Anatoly, I will take good care of your boss so you don't need to worry! As soon as he is on the mend I will call Mr. Corolev and let him know."

Dr. Tupolev dismissed the man and then prepared for what was to happen next.

~

"Shit!" Shit, shit, shit," yelled Stephan, once he realized that Amanda and Jeremy were gone. He'd searched the entire house.

"Sergei," he cried. "I need you to go out into the woods. See if you can find them. They can't have gotten far."

Sergei grabbed a flashlight from the glove compartment and headed out in search of the two escapees.

Amanda saw the flashlight and it was heading her way. With Jeremy in her arms she ran the last hundred yards to the lighted house. When she got there she rang the doorbell and then pounded on the door impatiently.

"Coming!" cried the voice and the door opened. An elderly man was standing in the doorway and Amanda heard a woman's voice asking her husband who it was at the door.

"Sir," she whispered hoarsely, her breath coming in quick bursts. "We need your help!"

The man looked at her suspiciously but she explained they had just escaped from their kidnappers who had kept them locked up in the house down the road.

"We escaped but there is someone coming this way, trying to find us! Please help us," she begged.

The woman came to the door and insisted that her husband invite them in.

Amanda quickly made her way over the threshold and closed the door behind her. She asked if they had a phone and the woman brought her cell over and handed it to Amanda.

She smiled at the old woman and looked at her son, grateful for human kindness.

She was safe!

⁓

He opened his eyes and he squinted. The lights above him were so bright! Confused, he struggled to understand.

Where was he?

He went to get up and realized he couldn't move!

"What the hell!" he said loudly. "Where am I?" he asked, lifting his head and looking around the room.

He was struggling with his bonds when the door opened and a beautiful young woman entered the room.

She smiled at him and moved closer, her soft hands caressing his leg.

He returned the smile and started to feel much more relaxed.

"Well hello," he whispered, seductively. "And what is your name?"

"My name is Irina," she told him whispering seductively in return. She moved her hand along his leg, then slid it under the sheet.

"I'm here for your pleasure," she said and moved in to give him a kiss, letting her tongue caress his lips before thrusting it in his mouth.

As she kissed him, her hand moved under the sheet, toward his swelling member and she held it in her hand, caressing it slowly. Her hand moved sensuously up and down his shaft causing it to grow.

"Oh Mr. Cherkov," she sighed. "It's so big." She moved her mouth, slowly running her tongue along his smooth stomach. Then she took him in her mouth.

He moaned loudly and closed his eyes taking in every sensation her mouth produced. He was in heaven. She had moved down the shaft and was tonguing his testicles when a male voice spoke.

"Hello Vladi," said the doctor. "Do you remember me?" he asked with a smile.

Vladi's eyes popped out of his head as he looked at Dr. Tupolev standing there. He was holding a scalpel in his gloved hand.

He moved closer to the bed and watched as the young woman continued to massage and lick the Russian's shaft slowly.

Dr. Tupolev smiled and directed the young woman to hold his penis at its base.

"Like this?" she asked, and held his rigid shaft tight. Dr. Tupolev smiled and told her she was doing it just right.

Then he leaned over and looked Vladi Cherkov in the eye. "This is for Vivian, you bastard," he whispered viciously and, with a single stroke, sliced off the head of his penis and watched it tumble to the floor.

Epilogue

One Month Later.

Chase Adams sat in the lounge chair soaking up the sun. He was in his friend's backyard sitting by the pool. Beside him lay Lisa, the girl of his dreams. It had taken some time but she had recovered fully from her broken wrist and the concussion she'd suffered. And since then Chase had never left her side.

He looked around the pool and was content. The backyard belonged to his good friend Matt Hanson. Matt stood by the barbeque cooking lunch for the group. His wife Amanda had just come out of the kitchen holding a tray of drinks and was passing them around. She didn't know it at the time but during her escape, from the house where she was held captive, she had broken her ankle. Her son Jeremy, who was frolicking in the pool, was her inspiration during their escape. The doctors could not believe Amanda did what she did because her foot was so badly broken. But as she often said since the day of that ordeal.

"A mother will do anything to protect her cub," and she always smiled when she said it.

Across the pool sat Melanie Wentz and her new best friend Anya Senkin. Melanie was still recovering from the bullet wound she suffered that eventful day but the doctors said she would eventually make a full recovery. Beside them and in deep conversation sat Julie Eskin, Lisa's little sister. Agent McVittie and his partner Jeb Stevens had found her later that same day. She had spent the afternoon with the woman named Marion and was just about to help Marion with dinner when the two men knocked on the door. They explained what had happened and assured her she would be safe with them. Chase thought often about Julie. It was her troubles that brought him and Lisa together.

It made him think about his sister Joanne. In the weeks before she died Joanne had changed her name. Her friends called her Luna. He had tried heroically but he couldn't save Luna from the clutches of that evil world. The world that lurks just below the surface. It was a world that, even at that moment, was trapping some innocent victim. But he knew he'd saved Julie from a similar fate and for now that was enough.

A commotion started behind him and he turned to see his best friend, and new business partner, Nigel Waters, walk through the patio doors. Holding his hand was his new friend, agent Heather Reardon. Heather still limped as she moved into the yard but the doctors assured her that with some intense therapy she would lose the limp. During her recovery Nigel kept vigil and was a big help in getting Heather back on her feet. Their budding romance was a joy to behold and, even though he had his doubts, Chase hoped it would last. These were the lucky ones he thought.

Sonja!

What a tragedy. She was such a lovely girl, with such promise. Killed by that monster Cherkov for no other reason than he enjoyed it. Melanie and Anya had attended her funeral and had put together the funds to pay for a casket and a burial plot. She didn't deserve to die like that! Nobody did. But they wanted her to have a proper burial.

Chase looked over at Matt and Amanda Hanson. And their son Jeremy, still in the pool.

Matt's career had taken a hit when he confessed his indiscretions to the Bureau. While they were sympathetic there was no way they could allow something like that to go unpunished. The Bureau suspended Matt without pay for two months and was now in the middle of his penance. He was using the time to heal the wounds his indiscretions had cause in his marriage, spending quality time with his wife and son. Chase could see it was helping.

The police arrested Stephan Corolev on kidnapping charges and he was awaiting trial. He had hired the top attorney in the city and the betting was that he would plead to a lesser charge to avoid jail time. But his organization fell into disarray and those who remained were so disorganized they caused little trouble for the authorities.

Last week they found the body of Vladi Cherkov. Fittingly, he was lying like trash in a dumpster. Someone had brutally tortured him and the medical examiner thought the torture had gone on for days. Based on the examiner's findings, Vladi Cherkov suffered in horrible fashion. And though there were no clues pointing to the identity of the killer, the authorities were certain the killer had some medical training. He cut up the body of Vladi Cherkov so he could, not only keep him alive, but inflict the victim with the utmost in pain. They were sure Vladi Cherkov was begging to die in the end.

THE END

Author's Notes

The writing of this book has been an interesting journey for me and I hope the result of that journey was enjoyable for you. My goal is to write a series of books, featuring my character Chase Adams and his sidekick Nigel Waters. I hope you, as a reader of this book will follow along in their journey. I promise the adventures I have in store for them will be an exciting ride.

If you enjoyed this book then I would ask kindly, that you please take the time to review it. Reviews are a key ingredient to a reader's decision to buy any book and I want as many people as possible to enjoy this work.

If you have any comments, good or bad, please send them to me. And if you would like to receive advance notice of my next book in the series and any beyond that please email me at thedonabma@gmail.com. I will personally respond to all emails and will keep a database to tell all of my readers what's coming next. I look forward to your comments.

Don Abma